As Best We Can

TESSA WEST

FOX BOOKS

As Best We Can

Published by Fox Books
South House, The Old Factory, Bells Lane,
Glemsford, Sudbury, Suffolk CO10 7QA

British Library Cataloguing in Publication Data
A catalogue record for this book is available from
The British Library.

ISBN 978-0-9543627-4-4

Book & cover design by Wordzworth Ltd.
*Front cover photo: The Camp, West Stow, 5857
from the Walter Burrell Archive,
Suffolk Record Office, Bury St Edmunds Branch
SRO B/K997/32/1*

Printed in Great Britain by Biddles, King's Lynn

For Joseph, Theo and Thomas

Other books
by Tessa West

Prisons of Promise, Waterside Press 1997

The Estuary, Fox Books 2002

The Reed Flute, Fox Books 2004

Companion to Owls, Fox Books 2008

The Other Vikings, Fox Books 2009

The Curious Mr Howard, Waterside Press 2011

Maps &Poems, Blurb 2013

Acknowledgements

Simon Parker-Galbreath's excellent website about the 25th (County of London) Cyclist Battalion was of key importance to me while writing this book, so I owe Simon my warmest thanks. I am grateful too to David Addy, webmaster of the St Edmundsbury Chronicle, for reading the ms. for historical accuracy. I must also thank Wendy Henningsson for her evocative *Sunlight and Blue Shadow* which, built around extracts of her father's letters, describes his time in the London 25th in World War One.

I was helped too by Peter Bance's books, notably *Sovereign, Squire and Rebel,* which is full of information about and images of the Maharajah Duleep Singh. Finally and importantly, I have perused numerous copies of the Bury Free Press in the Records Office at Bury St Edmunds, and want to acknowledge my particular debt both to the newspaper and to the efficient and friendly staff at the Records Office. Thanks also to Florence Cox, Geoff Markham and Emil and Robyn Kosviner.

As always, my partner has been a constant source of encouragement and support, so I award a special thankyou to Ralph.

February 1916

Lawrence was watching a boxing match. He had rarely boxed as a boy, and had never seen a real fight between adults, but here he was, one of a group of noisy soldiers crowding round a pair of bare-chested men on the deck of a ship in the middle of the ocean. He had thought it might be entertaining, but the grunts and the fists waving in their clumsy gloves hardly seemed to count as amusement or sport. Uninterested in who might win, he edged away and headed aft to a place he'd discovered a week ago. He climbed over a pile of rope and ducked down into a space near a couple of lifeboats. It was sheltered from the wind and just big enough for him to sit in if he drew up his knees.

He stared at the churning wake and the sea stretched out behind the ship. God, there was a lot of it. Today it was pale grey under a pale grey sky. Who would have thought, ten months ago, that he'd be on the White Star liner *HMT Ceramic* sailing across the seven seas, or some of them, at least? Who would have thought he'd be in the army? His life was changing each day. *Ceramic* was forging its way across the world. Each day was pushing him further away from the life he had had before.

By the time he reached his 18th birthday in the summer of 1915 his already weak intention to go to university had evaporated. He could study later, as others of his friends were deciding, for the opportunity to help protect his country would not come again. Or at least, it would not come again while he was young. Each time he passed the poster which said

THERE ARE
THREE
TYPES OF MEN

THOSE who hear
the call and obey

THOSE who delay

And - THE OTHERS

To which do YOU belong?

He wanted to rush off to the recruiting office, but when he asked his father about Kitchener's call to arms, still resonating despite already being a year old, his father hesitated. Lawrence, he said, should think long and hard about what he wanted to do. Yes, at eighteen he was now eligible to join up, but this did not mean that he had to. Britain, thank God, did not have conscription. Individual free will still mattered.

When, in September 1915, he enlisted as a territorial, his mother was anxious, but her sister's boy had done so too, and although her nephew Hugh was older, he was still quite immature. And somehow the fact that Lawrence was a Cyclist was reassuring, for obviously no Cyclists would ever go near real action. Being passionate about bicycles in general and his Marston Sunbeam in particular, Lawrence had opted for a cycling battalion.

He was the second of the Bailey boys to join the colours, still really only a schoolboy, and it was harder for his mother to let him go than it had been to let Conrad go. Conrad was different: bolder, well able to take care of himself though with a tendency to be impetuous. He was tall, too, and muscular. In the summer of 1915, soon after the sinking of the Lusitania, he and a few friends had enlisted in the 11th (Service) Battalion, Cambridgeshire. Seeing his parents' surprise, he explained that this battalion was, despite its name, part of the Suffolk Regiment. This had mollified them slightly, but Lawrence was shocked. Why would any Suffolk-born man join up in Cambridgeshire?

Within weeks Conrad was in khaki and on his way to a training camp in Ripon. A couple of months later his letters were coming from Sunderland, and then from Sutton Veny, near Warminster. In early December, he wrote to say it had been announced that they would be going to Egypt, and his mother gave a sigh of relief, for at least he would be out of the worst of it. Even better, he might be home for Christmas! But within days the decision was switched: they would be going to Boulogne on January 7th or 8th and there would be no Christmas leave.

Lawrence was an easy-going soul. Like his father, he found agreement easier than disagreement, and his mother worried about how he would get on with his fellow soldiers whom, she assumed, would be tougher than he was. Though Lawrence could be a clown at times, he was immensely and intensely proud of belonging to the 1/6th Battalion Suffolk Cyclists whose job was to patrol the East Anglian coastline in case it was invaded, and he put his heart into it.

Throughout the freedom of summer they rode between and around Lowestoft, Yarmouth, Southwold and Aldeburgh. They ranged the miles from Walberswick to Woodbridge and sprinted the short stretch from Bawdsey to Hollesley. They passed flint-faced churches, fruit-laden trees, pubs, gardens full of cabbages and carrots, acres of wheat. They went to Shingle Street and Snape. They waved at girls, waited for heavy herds of cattle to plod past, repaired punctures caused by thorns and stony tracks. They ate in the shelter or shade of elms and oaks, in church porches, on windy promenades. They dipped inland to Westleton and Eastbridge. They drank from pumps, bottles and their cupped hands. They raced and dawdled along the east of East Anglia, the eastern edge of England. Many of the men, like Lawrence, had never seen so much of the sea and it soon became their companion. It was to their right when going north, to their left when going south. It was always there.

When riding at night their lights were so dim they had to dismount to shine a torch on or even feel the raised letters of place names on the few remaining signs. While searching the sea and sky for signs of invaders, they saw the Plough, the Pole Star, Orion's Belt. Someone taught them to recognise Bootes and Arcturus, Castor and Pollux. Lying on their backs they looked up at shooting stars.

In October, after Zeppelins had come along the East Anglian coast and after the news of Nurse Cavell's execution, they summoned even greater energy and determination. They carried messages, sent signals, hid in hedges, searched for footprints and wrote reports. They were trained in fieldcraft and demolition work with explosives. They took their cycles to pieces, replaced parts, made repairs, put them back together and cleaned them so that they out-gleamed horse harnesses. Those were wonderful, joyful weeks for Lawrence, an amazing contrast to school and a vibrant introduction into a wider world. He counted himself amongst the most fortunate of boys, and Elly, his younger sister, could not have been more proud of him.

But after only a few months things changed. The first indication came when another Cyclist battalion, the 25th Londons, with whom the 1/6th Suffolks had often over-lapped on East Coast duty, was suddenly ordered to Chiseldon Camp, near Swindon, to prepare for service abroad. Nothing unexpected about that, of course, except for one important fact: they did not take their cycles with them.

It was the writing on the wall. The Londons were not the only Cyclist battalion being disbanded and amalgamat-ed with other regiments. The 1/6th Suffolks soon followed them, and they too had to surrender their beloved bikes. At least as unexpected and unwelcome as that order was the fact that they were drafted into the 25th (City of London) Cyclist Battalion, The London Regiment, thus losing their own name, so by Christmas they were no longer cyclists but infantry, and no longer Suffolks but Londoners, known as Londons.

A cheer went up from the foredeck. Someone must have landed a blow.

A flight of grey gulls cruised above the ship. The sea seemed endless.

They were at Chiseldon for only a couple of winter months but it seemed much longer. They were housed in C lines, a collection of temporary buildings made of wood and corrugated iron. Cold and damp though these were, they were better than the bell tents some of the troops had to sleep in. Lawrence and his Suffolk friends spent weeks digging trenches, using and cleaning rifles, fixing bayonets and charging at sandbags. In sodden clothes they marched with heavy packs for hours, often into the night, on lousy rations. And on the few occasions when they had time off they were not even allowed into Swindon where they might have found a bit of decent life, because of an epidemic of scarlet fever. Instead of the familiar East Anglian territory - shingle beaches, the slow Broads and the sandlings Lawrence had come to know so well, they became acquainted with the mud under the Marlborough Downs, Liddington Hill and the oddly named village of Snap. While the 25th London Cyclists' motto, *Tenax et Audax*, seemed very apposite for war, whoever thought of it clearly hadn't imagined the particularly extreme tenacity and boldness necessary for coping with mud.

Chiseldon Camp was one of the places from which battalions went to the front, but it was not always clear which front they would go to. It was also the place to which injured men were brought back from the battlefield. Trains sometimes carried over one hundred patients on stretchers, and as many walking wounded. When Lawrence went home to Suffolk at the end of 1915 for a short leave at Christmas he made the family laugh about the spartan conditions at Chiseldon, but he made no mention of the casualties being brought back from France, for Conrad was in France and his letters were cheerful enough, and the worst he complained of was boredom. *"We're just hanging around here, waiting for someone to decide when we should make our moves and where those moves should be. I've never played so many games of cards in my life. At least we've been told we'll get Christmas pudding and extra cigarettes!"*

But when Lawrence came home he was surprised to find that there were hospitals for sick and injured soldiers close to Bury St Edmunds and, indeed, all over the country, and that his own parents were being trained by the Red Cross to help with the wounded. Ampton Hall, only a few miles from West Stow where his parents were currently living, was being turned into a military hospital. The war and its casualties, he was discovering, were not confined to foreign zones.

When the 25th Londons returned to Chiseldon after their leave they were eager to know where they would be sent, for they had completed their training and wanted to get going. There were plenty of rumours, but it was a shock to learn that their destination was German East Africa. Each man was issued with his drill uniform and topee, some already marked "4th East African Brigade", and by the time these were stamped with regimental numbers, excitement was high. But suddenly plans changed, and they were told no, they would not be going to Africa after all.

As Lawrence sat with his eyes closed against the weak sun and felt the throb of the engine through his body, he recalled the mixture of disappointment and annoyance he and others had felt when they heard that. No bikes and no action and no decision were enough to depress anyone, especially after such a period of difficult training.

But then, only a few days later, in January, it was announced that the battalion was to proceed to India.

That was a surprise too - a good surprise, for he knew something of India and Indians from his father's stories about the Maharajah Duleep Singh. The Maharajah, now deceased, had been a favourite of Queen Victoria, and his home had been Elveden Hall, not far from where Lawrence grew up. He could recall his father's descriptions of the palatial interior of the Hall, and the fact that various lords (or were they even princes, Queen Victoria's sons?) used to visit for shooting parties. Though Lawrence had never seen the Hall himself he had often ridden past it on his bike, and in his mind the words *Duleep Singh* and *India* were synonymous with opulence. The Hall and estate now belonged to Earl Iveagh, and he did not think that his father had ever been there since Duleep Singh's day.

Yes. His father would certainly be intrigued to hear about this unexpected posting.

Within a couple of days the 25ths had been issued with slightly different uniforms and accoutrements to the ones they had just handed back, and they were ready to leave. In a final letter from Chiseldon, Lawrence told his parents where he was going but before they had time to reply his battalion was boarding a train for Devonport. On February 1st 1916 they embarked on *HMT Ceramic* with songs, bulging kitbags, and lively anticipation.

Now, sitting in his corner hideaway, it seemed to him that they were taking a long time to reach war. On the ship, after two weeks of little activity, Chiseldon and digging-in felt a lifetime away. They did exercises in an attempt to keep up their fitness, and they had inspections and drills, but broadly speaking they were passive passengers.

Lawrence was looking forward to posting another letter and particularly to receiving some when they reached India, or even Port Said. He wanted news from England, from Suffolk. He thought of Hardwick House, in whose grounds he had grown up. He knew that his father, who assisted Mr Gery-Milner-Gibson-Cullum with his library and collections, would be keenly following the news of the war, despite having no knowledge at all of actual combat. Lawrence had to admit that he didn't yet know about it either, but at least he had practised for it and was, at this minute, heading towards it.

He recalled his home, with the initials TGC for an earlier Thomas Gery Cullum, carved in stone above the front door. His father had always emphasized to him and to his brother that they should never take this imposing environment for granted, and they hadn't. Just before Lawrence returned to Chiseldon after Christmas he and Elly visited Mr Cullum who wished him well and shook hands with him. He remembered Elly bending down and stroking Mr Cullum's brown and white spaniels.

It was a good thing the family had moved to his uncle and aunt's farm in West Stow. A mile or two from Bury St Edmunds might make all the difference if it came to the worst, though it was impossible to imagine Germany actually invading. It felt good to know that, except for Conrad, the family was safe.

Lawrence thought about his elder brother. Conrad was more … more what, exactly? More direct? More confident? He never seemed to doubt what he was doing. Once he'd decided on something he went ahead and did it. He seemed able to make doors open, and, if one didn't open, he barged through it, grinning. Was that a good thing, or a bad? Anyway, right now he was somewhere in France with plenty of friends from Cambridge and Suffolk around him, lucky fellow.

As well as absorbing the Suffolks, the 25th Londons now included men from Sussex, Hampshire and Kent. Everyone was formed into new companies with new captains and they were still getting to know each other. Being at sea for a couple of weeks with not much to do meant that Lawrence made some new friends. He got on particularly well with Sidney Greenstone from Kensal Rise in north London and was glad to have someone sensible to talk to when it came to the business of writing wills. Neither of them had given their wills a thought until they were required to do so on joining up, and it sobered them. It sobered the whole lot of them.

He shook out the last cigarette of the packet and lit it. When it was as calm and warm as today and he was not obliged to be doing anything else, this was a good life. Well, perhaps it wasn't really life itself but more a gap between what had gone before and whatever would come next. He drew steadily on his cigarette. Part of him wanted to reach India as soon as possible, but another part wanted things to slow down and allow him to relax on this ship. Did that mean he was afraid of war? And if he was afraid, were the others? They didn't look as if they were.

He recalled the day when he left school, and the headmaster's speech about duty and purpose. If things had been different he might have been an undergraduate by now. His father, who had been to Cambridge, would have liked his sons to follow the same path. But Conrad had been hungry to enter the world of work. After leaving school he had found employment with Greene, King and Sons brewery and was looking forward to making his career there. Lawrence was left feeling some responsibility to live up to his father's expectations but he was not a natural scholar and it was openly acknowledged by his headmaster that he would struggle at Cambridge. It had been suggested that he might go to London University, but he did not want to be in London. Although he was uncertain about exactly what he wanted, he knew what he did not want. Right now he did not want to sit in lecture rooms and he did not want responsibility. Right now he wanted freedom.

He stood up and flicked his cigarette butt overboard. Anyway, things had changed in only a few months, and decisions about what to do next would have to wait.

February 1916

Aunt Bridget lit the saucer full of Potter's Asthma Cure on the kitchen table, pushed my neck down over it and put a towel over my head. I couldn't avoid breathing the smelly stuff in, and I knew better than to open my eyes. After a couple of minutes the spasms gradually began to ease up, and my aunt stopped pushing me and began to rub my back. Slowly, I calmed down, and she put her arm round me and squeezed me.

"There. Is that better? You poor girl, coughing like that. You'll be all right now." She stood up. "Stay here for a bit. Don't go running off. I'm going to leave this burning for a while."

My chest still hurt and I didn't feel like running off at all, so I spread out some old newspapers and settled down to do the polishing I was supposed to have done the day before. I liked cleaning the silver candlesticks with that thick yellowish liquid. If I used an old toothbrush to get into the awkward corners they ended up looking as if they were new.

Of course Mr Cullum had electricity at Hardwick Hall and Mother and Father said it was a boon that he had it put in our house too, but here at Aunt Bridget and Uncle Arthur's farm there were only oil stoves and oil lamps and coal fires and candles. Aunt Bridget spent her life cleaning things. Not just the fireplaces, but the rugs, the larder shelves, the mantlepieces, the stairs, the banisters, the windows, inside the cupboards. Mother said she cleaned things even when there was no need to.

Best of all I liked polishing the three cups Conrad had won for cricket. He won one in 1912, when he was still at school, another in 1913 for Ampton, and the last one in 1914, when he was playing for Icklingham. When he won the Icklingham one we all went to the presentation. His nickname at the club is Catcher Conrad, because he's very good at catching balls that go high. I polished the cups as hard as I could - they even got warm - so they would shine on the mantelpiece.

I left the kitchen grate until last. I hated this job but I loved the tin of Zebo because it had a picture of a Zebra on it. A black and white zebra on a red background.

I don't know how things get dirty just by sitting in a room, and I don't know how I get asthma. I can clean the dirt off the silver, and I can use Potter's Cure to get rid of my wheezing, but I wish there was something that could stop the dirt and the asthma from coming at all.

Father says that one day the doctors will invent something that will help me, but because it's the war they've got more important things to do. All the men who are brought to Ampton Hall have something wrong with them, and their injuries are much worse than my asthma, so I shouldn't complain. Anyway, Mother thinks I will grow out of it. I hope she's right. It's true that I've seen more children with asthma than grown ups, but perhaps that's because children have to go to school, while grown ups with asthma can stay at home and you don't know they're there.

I finished the grate and went to wash my hands. I've got used to living in this farmhouse now. I quite like it, except for the jobs. Father and Mother say it's much safer to be out of Bury, so we'll probably stay here until the end of the war. No-one knows when that will be, but I don't mind. It's not as if I haven't been here before. I've been here lots of times and I'm allowed almost everywhere.

October 1914

From "Eyewitness"

Since I had been at the front all the information I had gathered, whether from official reports, from the hospitals or from any other source – had seemed to me to consistently bear out the fact that apart from his artillery, the main strength of the enemy resistance – still only of an improvised nature – lay in his skillful combination of machine guns and wire. Throughout this time I had been racking my brains to discover an antidote; and within the last two weeks my vague idea of an armoured vehicle had definitely crystallised in the form of a power-driven, bullet-proof, armed engine, capable of destroying machine guns, of crossing country and trenches, of breaking through entanglements, and of climbing earthworks.

Ernest Swinton, Colonel

June 1915

Major General Sir George Scott Moncrieff to d'Eyncourt, Director of Naval Communications

SECRET. CATERPILLAR MACHINE GUN DESTROYER.

Suggested conditions to be adhered to in design, if possible. These are tentative and subject to modification.

Speed: top speed on flat not less than 4mph. Bottom speed for climbing 2mph.

Steering: to be capable of being turned through 90 degrees on top speed on the flat on a radius of twice the length of the machine…

Reversing: to travel backwards or forwards (equally fast?).

Climbing: to be capable of crossing backwards or forwards an earth parapet 5 ft. thick and 5 ft. high…

Bridging: all gaps up to 5 ft. width to be bridged directly without dipping into them. All gaps above 5 ft. in width to be climbed (up to a depth of 5 ft. with vertical earth sides).

Radius of action: to carry petrol and water for 20 miles.

Capacity: Crew and armament. To carry 10 men, 2 machine guns. I light Q.E gun.

February 1916

Tennyson D'Eyncourt, to Lieutenant Colonel Churchill, 6th Royal Scots Fusiliers

It is with great pleasure that I am now able to report to you that the War Office have at last ordered 100 landships to the pattern which underwent most successful trials recently. Sir D. Haig sent some of his staff from the front.

Lord Kitchener and Robertson also came, and members of the Admiralty Board… The official tests of trenches etc were nothing to it… Wire entanglements it goes through like a

rhinoceros through a field of corn… I strongly urge ordering immediately a good many to the pattern which we know all about. As you are aware, it has taken much time and trouble to get the thing perfect, and a practical machine simple to make; we tried various types and did much experimental work. I am sorry it has taken so long, but pioneer work always takes time and no avoidable delay has taken place…. The great thing now is to keep the whole matter secret and produce the machines altogether as a complete surprise.

February 1916

Dear Mother and Father,

Thank you for your letters and the newspaper cutting about Hawstead House. What a terrible shame. Do they know how the fire started? Can it be rebuilt? I hope Colonel and Mrs Booth are safe.

Well, we've been strengthening a bridge today, lugging logs, digging. Luckily, this kept us warm. It's FREEZING here and we poured water down a slope last night to make a slide. We ran and slid like Lawrence and I used to do on that slope at Hardwick, and I got hold of a plank of wood and some strips of packing cases (for runners) and I made a sort of sledge. Soon everyone wanted one!

It was good fun until one man fell and broke his arm, and then we weren't allowed to do it any more. Have you had a chance to skate at Isleham this year?

It's cold and there's a strong wind, so we try to create shelters from wood, canvas, and bricks. But most of the time we're moving equipment and supplies from one site to another. Most of the roads would not support the heavy vehicles and the number of troops who'll be using them, so we have to mend holes, shore up edges.

We look forward to arriving at villages, because sometimes we're welcomed with things to eat or drink. But many of the villages are almost deserted – the people have gone away to somewhere they hope will be safe. But who knows where that is? Only the old people are left.

If we have time, we check the houses to see if there's anything we want. Yesterday we found three chickens and eleven eggs, and last week someone came across some bottles of wine in a cellar. My best find so far was a clamp of carrots! It feels bad just helping ourselves to other people's things, but that's what happens.

Well, we still don't know what the plan is. Will we stay here? or move? and if so, when? will we get any leave? Of course, if I knew the plan (or even if I knew there was a plan) I wouldn't be able to tell you about it.

Obviously, I can't mention placenames, and anyway they probably wouldn't mean anything to you. I've never heard of any of the towns we've been to.

Sometimes those of us who are from Suffolk talk about places we know, but most of the others don't believe us! They can't accept that there really are villages called Kettlebaston and Dallinghoo and Eye!

I've had a bad stomach this week. Most of us have. We're getting over it but I can't tell you the problems such a common illness causes. At best, there's a hole in the ground somewhere out of sight but not out of smell. And though it's winter and there aren't many flies around now, I dread to think what it'll be like in the summer. But I'm sure we will have moved on by then.

Well, tomorrow we should get that bridge finished. Then it'll be on to the next one.

So things aren't too bad for us, and when we hear what's going on elsewhere we don't complain. And it's good to be together and doing something important.

There's not much more to tell you about and it's time to eat so I'll finish here.

Your loving son, Conrad

February 1916

Dear Mother and Father,

We're in the Mediterranean now, and the skies are as blue as blue can be, and the sea is another shade of blue, but it keeps showing slanting slabs of white as it catches the sun. We're not alone, for as well as the armoured cruisers and destroyers escorting us, there are little fishing boats around. It's an amazing sight and I wish you could see it. Yesterday we saw porpoises again! I watched them for nearly an hour until some idiots decided to shoot them which of course scared them off. This morning we had a medical inspection, because there is a constant fear of disease, and last week a man on a troopship died from spotted fever and was buried at sea. We saw the ship flying a yellow flag. We've been given stuff to gargle, but I'm not sure what it's for, and we've been inoculated against typhoid so we've all got sore arms.

The people who were being sea sick have got over it now. I was lucky to have only two days of it, and I should have expected it in the Bay of Biscay, what with all the zigzagging we did to avoid the enemy who might or might not have been there.

We have a parade every day which we all think is pointless, but I suppose it occupies us for an hour or two. There's a boxing tournament in progress but some of us have invented a better sport called Spud Dropping, where you drop spuds from an upper deck onto the heads of the men below. Direct hits score points, and I'm pleased to say that so far I'm in the lead with 21 points!

And on this ship we have millions of tiny and unwanted passengers. Lice. They're a d----d nuisance. I don't see how we'll ever get rid of them. Several canvas baths (definitely better than no baths at all) have been rigged up, but even soap and scrubbing don't shift the little b... ...s.

We all had to listen to a lecture about India. I thought it would be about the history or the geography of India, but it turned out to be about disease, and what we should and should not do. For example, we're not supposed to eat strawberries, but I didn't even know strawberries grew in India.

The ship is full of rumours. That water is leaking into the hold. That there's not enough coal to get us to Port Said. That we will have stew every day for the entire journey. Sometime we talk about new potatoes, roast chicken, apple tart, proper tea with plenty of sugar and fresh milk, but I'm making a mistake even by writing these words.

And just now a small shoal of flying fish went by in a shiny flash. Beautiful. They're like silver daggers streaking above the water. I didn't even know there were such things. There are clouds on the horizon now, and I think we may have another thunderstorm. We had one last night and I went out onto the deck to see it. It was quite extraordinary. The sea wasn't particularly rough, but every now and then thunder blocked out the sound of the engine and lightning lit up the water. I stayed outside until it started to pour in torrents.

I've now got to know plenty of the Londons. I like them. I'm one of the youngest here, and there are people with fiancées and wives and even children. It must be very hard for them, but we're all feeling cheerful at present and can't wait to get to Port Said. When we get there we'll feel we're properly on our way. As soon as I've posted this letter I'll begin another one. Some men are keeping diaries, and I wondered if I should, but if I did I'd be writing it all again to you which would take a long time.

A special hallo to my little sister Elly. What's happening at school? Are you doing another play? You were good in the last one, when you were that fairy. Write and tell me what you are doing. Have you still got your pet rabbit?

It's good to know you're safe in Suffolk and a long way from the war. Mind you, we're even further away then you are! But some of the men here who live in London are worried that the Germans will bomb their houses, and they won't be there to help their families. But most of us don't believe that the Huns would deliberately target civilians.

Have you heard from Conrad recently? I should think he's finding France a very crowded place now that so many troops are being sent there, or so we've been told.

Don't worry about me. I'm fine. In fact, though there are many boring hours, there are plenty of times when I feel it's good to be alive. Like now, when I'm thinking about you while sailing along on this beautiful sea under an azure sky.

Your loving son and brother,
Lawrence

February 1916

Dear All,

There's so much to tell you! When we berthed at Valetta in Malta we were all ready for a change from the routine of life on board. Though not allowed to disembark, it was marvellous to be close to land, to see the forts, to be surrounded by numerous small boats. Everyone was trying to sell us peaches, melons, fruits I don't know the names of, even pottery and embroidered cloths. There were things I've never seen at home. People spread out what they were offering and held up their fingers to indicate the price. When a deal was agreed, they sent up a basket for us to put the money in, so we wrapped the coins in a cloth and lowered it down to them. Once they had the money they put the goods in the basket and we hauled it up again! Much more fun than going to a shop! I loved the shouting, the foreign-ness, the heat. It beat market day in Bury St Edmunds hands down!

And the women! We've not seen a woman for ages, but here were dozens of them, all in vivid red and orange and green clothes, all smiling and waving at us. I tell you, if Conrad was here it would be hard to stop him from jumping overboard and swimming to them! All thoughts of that girl Daisy, from

Fornham St Martin (or was it St Genevieve?), would be forgotten! I loved it because everyone was yelling and waving and laughing.

But we were soon on our way again, and we reached Port Said within a day or two. There was as much stench here as colour and bargaining, but what impressed us the most was the amazing way they re-coaled Ceramic. Barges laden with coal came alongside the ship, and hundreds of men, each dressed only in a single dirty piece of cloth, scooped up coal in a basket and swung it up onto their head. Then the poor blighters set off for the deck at a fast barefoot run along narrow planks, tipped the coal out into one of the ship's holds, and ran back for another load. It took them hours. At night the scene took on an unreal dimension. It seemed a vision of some underworld full of dark glistening beetles. Amazingly, no-one fell into the dock, and no-one spilled their load of coal, but by the end the entire ship – and its occupants – were covered with a layer of black dust.

The days are bright and blue as we continue our way along the Red Sea. So much sea, so much sky and sun. It makes you think about this huge universe, and about our small world sailing through it like a moving island. Everything is new to every man. Only a few men here have ever been overseas before and no-one has been to the east, so we were very impatient to reach India.

And here we are at Bombay. Bombay is certainly India. I've been to London a few times in my life, (remember when you took me and Conrad to see the Tower?) but London has nothing like these vast numbers of men and women, nor these thousands of children, many of whom stare at us, call out to us and even pull at our clothes. When I looked down on the scene

*from the deck it all seemed exciting, but when I got onto the
dockside I didn't like it at all. It almost felt as if I was being
assaulted. I hate the heat that hits you like a hammer, the
squalor, stench, light, noise, crowds and cows. Even though
nearly four thousand troops disembarked, I was worried that I
might be swallowed up by these foreigners. Every one of their
alleyways is unique yet the same. It would be so easy to get lost.
I cannot understand how some of the troops, including Sidney,
seem to want to drink India in. Even as they walked off the ship
they looked at home, irrespective of what they came across –
people with no legs, or only one eye, cows shoving at market
stalls spilling all the goods, children begging, men selling food
covered in black flies, dirt everywhere. Father, how could you
ever have wanted to come here, or imagined that I would like
it?*

*And then we got on a bone-shaking troop train for a thirty-six
hour journey east to Bangalore. Even after a couple of days in
this climate we were suffering from red and blistered necks and
knees. On that journey we saw so much we had never seen
before: palm trees, monkeys, exotic birds, ox-carts, bright
coloured clothes and costumes quite unlike ours, rice fields,
huts, temples, completely lightless nights.*

*You should see the railway stations here. People wait for days
for trains. They sleep, eat (and more) on the platforms. They
try to sell us tea, water, cigarettes, food I've never seen in
England. And they beg from us. One old woman wouldn't leave
us alone, but followed us around with her dirty naked baby in
one arm while waving the ugly stump of her other arm at us. I
gave her some money, but I'm still not sure how much the coins
are worth, so I've no idea if I gave her a lot or a little. And when
a train comes the Indians clamber in with their baggage,*

crowding into the carriages, and even onto the roof! Children try to squeeze in too, and I saw a train setting off with several boys clinging onto the windows. I was exhausted by it all, and couldn't wait to reach our destination.

Baird Barracks is the nearest thing to England in terms of accommodation, thank God. It has big bungalows with proper beds, showers, a swimming pool, familiar food, even a concert hall. There's room to sit and read or write comfortably. The whole place feels very English, with the advantage of there being Indian servants who clean our boots and wash our clothes for next to nothing. We're confined here for three weeks, in quarantine, but no-one's complaining. I could stay here for twice the time.

I know that back in Suffolk it won't be long before the wheat will shoot up, trees and hedges thicken, and swallows zip through the air. I imagine Mother cutting roses and sweet peas. I think of Elly with her skipping rope. And Conrad. What's happening to him? Poor s-d, he certainly won't be lounging in the sun and calling to a chai wallah for another cup of tea.

After all this dryness, noise and activity I would love, just for ten minutes, to see the River Lark between its green, damp banks, and to lie on the grass looking up at the sky. That would be so good, so very good. I'm thinking of a particular spot near Hengrave where Conrad and I were once so busy trying to construct a bridge from bits of wood we had "borrowed" from Uncle Arthur that we did not notice cows approaching us at a lumbering run from the field behind. Not trusting our half-built bridge we had to wade across to get away. I remember Mother's face when we arrived home in soaking wet shoes and trousers.

23

Father, I ought to know more about the Duleep Singhs for since being in India almost everyone I have seen is desperately poor, and apart from a few temples we've only seen the most basic of buildings. By now I'm getting a sense of the vastness and variety of India. I realise that the continent must contain rich as well as poor, but apparently not in this part of the country.

In the three weeks we've spent at Baird Barracks, a Chiseldon-like life has returned, minus the digging. There are parades, route marches, sports. We all look forward to the post and to the shillings we receive on pay day. When marching we even sing, as we used to. Several men have managed to get hold of boxes of paints and sketch books. Some have begun to embroider the battalion emblem, with its wheel and spokes and complicated crown. I'm fascinated by the variety of flowers and plants we see, and so I'm going to note down and draw what I find. A decent notebook and some coloured pencils would be more than welcome, if you can manage it, please.

And now we're heading to Hebbal.

All my love, Lawrence

March 1916

I was sitting on the rug in the sitting room, doing a jigsaw of people on a beach. I have only been to the seaside twice. Once we went on an outing to Lowestoft, and a boy went too deep in the sea and had to be rescued, and another time we went on the train to Felixstowe and I was stung by a bee.

Uncle Arthur was reading the Bury Free Press. Suddenly he called, "Bridget, come in here. Come and look at this.

Just look at this."

Aunt Bridget hurried in from the pantry, her hands raised and covered in flour. Uncle held up the paper so she could see a big photo.

"It's a crying shame. They're killing families now. Listen. '*Innocent victims of Friday night's air raid. German baby-killers at work. Women and children ruthlessly slaughtered.*' "

"What? Here in Bury?" Bridget was shocked. With her hands still raised, she shook her head and went back to her pastry.

"You should see this too, Elly," said Uncle. "You need to know how cruel the Germans can be. Listen to this: '*While the father was away serving his country on military duty, the sky Huns came and murdered his young wife.*' "

I stared at the photo. It showed a soldier in uniform, his wife seated beside him, and their five children. Words had been printed on the people, like labels, saying what had happened to each of them. On one girl it said *Eyes injured*, on a boy it said *Nearly suffocated*, on a very little girl it said *Injured* and on the mother and on two more children was the word *Killed*. I imagined the family sitting down to their dinner, and suddenly everything blowing up, and the knives and forks and peas and potatoes flying into the air.

I looked at the soldier and his family carefully. I was sorry about what had happened to them. I was very glad it was his family and not ours which had been hit by a bomb, but then I felt guilty for thinking that so I said a quick sorry to God. There was a dog in the photo too, and I wondered what had happened to it.

"Do you know that man and that family?" I asked. "Do they live in Bury?"

Uncle Arthur looked more closely to read what was written under the picture. "No, they don't. It just says *Daily Sketch* underneath. This picture's probably in papers all over the country. But it could be here in Bury. That family could be in Bury."

Aunt Bridget came back in, drying her hands on a tea towel. "So we're not as safe as we thought. Who would have thought there'd be more Zeppelins?"

"Uncle, if Mother and Father died or were killed, who would look after me?"

Uncle Arthur looked at me over the top of the paper with a smile. "We would, of course. Aunt Bridget and I. We'd look after you."

I thought of all the jobs I'd have to do if I lived here, in West Stow, until I was a grown up and got married. I didn't think I'd like it, but I didn't want to seem rude, so I just asked, "Would I stay in the little bedroom?"

"Yes, you probably would. But it won't happen, Elly, so there's no need to worry about it. You're safe here. We're all safe."

I went back to my jigsaw. When I got to the end I was disappointed because two pieces were missing which meant there wasn't a flag on the top of the sandcastle.

That night I dreamed about Sky Huns. They had big teeth, and wings made out of German flags.

March 1916

Dear Mother and Father,

Well, you'd be surprised to see where we're billeted just now. In some WOODS! It's better than I thought it would be, but it's impossible to put a tent up. However, as we need fuel and are allowed to have fires, it's a good place to be!

We're hungry, so even bully beef and old bread tastes good, but today what we need most of all is CLEAN WATER. *Hopefully we'll get a supply this morning.*

And at least there's a hint of sunshine now that it's spring, and today I hoped that it might be possible that one day in the future these fields would be free of troops trampling down the crops (mostly barley and wheat) and that the trees would grow up again.

There are stories and rumours about what might happen in the next month or so, but the only thing we can be sure of is that all of them will result in us having WET FEET.

And I've just remembered I forgot to thank you for the socks and the cigarettes. Each sock and each ciggie is, or was, a treat. I'm sorry if I've not thanked you properly for other things you've sent, esp the magazines.

And another request, please. Can you send some CROSSWORDS? *I'm getting quite keen on them, and doing them helps me relax.*

So, you must imagine me sitting by a warm fire and trying to dry my boots, while drinking something that's supposed-to-be-soup but who knows what sort of soup it is? However, two fellows from March shot a couple of rabbits, and these will be our second course. We're using a bayonet as a spit, and the bunnies are roasting. They smell wonderful.

Sorry, Elly! I didn't mean to upset you. Have you still got your pet rabbit? I hope so.

Well, tomorrow we'll be loading equipment onto trucks. It's needed up the line. That's the direction almost everything is going in - up the line. We've seen men coming back this way, of course, en route to field hospitals or back to Blighty. What bad luck to be wounded. When I see them I thank God that I'm still in ONE PIECE.

My love to everyone at home. Thank you again for your letters and parcels.

I'll write again soon.

> *Your loving son, Conrad*
> *PS Please give my regards to Mr Cullum.*

April 1916

I was walking home from Ingham station. I was wearing my new Red Cross uniform with its peaked cap which is slightly too small, but which I'm relying on to stretch with use. When I presented myself to Hattie last Monday morning, my first morning, she said, "Eric! You look marvellous!" This gave me confidence and after only a few days I was already looking forward to meeting each convoy of sick and injured soldiers from the front. At Ingham station, those who could walk disembarked from the train first, and then those on stretchers were carried out. On the platform ladies supervised urns and handed out cups of tea. The men accepted them eagerly and warmed their hands round them. The air was thick with cigarette smoke and the cooling engine's steam. I noticed several men having to drink from cups held by a friend because their own hands were holding crutches. I wondered why one man, standing firmly on his own two legs, drank from a cup held out to him, until I saw that he had only one hand, and that was as thickly bandaged as a boxing glove.

Gradually, we helped the men to get from the platform and into one of the assorted vehicles waiting outside: a couple of vans from the Victoria Laundry in Bury, several Red Cross ambulances, two lorries and a smart horse-drawn carriage.

There was not room for everyone, so some had to wait. A few Red Cross workers travelled with the sick and injured, but I and some others walked the mile or so to the military hospital at Ampton Hall. We arrived to help carry the last patients out of the vehicles and transfer them to the care of the nursing staff. Then we rode back to Ingham station to collect a second and then a third batch, each numbering some dozens of men.

I and the several other new volunteers were still getting used to seeing damaged and depressed tommies. The men uttered as many grunts as words, and many seemed to have lost their ability to do more than accept what others did for them, though there were those who expressed their gratitude by a gesture. Some men had lost limbs, while some were wearing bandages round their heads, and still others seemed to have no wounds. I thought of the injuries which would be exposed when the clothes stiff with blood, mud and vomit were removed. Occasionally I saw a handful of soldiers who were mere boys – boys who should have been on football fields not battlefields. Boys like Conrad and Lawrence. I still can't help wincing inwardly when I recall seeing each of our boys off at Bury station.

Why were so many of these patients in such a poor state? Surely the field hospitals had been caring for them?

Surely they should have been issued with clean clothes? The foul smell they gave off indicated that infection was festering. Few looked well nourished, and why did none of them have more possessions than a small bag or knapsack?

After less than a month of doing this work I was reluctantly forced to conclude that the best the British Army could do for the sick and wounded in the field was not enough. There were just too many patients, and too many injuries needing specialist attention. What must it be like out there? Probably worse than the things Hattie was telling me about men here at Ampton who gibber or won't stop laughing, and their pleas to be allowed to die, or their determination to live.

I have become extremely proud of Hattie's work as a VAD. She trained at the beginning of the year and was soon entitled to put on her blue uniform with its red cross. At that stage I had not realised exactly what she would find herself doing – I had supposed it would be a spot of bandage rolling, and bed making, and perhaps dealing with some superficial injuries - but after only a week or two she was giving injections, changing dressings, checking medicines and writing letters for those who could not write. Straight away I could see that this work was going to be extremely important to her, and she was telling everyone – even Bridget whom she didn't talk to much - about Ampton.

However, she didn't tell anyone other than me about the amount of venereal disease among the patients, for Bridget was already worried about her bringing diseases home. I was astonished to learn that the illness was as prevalent amongst officers as it was amongst the troops. I just hadn't thought about it, and, I have to admit, I didn't want to.

I only entered wards to deliver new patients, and, after hearing some of Hattie's accounts, I was not in a hurry to spend more time in any of them. Perhaps women were made of sterner stuff than I supposed. And thank God they were doing what they did, for there were few men to do it. On the whole, the patients I met at Ampton were those ambling or being pushed round the grounds on fine days in search of fresh air, privacy or the droves of bright daffodils near the long lake. They were seeking, as I would in their position, whatever might nourish and heal their damaged bodies and souls.

That evening, after delivering the last patients to the hospital, I walked back to West Stow alone, sometimes greeting pairs or small groups of men strolling along the lane enjoying a cigarette in the dusk. Most were from the lines and lines of pointed tents which had recently been erected to house yet another battalion, while the luckiest lived in wooden huts which had been put up hastily a year ago. Officers were billeted in many houses and outhouses, and if Hattie, Elly and I had not moved into Arthur's farmhouse, the spare rooms would have been given over to the army. The newcomers spoke with an unfamiliar accent. They were from somewhere in the north, I guessed. This almost bare and flat part of Suffolk was perfect for training, and the arrival of troops more than tripled the local population.

After another fifty yards or so a pheasant scuttled along the hedgerow in front of me. It was one of the species which had managed to survive and breed despite the fact that years ago its ancestors had been brought here from the other side of the world. I stopped walking, and it slowed down before turning its body as if to show off its red and yellow feathers in the sun. It took its time to find a hole in the hedge and disappear, trailing its marbled golden-brown tail.

I walked on more slowly, thinking again about how, only a matter of days ago, a Zeppelin had bombed Bury, damaging Hattie's mother's house in Mill Road. Hattie had therefore taken a few days away from West Stow to help her mother move into her other daughter's home in Downham Market while repairs were carried out. She wasn't far away and she'd be back soon, but the incident emphasised the feeling I was experiencing more and more: here, even in an ordinary English village, we could no longer count on being safe.

I thought of Conrad in France, wet, bored and impatient for action. Somehow I had come to terms with his situation, but not with Lawrence's. Like Hattie, I thought of my eldest son as self-sufficient and mature, even though his last letter hinted at the pressure he was experiencing. As for Lawrence, though he seemed too young to be in uniform he was excited about his journey to India, and that gladdened Hattie and me. He would definitely be safer there than in France.

He had told us the Londons travelled north by train. But where were they heading? A few days ago, on a brief visit back to Hardwick House, I took the large Pinkerton atlas from its shelf in the library and opened it carefully.

A Modern Atlas
from the
Latest and Best Authorities
exhibiting the
Various Divisions of the World
with its chief
Empires, Kingdoms and States
in Sixty Maps

I polished my spectacles before turning to the Introduction. It began with these words:

Geography is a study so universally instructive and pleasing, that it has, for nearly a century, been taught even to females, whose pursuits are foreign from serious researches.

The atlas had been published in 1815. My goodness! How things had changed!

India was not mentioned in the Contents, but there was a big plate of Hindostan. I put my finger on Bombay and hesitantly moved it northwards, but I had no idea where I was looking for. I found regions such as Madras and Mysore, Calcutta and Delhi. But where was Amritsar, the place which was, for Duleep Singh and his family, and for all of Sikhdom, the Holy City and spiritual home? Surely I could find that? But I couldn't, and there was no index. I could only think that Amritsar had had little importance at the time of the atlas's publication.

And where exactly was Lawrence's destination? And why? India, British India, was not at war, so the fighting must be against people on the borders. But who were they? What nationality were they? Were they the Afghans Britain had fought against twenty-five years ago? My finger wavered over the map as I read the words Cabul, Candahar, Great Sandy Desert, Himmalaya or Snowy Range of Mountains, Desert of Cobi. And there was the Indus. Of course I knew of the Indus, at least. With a magnifying glass I traced it from its beginnings near the mountains of China, through flat plains and so down to its many mouths and out into the pale Arabian Sea. Using the glass made the map come alive, and I revelled in following the river between the enlarged letters of place names. The scale, I noticed, was forty-four Hindostan and thirty-two Rajepoots Cosses to a degree.

Then I took the Cambridge Modern History Atlas from the shelf, and looked up Amritsar. The maps were much smaller, but there was an index. I found the city at once, up in the Punjab.

I decided to ask Lawrence to explain the situation, for there must be some vital military reason for them to be going to such a far off and little known place. But of course he would probably not be allowed to write about it.

My interest in India stemmed from childhood. As the son of a doctor who was occasionally called to Duleep Singh's household at Elveden Hall, I had accompanied him there on several visits. Usually a uniformed footman appeared as soon as we arrived, but one day we found the Maharajah waiting in the garden where bright green and red parrots were pecking at the grass as comfortably as crows. Dressed in a formal suit, a velvet turban and a necklace of large pearls, Duleep Singh made a huge impression on me. I was ten. Through the window of the gig I watched him hurry towards us, open the door for my father, greet him and tell the driver to take me to wait in the stables.

When I jumped down from the gig I smelled the familiar smells of hay and manure, and someone asked me, "Do you like horses or hawks best?" When I replied that I'd never seen a hawk close I was led off to the mews where another man, who I learned later was the head gamekeeper, asked if I would like to have a falcon on my wrist. With some reluctance, I did so, and I never forgot its solid weight, its glossiness, its silver bells. It was hooded, but after a minute the gamekeeper took the hood off and offered it morsels of meat while quietly whistling the same few notes over and over. I watched the falcon's eyes and its beak as it took them. I had often seen wild birds close to, but never one like this.

That visit meant so much to me that whenever I heard my father was going to Elveden I tried to go with him. I managed three more visits and though I never saw the birds of prey again I was not disappointed, for on the first of those occasions I saw an ostrich, and on the second I saw monkeys in the trees.

The third time I went to Elveden Hall I was told to remain near the gig, but as the horse had been tethered to a fencepost I risked wandering around a beautiful lawn. A few minutes later two girls of about my own age appeared. Astonishingly, they were wearing breeches, not skirts. I had never seen any woman or girl wearing breeches, but I had to believe my eyes. I sidled back to the gig without them seeing me.

They looked as if they were sisters, and I was even more surprised to see that one was carrying three cricket stumps, and the other a cricket bat and a tennis ball. I watched them measure their pitch, make creases, and push the stumps into the ground ready for a game, just as I did at home with my brother Arthur and the rector's sons. They even had bails. I had seen girls try to play cricket before and knew they were useless. The one who was going to bowl had her black hair tied back off her face, but some kept blowing loose. It seemed as wild as a horse's mane. The one who was about to bat had hers tied into a single, thick rope which hung down her back.

I watched the bowler walk a few paces away from her crease, scrape a mark on the ground with her heel, turn, run and deliver an accurate overarm ball. The girl batting gave the ball a good whack into some shrubs. I was amazed. While the bowler went to retrieve the ball, the girl with the mane ran fast from wicket to wicket three times.

I couldn't wait for Father to return. "Look!" I said, "Look at those girls! They can play cricket properly! I didn't know girls could play like that! They're better than Arthur! Watch the one who's bowling. See, she's good, isn't she?"

Father said nothing but smiled and watched while a few more bowls were bowled until the ball hit the wicket.

"They're boys. They are the Maharajah's two eldest sons, Frederick and Victor. Victor is named after Queen Victoria. She's his godmother."

I was confused and I said, "They can't be boys. Not with hair like that."

So, aged eleven or twelve, I learned about Sikhs and their hair and their turbans, and began to be interested in India.

Victor and Frederick were about the same age as me, but they did not attend King Edward VIth School in Bury St Edmunds as I did. They went to Eton. But I had heard they were up at Cambridge at the same time as me, and one evening, when I saw two tall young men in cricket whites and turbans practising in the Trinity college nets, I guessed who they were. I introduced myself and found them friendly. But when we all returned to Suffolk for the vacations the brothers made no contact with me, even though they only lived a few miles away. Of course I understood perfectly well that, though a fellow student, I would never be invited to a household which entertained members of the royal family. I was pleased merely to shake their hands and play cricket with them in the Easter Term, for they were good-natured fellows.

My father had told me that their father, the Maharajah, was the last crowned emperor of the Sikh empire, and that when the British Empire annexed the Punjab he was exiled while only a boy, obliged to relinquish his inherited authority and wealth in India and to live in England. The British confiscated from him the Koh-i-Noor diamond, the most treasured jewel in Sikhdom, and gave it to Queen Victoria.

As he grew up, Duleep Singh became the epitome of an English gentleman, a personal friend of the Queen, and a Christian. He was baptized with water from the Ganges. But he built up huge debts, fell from grace and died in poverty in France in the 1890s. He was only fifty-five. It was sad story. He had had two wives and fathered eight children, but where were they all now? Frederick and Victor were the only survivors I knew anything about. The last I had heard of them was that they had both joined the army. Perhaps they were still in it.

Two soldiers clattered past on bikes and called out a cheerful "Good evening!"

And then I found myself thinking about the war again, and the wounded men, and I imagined Lawrence being injured, and the terrible journey he would have to make to get home to an English hospital. Being brought home from the other side of the channel was bad enough. But soldiers wounded in India wouldn't be brought home, would they? They would be cared for in India until they were well enough to travel. But what if …

A movement at the side of the road caught my attention. I paused to watch a hedgehog snuffle in the verge. It was unusual both to see a hedgehog in this sandy soil, and for one to be out of hibernation so early. Perhaps the weather was warming up.

I pushed away the fear I felt about Lawrence and made myself think about Elly. It was a pity her schooling had been interrupted, for she was doing well. In fact, her teacher had told Hattie that she was "a girl with particular promise". But since the outbreak of war there were thousands of boys and girls who had changed schools or whose schooling was interrupted. We didn't want her cycling in and out of Bury every day. Anyway, she would catch up easily and so although there was no sign of the war ending we had decided not to evacuate her. If children were being brought to Suffolk for safety, surely there was no need to send our own child further away? And what if her asthma worsened and she were to go to someone who knew nothing about the condition? What mattered now was that Elly was as well and as happy as she could be. The bombs which fell on Bury were proof that living at West Stow was definitely the best option. Even though I've little in common with my brother and his wife I reminded myself that Arthur was very generous in letting our family move into his home for an unknown length of time. There was no-one else I could have asked, and his agreement had been immediate and warm. Being brothers certainly counted for something, and I found myself hoping that Conrad and Lawrence would help each other in the future.

I wondered whether I should set Elly some more schoolwork, but my Red Cross commitments were taking more time than I had expected, and, in truth, the injured men needed me more than she did. She seemed to be able to occupy herself perfectly well, and Bridget found her jobs to do. It wouldn't do her any harm at all to learn about life in a house that, like most, had no electricity or running water. Indeed, living here would make her appreciate how lucky she was.

Just then I heard a horse and cart approaching from behind, and George Abley offered me a lift for the last few hundred yards. We pulled up outside Bridget and Arthur's farm in the gloom. I thanked George and opened the garden gate. Before entering I checked that no jot of light was visible from outside.

May 1916

I couldn't wait to show it to Father. It was the best find I'd ever had, and I hadn't even been looking. It had almost jumped out at me from the ground. Father would be astonished and delighted, and so would Dr Sturge. I imagined each of them examining it with their magnifying glasses, turning it and holding it to the light, studying it for clues about how old it was or what it'd been used for. I might get one and ninepence or even two shillings for it if I was lucky.

It was safe in my bag as I took a short cut through the pines on my way home, but suddenly my way was blocked by a sheet of canvas stretching from tree to tree and post to post, like a sort of taut but soft fence. It started by the flint wall, making it impossible to cut through the edge of the Elveden estate, which is what I usually did. What on earth was it?

Obviously it was something to do with the war, for the only animals around here were a few horses and sheep, unless you counted rabbits, which were everywhere. No-one could possibly count rabbits or keep them in one place. And horses were kept in paddocks and sheep wouldn't need a fence like this one, especially not here on the edge of the brecks. And why canvas rather than wood or wire, like most fences I'd seen in my life? This was like a heavy curtain. It continued ahead through the pines, where bits of bushes and branches had been sawn off to create a corridor for it. Where there were no trees, it was fixed to new posts. It was like a road the Romans used to make - straight through everything.

The Zeppelins in Bury meant that war was getting nearer, but was it really as close as this? Only half a mile or so from my aunt and uncle's house? Surely not. But my grandma's house had been damaged by a bomb, and everyone was saying she was lucky to be alive.

I wondered again about what I should do if I saw German soldiers. I thought that if I spoke even a little bit of German, they would be less likely to kill me, but so far I only knew how to count to twelve and say *Guten Tag, Auf Wiedersehn* and *Was is los?* (which Alison told me means What's the matter?). I had told myself to learn some German words, but I didn't know anyone who spoke German.

The fence hadn't been there yesterday afternoon, so it must have been put up yesterday evening, or more likely, today. I hitched my bag up onto my shoulder and began to hurry along it, keeping it on my right and heading, I was sure, in the right direction.

It was high – much higher than a tall man - and it had a particular smell. Quite a pleasant smell, not like creosote, or hay or manure or any of the other farm smells I knew. More like wellington boots. As I walked I ran my hand along its smooth grey surface. There was a wide seam with a thick edge along the bottom, and every few yards there was a join. In places it was attached to a tree trunk or to a newly dug-in post. The canvas had been nailed from the side I was on, but the bottom of it seemed to be fixed from the other side. I thought planks or stones must have been attached to weigh it down, for when I tried to push it, it hardly budged. Could it be to keep the Germans out? No, because anyone could cut through canvas if they had a really sharp blade, but it could certainly slow them down.

It was late afternoon by now and despite shifting my heavy bag, the strap was digging into my shoulder, and I was wondering where and how the canvas curtain would come to an end. And then it stopped. Just like that. For no apparent reason. But straight ahead were piles of earth which showed where there were newly-dug holes for the posts. Clearly, the curtain was going to go further.

The land was no different on the other side, just heath and pines, and soon I recognised the proper footpath which took me to the road. And as I approached the road there was something else new.

A huge sign had been put up.

ELVEDEN EXPLOSIVES AREA
KEEP OUT

Nearby, some soldiers were unloading huge rolls of canvas from trucks while others carried piles of posts from a lorry. They were probably from the West Stow camp.

I raced home to the farmhouse with my bag banging on my back. Uncle Arthur was putting polish on his boots and looked up briefly when I came running up to the back door, out of breath.

"Uncle, have you seen the big sign by Weatherhill Farm? "

"Yes," he said, as he inspected the heels and soles of his boots.

"It says there are explosives."

"I know."

"Why?"

"More training, I suppose. More practising for war."

He leaned over and brushed the heels vigorously. "Keep away from there, won't you? It's very dangerous. No-one's allowed inside that area."

"Is it something secret?"

"Probably. But what's important is that explosives are dangerous."

While I washed my hands in the sink he gave a final rub to his shoes, and by the time I turned round he had put them away under the dresser. The toes faced forward, as brown and shiny as conkers. How could he be cleaning shoes when war was round the corner?

Father was still out, so after tea I washed up, went upstairs to my room, took my shoes off and sat on the bed. What if war came here? What if I looked out of the window one day and saw German soldiers marching down the lane and stopping here? Would they kill me, even if I said *Guten Tag*? By now I had seen hundreds of British soldiers and although their uniforms had different badges and things, I was certain I'd know a German soldier when I saw one. Their helmets were very different, for a start. Everyone said it wouldn't happen, but they'd been wrong about the Zeppelins.

To stop myself worrying I inspected my flint properly. Part of the outside still had cortex on, like cement. The flint itself gleamed blue-black, but it was not as bright as it had been in the sunlight. On one side it had a distinct bump, and Dr Sturge had told me the proper name for that was "the bulb of percussion", and that was where whoever had worked it had hit it to chip off sharp flakes which they could make into cutting tools. This flint was one of the ones with lines of scratches over it. Some went long-ways, like blades of grass, and some went cross-ways. I kept forgetting what they were called.

Occasionally, Lawrence had cycled over to Icklingham Hall with me and my finds for Dr and Mrs Sturge. They collected flints and they even had some stone axes, though they looked more like hammers to me. Aunt Bridget had never been there but said they had a whole room full of them in the Hall. Someone had told her they were all spread out on tables and shelves, each with a label.

Flint-hunting was a good thing for me to do because it stopped me from being bored, and it didn't make me wheeze. I wished I was back in Bury near Alison and Lisby, but even before my grandmother's house was bombed we had moved away from our home in the Hardwick House grounds. Father had asked Uncle Arthur if we could stay with him and Aunt Bridget for a while, and they said yes, and at the same time Mr Cullum said that he didn't need Father at present. So we all came to West Stow near where my father grew up. Luckily, we were able to bring Bran too, even though Bran is not a working dog and my uncle thinks there's no point in having a dog unless it's a working one. And now Mother's away helping settle Grandma at my other uncle and aunty's in Downham Market. I didn't go because Mother said it was on the edge of the fens and would make my asthma worse.

It feels much better to be here at West Stow. No-one would bomb fields, would they? And I don't have to go to school and anyway it's nearly the holidays. To begin with Father made me do some schoolwork. He gave me books to read and I had to answer questions about them and learn spellings.

But sometimes we do other things. When he can borrow a horse or get a lift, he takes me to visit some of the friends he's known since he was a boy growing up at Retts House near Elveden. Some of the men we see are quite old, and some have sons or grandsons away at war. Father always comes away from seeing these friends feeling better about Lawrence and Conrad. Now he says it's good to be reminded that they are not on their own: thanks to Kitchener, he says, they are with thousands and thousands of other strong young men.

Father has explained to me about conscripts. Conscription is when the government says men *have* to go to war. Father's changed his mind about it. Now he thinks that England needs more soldiers and that if not enough men volunteer they should have to join the colours even if they don't want to. Uncle Arthur thinks the same. He has no time for men who say they don't want to go into the army. He says they are probably either cowards or lazy, or both.

Whatever Father and his friends are talking about, when it is time for us to leave someone usually mentions the Maharajah or Earl Iveagh or Elveden Hall. That holds us up for another quarter of an hour at least, and afterwards Father will occasionally suggest that we make a detour to visit Elveden Church to see the Maharajah's grave. I always agree because I love that church.

First we look at the three graves of Duleep Singh, his wife and one of his sons, and then we go inside.

It's very big indeed, and Father says that's because it's actually two churches, St Andrew's and St Patrick's. St Andrew's was built first, and when Earl Iveagh moved into Elveden Hall after the Maharajah left, he had the second church built. Behind the altar is a wall of wooden statues. The roof is wooden too, and it has lots of angels. Some are holding musical instruments, like harps and pipes, and some have one of their wings folded. My neck gets tired from looking up at them. And there are pictures on the floor tiles. I like the snakes best, but the fish are good too.

At the back there is a sort of long corridor leading to a bell tower, and if Father lifts me up when there aren't many leaves on the trees, I can see the Hall.

It's more fun to be out with him than back at my uncle and aunt's, but now that he's a Red Cross ambulance man, I can't spend as much time with him as I want to, so when we go to Elveden, I always try to make him stay as long as I can.

That evening of the day I saw the KEEP OUT notice I was worried because Father did not come in when it got dark. The spare horses had been taken from all the farms months ago, and we had to walk or cycle almost everywhere. But then, when I heard a wagon slow down outside the house I guessed Father had managed to get a ride from a neighbour. As soon as I heard him I rushed downstairs with my precious flint.

But instead of taking his boots off as he entered the house and calling out a friendly hallo to whoever was around and taking time to stroke Bran, he was already with my uncle and aunt in the kitchen. He looked tired out and unhappy. Straight away, I wished Mother would come back soon.

"Is there anything to eat, please?" he asked. "I'm famished."

"I'll get you some carrot soup and bread."

"Thanks, Bridget. I'll just go and wash," said Father. "Is there a letter from Hattie?"

"Afraid not. But there's something as good."

Father looked at Bridget with interest.

"A letter from Conrad."

Father's face changed at once to a big smile, and he eagerly took the letter she held out.

"I'll read it while I eat my supper. What a treat."

May 1916

Dear Mother, Father and Elly,

Well, before I forget, thanks for the crosswords. You'd be surprised to know how thinking about 6 Down or 12 Across can stop you from worrying about other things.

Well, the way we're moving now is backwards and forwards. Every so often we take our turn closer to where we expect we might meet Fritz. Then we retreat from wherever we've got to and another bunch like us takes over for their turn. We have a bit of a rest, and then we're back there again.

It's no secret for me to tell you that we're in THE SOMME. *The Somme itself is actually a big* RIVER, *but we've not seen it and I've no idea where it is. By all accounts it's very beautiful, and a few days ago I saw a heron heading west. I hoped it was flying to safety.*

46

In order to extend the trenches we're moving sideways like crabs rather than directly forwards. It doesn't feel dangerous, but I can't deny I'm ACHING and WET and TIRED.

But on the good side I'm proud to be part of a battalion of remarkable lads. You wouldn't believe how much we laugh! We make jokes about things I would never have believed anyone could laugh at. And sometimes we SING.

I'd rather be with you in Suffolk than here in this crowd, but, if the possibility arose, I don't think I could walk away from these fellows now. We belong to each other, and EVERY MAN JACK OF US has sworn that once the war's over we'll stay in touch for ever.

I belong to our family too, of course, and I think of you all often, and thanks so much for your letters. They always cheer me up. I've had two from Lawrence.

His war is very different from mine. It almost feels as if he's on a Boy Scouts adventure, doesn't it? But I wouldn't swap places with him, and anyway, who knows what will come his way in the next few months?

Well, it's late now and there's no daylight to speak of, so I'll sign off. We've had a quieter day today and are told that we should have a quiet night.

I've managed to find a plank and a flattish place to put it, so I might get some sleep, although I'll be sharing it.

I'm sending my love to you all, and hoping that the Zeppelins stay well away from Suffolk.

Your loving son,
Conrad
PS I'm glad the Red Cross work continues well.

May 1916

The next evening I waited until Father was sitting down for his meal before I produced my flint. I was excited while I waited for him to say what he thought of it.

"It's a beauty. Dr Sturge will be very interested."

I wanted him to look at it properly and say more, but he was thinking about something else, and then when he began to eat he opened up the paper and began to read. I was disappointed, but of course he was more interested in the war than in my flint. And Conrad's letter had made him sad. Yesterday, when he'd finished reading it he cried, and I'd never seen him cry before. I thought it meant that Conrad was wounded, but Father said no, he wasn't, but that he had changed. He had been away for eighteen months, and in that time he had changed. I expect he'll probably be even taller when he comes home. And perhaps he's grown a proper moustache, not one that Lawrence used to say looked like a tired toothbrush.

"Tomorrow I'll go back to where I found this flint and look for more good ones."

Father looked up, his spoon halfway to his mouth. "You know they're closing off some areas? You may not be able to go where you usually go."

Even though I knew the reason for this, I asked, "Why not?"

"Tests. More tests. I don't know what exactly, but they're bringing in more troops to guard the training area. Remember, you mustn't go beyond the safe places I've shown you. You know, the places we've talked about."

I was passing my flint from hand to hand as he ate, and it had become quite warm. I looked at it again, ran my finger over the scratches, thought of the dry ditch where I had found it.

At first I had found it hard to pick out flints but when I was quite little, only about seven, Lawrence showed me how to do it. There weren't any flints at Hardwick, but we always found them in the fields at West Stow. The first thing I learned was to search for chippings in the soil. Of course no-one wants chippings, but if you found those you knew that someone had been working flints in that place. Then, when we'd found chippings, Lawrence would choose a section of a likely field and mark out a bit of it about five feet by five feet. He always had a knife with him. He told me that it was always useful to carry one on expeditions, in case you wanted to cut or sharpen sticks, or dig.

Then, promising me that there were several good flints inside the place he'd marked, he'd set me to search. To begin with I just guessed and picked up a few shiny stones, but he said none had the signs to show they were used by early people. Then he showed me what he meant and gradually I began to see what mattered: little scoops of the same size, straight edges, sharp points. Lawrence said I was good at finding them, and I've got even better since I've been here at West Stow. Mrs Sturge said this part of Suffolk is covered with flint, and she's right. It's all flint and chalk. The brecks are best, but she said it's also worth looking along old water-courses and, at this time of year, on field headlands where the crop is still close to the ground. Once the wheat or barley is up it will be impossible.

Clumsily, I let the flint fall from my hands onto the stone tiles with a loud crack, making Father look up with a start.

"Sorry."

Father checked his watch and folded the paper neatly. My aunt and uncle came in from the kitchen. Aunt Bridget sat in the armchair and Uncle Arthur stood by the window with its carefully drawn curtains. They talked about what was in the paper, and I listened for a few minutes. I didn't know the places they mentioned, but I understood that the war wasn't going further away. In fact, it was coming nearer.

I stayed and talked while father ate an apple because otherwise Aunt Bridget might find a job for me. When I first came here I did whatever she asked. She expected me to do some of the jobs, and was shocked that I didn't know how to wash and clean and cook.

"How will you get on when you have a home of your own?" she asked. "You're already nine. When I was nine I had to look after my two little sisters, and keep the fire going and run errands."

I pointed out that I often ran errands, but I didn't dare say that I expected to have a maid, and an outside man, as my parents had done for all my life at Hardwick. Uncle Arthur was older than my father, but he had not been to Cambridge as Father had. Father said he seemed perfectly content running his small farm. When I was little I used to love the calves, and I'd traipse round after the cowman, Lennie, helping when I could. I still go with Lennie sometimes.

If I remained around the house and tried to read, Aunt Bridget would set me a task, but usually she didn't complain if I disappeared once I'd made some sort of effort, such as peeling potatoes or dusting. Wash day was hard work, so I couldn't really not help, and it was true that she had a great deal of extra work because we were staying. When we were at Hardwick, my mother would sometimes sit and read a book with her feet up, but Aunt Bridget never does that.

One day, when I was in the privy with the door shut, I heard Aunt Bridget say to Uncle Arthur, "I just can't understand why Hattie hasn't taught her girl how to do even simple tasks. She can't knit and can hardly sew."

"But she's a bright little thing," said my uncle, "She can read anything, and she can climb trees as well as any boy."

"And what use will that be when she's older? Who wants a wife who can climb trees?"

"Probably no-one, I agree. But she's doing well at school, and there's time enough for her to learn the other things she needs."

I stayed in the privy till I heard them walking up to the house, though I usually got out from there as quickly as I could because of the horrible smell.

June 1916

Everything was ready. Everyone had worked to the utmost of his ability. Now they were waiting on the brand new platform at Barnham station for their first delivery. Colonel Swinton was feeling both optimistic and slightly on edge. So much had happened in four months, more than he had hoped for. Moreover, equally importantly, there had been no breach in security. Even though hundreds of troops were involved, no outsider knew what was happening. So far so good.

Once it had been agreed that Earl Iveagh's estate in Elveden in Suffolk was the best place for the task, and permission had been sought and granted, work got underway.

By the end of April a mock battlefield full of trenches had been created. These were hardly distinguishable from real ones except that, although full of wire, water, boards and metal, they were empty of men. But a month later there were plenty of soldiers in them, engaged in staged assaults. Swinton was amused by the fact that these extraordinary and unexpected operations enabled the estate's pheasants, partridges and rabbits to live much longer than they would have done if the usual shoots were being held. Not only had Earl Iveagh held highly successful shooting parties before the war, but Elveden Hall's previous owner, Duleep Singh, was renowned for the excessive numbers of gamebirds he personally shot on a regular basis. Once, it was rumoured, he had killed nearly a thousand in one day. Swinton's staff were appalled by such unnecessary slaughter and considered it clear evidence of the cruel nature of Indians.

The countryside around Culford Lodge Siding where Swinton and his officers stood was completely black and almost silent, but there was noise in the sky, for planes from Thetford airfield were active. The waiting men were listening intently for different sounds, and at last they distinguished the low rumbles and hissings that heralded a train. Something was appearing from out of the darkness. Swinton approached it as it slowed to walking pace alongside the long platform and its special ramps.

And there was the precious cargo. Not identifiable, of course, for it was well covered in tarpaulins, and its bulky shape suggested a huge tractor, or a container of some sort, or even supplies of some large equipment.

As soon as the train came to a stop soldiers jumped out of nearby trucks and ran onto the platform. Swinton watched his staff supervise the actions they had carefully planned and practised. There was urgency in what they did, but they did not rush as they brought forward lifting equipment, wires, clamps. Occasionally a flare lit up the scene, drawing Swinton's attention to the branch of a tree beyond the station, or the gleam of a guard's weapon, or a man grimacing with effort as he attended to his particular task. *No-one has ever done what we are doing,* Swinton was thinking. *This is something completely new.*

Within two hours the massive object was safely inside the restricted area, the train on its way back to Bury and the station at peace. While Swinton and his senior officers retired to their quarters and drank to the success of their project, several hundred sentries were already in their places making up two defensive cordons round Elveden. Those in the outer cordon, who were almost within speaking distance of one another, had no idea what they were protecting.

May and June 1916

Today is my 10th birthday! It rained all morning but I didn't mind because I was making a cake. It's a sponge cake and I decorated it with some daisies, but they drooped. Aunt Bridget and Uncle Arthur, Mother and Father sang Happy Birthday, and I blew out just one household candle in a candlestick because we have to save them, and no-one has cake candles any more. I did not expect presents, but I was given a new blouse, a book about geology (it has lots of pictures) and a box that locks. I wasn't sure what could go in it, as I don't really have anything special, but then Uncle Arthur gave me half-a-crown, which was very generous, so it'll be a good place for that and my flint money.

Mother told me that some people write their secrets down and put them in a safe place, but I don't have any secrets, and if I did I'm not sure if I'd write them down. I decided that the best place to hide the small key for the box was on a little ridge behind the Lord's Prayer which is hung up on my bedroom wall. You can't see it so you have to feel for it. It'll be quite safe there.

I've tried to find out more about the canvas curtain, but everyone I ask says that it's something important to do with the army, and I should keep well away, just as the notices say. But the day before yesterday I followed it away from here, to the north, towards Elveden. There are no gaps at all, so I climbed up a tree with quite easy branches (Father hadn't said I shouldn't climb trees), and I could see over the top. I thought it might go right round the Elveden estate, fencing it in, even though the land looked exactly the same over there as here – just pine trees and bushes, then heath, but later I found out that it didn't. It was only put up where tracks and paths went into the estate. Anyway, I got down and went on walking and then I heard talking and smelled smoke. Only a few yards away from me, on the other side of the curtain, two men were having a cigarette. Because I could hear them I thought they might have heard me, so I stopped pushing through the bushes and stood completely still. After a few minutes, I heard them set off noisily, and one said, "Watch out for nettles!" loudly.

The explosives must be for blowing up Germany. The soldiers must be experimenting with them. You don't often hear them in the day, but you can at night. Sometimes I lean out of my bedroom window and look at the stars in the blackness. If I shut my eyes and listen carefully I can hear other things too, like night birds, and that dog of Mr and Mrs Naylor's which barks with a wheezing bark. Can dogs have asthma?

And yesterday evening I heard a very different sound. It sounded as if something was in bad pain. A sort of wailing that started and stopped. Could it be a fox caught in a trap? I shut the window because I didn't like it.

Next morning, when I came into the kitchen Aunt Bridget was talking to Father and Uncle Arthur. "It's pitiable," she was saying, "How cruel to do that to men who're doing their best for their country. Poor fellow."

"Field Punishment Number One," said Uncle Arthur. "They've got to have discipline. You don't know what he'd done. For all you know he…" Uncle stopped talking when he saw me.

I poured myself a cup of tea from the pot, cut a slice of bread and put it on the hottest hotplate to toast it. No-one said anything else. Then Father asked, "Elly, what are you up to today?"

"Not sure."

"There's a job you could do for me," said Aunt Bridget. "You could run up the road to Mrs Firth with some jam jars. She's managed to get hold of some sugar and is going to make rhubarb jam, but she's got no jars, and I've a stack of them."

So after breakfast I set out with a string bag full of jars. Perhaps Mrs Firth would repay us in jam.

There was quite a bit going on: a couple of boys were leading a cow down the road on a halter. Two ladies I knew by sight were walking along with brooms, on their way to clean the church. Several men passed me on bicycles and made me think of Lawrence. When he was home on leave before Christmas he went to have a look at his bike in the tack room at Hardwick. He cleared off the cobwebs and oiled it and pumped up the tyres, just so he could have a couple of rides before he left England. When he went away again, Father decided he'd borrow it, so he rode it over here and now it's in Uncle Arthur's woodshed, but Father hasn't used it much.

Mrs Firth was delighted with the jars and gave me a biscuit.

"And what news of your brothers?"

"Conrad's in France."

"How's he getting on?"

I spoke with my mouth full. "He says they only do three things: waiting, getting ready and moving from one place to another. And Lawrence is in India."

"India?"

I nodded. "He's seen a circus!"

"A circus?"

"Yes. There was a man on a tightrope, and monkeys, and tricks with flames."

"Where exactly is he?"

"I've forgotten the name of the place. Father showed me on a map. It's up towards the top of India." I ate the last of the biscuit. "I wish I could go there."

"You're much better off here, Elly. It's safe in Suffolk."

"But what about the Zeppelins? My grandma was nearly killed by a Zeppelin."

"I know, and thank goodness she wasn't. But it's still much safer here than in India."

I thought about this as I walked back. Was Mrs Firth right? Was it safer here than in India? It didn't feel like it. Lawrence hadn't mentioned Zeppelins or bombs or fighting, so India sounded safe to me except for all the dirt. Aunt Bridget said they must get lots of diseases. Lawrence didn't say why the Indians don't clean things up like we do, and Mother said Aunt Bridget should go there and show them how to do it.

And what about the Danger notice? Uncle Eric and Father had warned me several times about Elveden being a dangerous area, and I had only half believed them. I realised now I'd taken a risk by going close to that canvas curtain, and decided to keep away from it from now on.

But those men I had heard talking had sounded quite ordinary. Surely they weren't anywhere near explosives? They sounded more worried about stingers than explosions.

I decided to ask Father if India was dangerous, and I'd ask him what Field Punishment Number One was. But when he came home at lunchtime I didn't get a chance to because he and Uncle Arthur were talking about Earl Kitchener who was on board a ship when it was attacked by the Germans, and he was drowned. Later, I saw a headline in the newspaper about the attack. More than six hundred men died. There was lots of writing about the Earl but all it said about the other men was that they had been drowned too, or lost at sea. I think that being lost at sea must be terrible. You would be under the water, not knowing which way to go because once you had fallen off the ship all you'd be able to see would be waves. And your clothes would become so heavy that you wouldn't be able to swim, like that boy who fell into the Lark and nearly drowned somewhere near Mildenhall last year.

July 1916

Standing orders for the 25th (County of London) Cyclist
Battalion, The London Regiment, August 1912

Appendix A Instructions for Pitching tents

*One N. C. O. and six men (one file as polemen, one as packers,
one as pegmen) are required to pitch each tent.*

*The whole of the tent party, with the exception of the front rank
poleman of each tent, will march off under a Subaltern from
each Company, unpack the wagon and bring up the tents.*

*The Officers Commanding Companies will parade the front
rank polemen in single rank. The polemen will then receive the
word of command. "From the left (or right), --- paces, Extend."*

*The Officers Commanding Companies will dress the men from
left to right of Companies (or vice versa), an Officer covering
them in succession from the front.*

*Each tent squad will bring up a tent, pegs and pole, open the
tent bag, and drive a peg between the heels of the polemen who
will grasp the pole; the tent will then be opened and placed on
the pole. If the tent has storm guys, they will be fixed, and the
ends placed over four pegs driven at right angles to one another,
marking four corners; if the tent has no storm guys, the four red
runners will be held each by a man, the N.C.O. seeing that the
door points the proper way and that the fly is fastened.*

*On all being reported ready the bugle will sound one G and the
whole will be raised at once, the guys fixed, and the pegging
down completed.*

July 1916

The 25th Londons were getting used to India. They ambled around bazaars, smelling pungent spices and raw sewage, sucking sticky sweets and trying out betel. By now they trusted local barbers to shave them with sharp blades and were used to women with marks painted on their foreheads, hands and feet; holy men in prayer covered in ashes; limbless beggars; swaying boxes piled on the heads of men on bicycles; homes built from almost nothing; crops growing in little more than wetted dust.

In June, in Hebbal, they focused on perfecting their musketry. The camp there consisted of nearly three hundred tents. When they saw that some of these had names like *Nick's Nook* and *The Jolly Roger* they thought it promised to be a friendly and relaxing place, but it was from here that they began serious route marching across inhospitable country. Laden with weapons and accoutrements they marched in heat they had never experienced before. The sun, such a friend in England, had become an enemy from which escape was impossible. Every man was exhausted and some became seriously ill, but gradually the troops' ability to cross watercourses, clamber uphill and cope with flies, sand and wind increased to the point where they all recognised they had made improvements. Lawrence was amongst those many men wondering when they would see active service, and impatient for it.

When he had the chance he explored the local area looking out for flowers and plants. From boyhood he had picked and collected all sorts of growing things, and now he carried his sketch pad and pencils when he and Sidney went off in their spare time. Lawrence drew what they came across, and noted dates, weather conditions and soil types, while Sidney made sketches of the landscape. On their wanderings they found rivers, temples, caves, patches of unknown crops and groves of sweet mimosa. All this wasn't what they'd come for, but it wasn't bad.

July 1916

Eric was studying the local paper. He read

The War
The Great Advance
Germans Driven Back
Thousands of Prisoners Captured
Enemy's enormous losses under terrific shell fire

The long expected British and French offensive on the Western Front has begun, and begun well. The feeling of satisfaction with which the news was received on Saturday, when it was stated that the day was going well for the Allies, was confirmed last evening when, in a dispatch printed below, Sir Douglas Haig reported substantial progress, adding that Fricourt, round which furious fighting had raged, had been captured by British troops.

The attack began at 7.30 on Saturday morning north and south of the River Somme, on a front of about 25 miles. North of the river the British captured a labyrinth of German trenches on a front of 7 miles to a depth of 1000 yards and stormed and occupied the fortified villages of Montauban and Mametz.

Farther to the north, on a 4 mile front, the battle on Saturday was most severe and our troops were unable to retain some of the gains made.

The words thudded round Eric's head and he had to read it again. A few days ago, knowing the Push was in the offing, he had not dared to hope, so this news was better than he could have imagined. Of course there was no certainty, but at this minute it seemed more likely than not that Conrad would survive, walk in the door, drop his bag in the doorway and shout, "I'm back!"

"Look, Hattie. Things are going very well."

Hattie put on her glasses and read the brief paragraph for herself. "It doesn't tell us much. There must have been some British casualties, surely?"

"Yes, of course that's likely. But it could be much, much worse, couldn't it?" He got up and put his hand on her shoulder. "We have to keep … oh Hattie, we … "

Since Conrad had been in France Eric had swung between two extremes: longing for the best and, as some sort of preparation for the disaster he dreaded but which might never arrive, making himself think the worst. He could not prevent himself imagining a variety of positive futures for his eldest son: a future in which the war ended tomorrow or one in which he came home only slightly injured and picked up his life from where he had left off.

He was finding that his most vivid memories of Conrad were quite specific; he recalled him as a boy making a trolley and scooting off down that slope at Hardwick House, or complaining about having to do his share of jobs. He remembered the time Conrad cut himself on a nail sticking out of a shed door, and the day he came home triumphant, having secured a job at Greene King. Why was it hard to recall him doing everyday things like walking to church or eating a meal? It seemed that when he tried to summon up a picture of his son, Conrad kept moving just slightly out of view.

" 'Furious fighting,' " said Hattie. "It says there was 'Furious fighting' ".

"There must have been. But we've got to expect that, haven't we? It's war. That's what happens."

Hattie pulled out her hankie from the cuff of her cardigan and blew her nose. Eric leant towards her and stroked her arm.

What was there to say? Their two sons were doing what they should be doing, doing what so many other people's sons were doing. But. But they might be killed. They might both be killed abroad and not come back. And he and Hattie hadn't seen them for months and months. The last time they saw Conrad was in May or June 1915 – nearly a year ago. And although they'd seen Lawrence more recently, last Christmas, it seemed just as long.

Bridget came into the room. She saw at once that Hattie was upset, and bent down to pick up the paper which had fallen to the floor, breathing, "Oh no ….?"

Eric shook his head. "No. No. It's not that. The news is positive. Very positive, as a matter of fact."

Bridget put her arm around Hattie in an unfamiliar but genuine gesture.

Hattie believed that her life would have far less meaning if she had not had children, and over the years she had often felt sorry for Bridget and Arthur because they had none. But now she found herself half envying the fact that they had no-one to lose. And even if the boys … even if the boys didn't come home, she made herself say, she and Eric would still have Elly. Thank God they had one girl. Mr Aitkin, one of the gardeners at Hardwick House, had three sons, all of whom had volunteered. He and his wife were devastated by the death of their middle one a couple of months ago. She must go and see them.

"I need some fresh air." Hattie got up and touched Eric's hand before going out of the room into the kitchen.

Eric heard the latch click on the back door. He didn't follow her, for at times like this she preferred to be on her own. She would be going round to the back of the house to walk a little way along the lane towards the old cattle shed and look across Buttons Acre towards the north. It was a peaceful place and since her arrival at West Stow she went there when she needed some time to herself. First she had been worried about her mother, and now she was in anguish about Conrad. She was usually quite confident about their eldest, for he was the one who dealt with setbacks as if they were challenges, but today Eric saw that she was unable to be optimistic. He thanked God that they did not have to worry about Lawrence too. The worst thing he had reported was bad blisters.

So Conrad might well have reached the Somme, albeit while fighting. After the reference to it in a letter, Eric had looked in Mr Cullum's atlas, as he had looked up the Indus. And there it was, a river he had never heard of before, flowing north-west across a plain. He wondered what name this most recent battle would be given. The Battle of Fricourt, perhaps? Or after one of those villages beginning with M? Or perhaps just Somme, like Gallipoli.

Elly came into the sitting room with her new geology book. "There's a whole chapter on flints."

"Is there?" said Eric.

She felt the emotion in the room but, not knowing what was going on, said, "There's lots about Grimes Graves. Do you think I could go there again?"

"One day, yes. I'm sure you can. I'll take you there, after the war."

"I loved it when we went before. All those little humpy hills. Will we be able to go inside the ground, down into the place where they found the flint?"

"I don't know. We'll see."

"The war's been going on for a very long time already."

Eric nodded. "Nearly two years, and it's not over yet. But things are a bit better for us now, because here in the paper it says that last week our soldiers stopped the Germans from taking more of France and pushed them backwards. We've captured lots of prisoners, too."

Elly held the closed book against her chest and asked, "What happens to the prisoners?"

"They're locked up till the end of the war."

"Where?"

"Some in France and some in other countries where they've been captured. Some are brought here."

Elly stared at him. "To England? Why? We don't want Germans here, do we?"

"Well, we don't want them to escape and go back to join their army again. If they were near where the war is, they might manage to do that, or they might be rescued."

"You're right to be worried, Elly," said Bridget, "I agree entirely. We don't want any Germans here. We only want Englishmen."

"Mother said there are men from other countries at Ampton. She showed me a photo in the paper. There was one from Scotland, one from Canada, another from Russia and even one from India. And I think another one too, but I can't remember where he came from. Mother said they all looked the same when they were in pyjamas and bandages. It was just the Indian who looked a bit different, but not very different. And she said that all of them were fighting for England, and all of them were nice."

Bridget said nothing to this, but her expression caused Eric, in a voice he recognised as overly pleading, to say, "Look Bridget, there's people from all over the place, and a good thing too. We're all human beings, aren't we? We *need* them."

"Well, as long as they're our friends."

Elly opened her book and looked unseeingly at the illustration of a half-clothed man using an antler pick to mine flints.

"Do the Germans ever capture our soldiers?"

"Yes."

"Could Conrad be captured?"

"Elly, it's possible, but I'm sure it won't happen."

"I don't think it will either. He's a fast runner, so he'd probably get away, wouldn't he? He'd zigzag like Lawrence's ship. Then no-one would be able to catch him or shoot him."

Her father did not reply. At his feet Bran yawned, stretched, and curled up again.

Elly asked, "What's Field Punishment Number One?"

"It's a punishment given to a soldier who does something wrong. Like disobeying an important order."

"But what is it? What happens?" Elly held the book horizontally, the edge against her stomach.

Her father took off his glasses and polished them with

his handkerchief. "I don't want to tell you because it's horrible."

"Tell me."

"They tie the man – the man who's done wrong – to the spokes and rim of a big wheel."

Elly waited.

"And they leave him there for a long time – hours sometimes, and of course it hurts him a great deal to have to stay in that position."

"Do you think it would stop him doing anything else bad?"

"I don't know."

"It might not. There would probably have been a reason for him doing what he did. No-one would risk getting such a bad punishment, would they?"

July 1916

This last month at Elveden has been extraordinary. While the mechanics and engineers were perfecting and developing our new machines, others were creating a mock battlefield. We needed German style trenches, abatis, wire entanglements, grenade stores, notices in German, shell craters, exploding mines, breastworks, and enemy troops. We have had to deal with expressions of astonishment from the suppliers of some of our purchases. They can't understand why we need literally hundreds of thousands of sandbags, and vast quantities of petrol. We also need a ready supply of water, which meant we had to drill our own Artesian well.

Hopefully, the writing we've had painted on the land machines in Cyrillic lettering will confuse the enemy. And

I've now employed a camouflage expert. Apparently he's ordered gallons of pink paint, so I hope he knows what he's doing. All this progress has been achieved in a surprisingly short time, and it's been achieved by men who do not know our true purpose, but nevertheless worked like Trojans. I particularly valued the Welsh troops who came here. They were miners to a man, and they sang their way through their work with spirit.

We've had to let the officers know what we are up to and now we've told Earl Iveagh. Having requested a meeting with him, he invited us into his magnificent Elveden Hall. It has a copper dome, scalloped onion-shaped arches and tons and tons of marble exquisitely carved by Italian craftsmen. There's a vast, lofty room decorated in ornate, opulent style by the Hall's former owner, Duleep Singh, an Indian. We spread maps out on the billiard table and outlined what we intend to do with our tanks. Everyone was sworn to secrecy.

And yesterday the Secretary of State for War came to inspect our progress, and we set out to impress him. The machines and their crews paraded in front of him before going into a mock battle, and a flag was raised and a smoke rocket set off. He was fascinated as he watched our monsters climb ramps, reach across trenches and remain unaffected by violent assaults. According to the terrain and what they faced, the huge things reared up, swung round and reversed, all the while making their distinctive and infernal noise. The platform we had prepared for Lloyd George shook slightly when the bombardments were heavy, and I noted him pull his hat down solidly on his head and tug his trademark cloak firmly round him.

The day was a great step forward. I retired exhausted

but entirely satisfied. Our next guest will be His Majesty, and I now feel confident that we can put on a show which cannot fail to win him over.

July 1916

In yesterday's paper one of the reports of a soldier's death said

We record with sincere regret the death of Prvt R O S Walpole, only son of Mr HOC Walpole, solicitor, of Bury St Edmunds, who was killed in action in France on July 1st, the date of the initial stage of the great and successful British advance against the Germans.

The deceased has the distinction of being the first member of the Walpole family to give his life for his country and the field of battle.

I wondered about this. The report seemed to be saying two things at once. Obviously it was a bad thing to be killed in action, because it meant you were dead. But did being dead also mean that you were special? I've never heard either Father or Mother say that they want Conrad or Lawrence to be special. They're special anyway. Everyone's special to their family. What families want is for soldiers to come home safely.

Recently I have noticed two things that have changed from the way they were. The first is that in the paper the list of men who have been killed is getting longer and longer. The second is that until very recently, no-one, not even Uncle Arthur, was saying anything about this, but now they are. I think the war is definitely getting worse.

Today, when I'd read the parts of the paper I usually look at, I decided to escape before Aunt Bridget could find me a job. Things were a bit boring now, because my parents were often at Ampton Hall or Ingham. Mother especially seems to be out most of the time, and a few days ago I heard Father tell her he thought she was working too hard. But she answered that she needed to, and that everyone needed to while there was a war on.

"But you're not used to it, and you hardly sit down except on Sundays."

"I'm quite all right. It's true that I've never been so busy in my life. I've been lucky – I've never had to earn my living, but now I've a chance to help people, and I want to do as much as I can."

"Don't do too much, Hattie. I don't want you to get ill. Physically, women aren't as strong as men."

"Eric. Please believe me. Although I'm on my feet all day I'm not lifting big loads or doing anything really strenuous."

I liked hearing about Ampton, and Mother told me that the next time they had a concert or tea party when visitors were allowed in, she would take me, as long as my asthma wasn't bad.

One afternoon I set off walking towards Icklingham without Aunt Bridget noticing. I was thinking again about Dr Sturge's flints sitting on the shelves with their labels, and I planned to ask if I could cycle over to his house, but there wasn't enough time to go today. One day, I thought, I would walk to Icklingham along the River Lark with Father. He had shown me on a map how once he went as far as Mildenhall, and then on to where the Lark met the Great

Ouse. He said the Lark was very small compared to the Ouse, but in those days it carried plenty of boats carrying coal. Now it was rare to see anything bigger than a rowing boat.

The heath was on one side of me and the river on the other. I counted four herons, and the sky by the church was full of swifts. I was missing Alison and Libby and wondered whether Father would agree to take me to Bury on a Saturday when someone was giving him a lift there or whether either of my friends could be brought to us. Opposite me a wide, damp meadow sloped down to the river, past clumps of bushes and a line of trees. The hedges I passed were noisy with small birds.

Ahead, I saw a boy fishing in the river, and the path I was on meant I had to walk right past him. He noticed me coming, and I thought perhaps he was from the Hunt family I'd heard about. They had four boys. I wasn't sure whether to go near him or not, but it'd seem silly if I just turned round and went back the way I had come, so I carried on. As I approached, he caught a fish. He was so pleased that he shouted and I watched him wind it in.

"It's big! Look!"

I went up closer and looked at the fish. It wasn't big at all, and it was wriggling and flopping about as the boy lowered his rod to the ground. It was gasping like I do when I wheeze, and the boy hit it on the head with a stone until it bled and was still.

"What did you do that for?"

"To make it die quicker."

"It would have died more peacefully if you'd left it."

"It was in pain." The boy loosed the fish from the hook and put it in a bag. "So I put it out of its pain."

I didn't say anything, but *I* wouldn't like to be hit on the head if I had a hook in my mouth and couldn't breathe. Several dragonflies zoomed across the water in their coupled flights. The surface, reflecting the sky, was a very blue blue. As blue as cornflowers.

"It's only a *fish*," he said.

I stayed to watch him open a small tin, pick out a couple of wriggling worms and push them onto the fishhook. Then he cast his line again and when the little float was bobbing up and down he turned to look at me. He was a year or two older than me.

"You're staying at West Stow, aren't you?" he asked.

"How do you know?"

"Are you?"

"Yes. It's safer here than in Bury."

"We had Zeppelins here in February," said the boy. "Do you know what they killed?"

"No."

"Guess."

"A person?"

He shook his head.

"A horse?"

"No. Hens. They dropped bombs on fields over there, and all they hit was two hens!"

I decided not to say anything about Grandma. I just kept my eyes on the wavering float.

"My uncle's fighting in France," said the boy.

"So's my brother. And my other brother is in India."

"India? What's he doing there?"

"He's a soldier too."

"But there's no Germans in India!"

A lark rose up above us in full song and I tipped my

head back and searched for it. I had to half-close my eyes against the sun.

After a bit the boy asked, "D'you know when the tunnel will be finished?"

"What tunnel?"

"The one at Elveden."

"Elveden? I don't know what you mean."

"The tunnel they're building to France."

I had no idea what the boy was talking about and he could see that, so he said, "You know those notices telling people to keep out?"

I nodded.

"Well, the reason they want people to stay out is because they're digging a tunnel to France."

"But France is miles and miles away. It's on the other side of the sea. They'd have to dig under the sea. That's impossible."

"They're making some special machines to do it. It won't be finished for a year at least, but then our soldiers will go in and surprise the Germans and kill them all."

I stared at him. "That's not true."

"I'm telling you. It's true. My father told me."

"How does *he* know?"

"One of the officers told him."

Then the boy asked, "Have you heard the war at night?"

I shook my head. "They don't fight during the night. In my brother's letter he said that they try to sleep at night."

"Some do, but not all of them. You should listen. You can't hear the booms in the day time, but you can at night when there's not many other noises."

I said, "I've never heard them," and turned to go back.

"Where are you going?"

"Home."

"Don't tell anyone about the tunnel, will you? It's secret. If you tell anyone my father will get into trouble, and so will you. You might even start a war here."

I was about to walk away, but he called out, "Promise you won't tell anyone. Go on. Promise. You don't want to make the war worse, do you?"

I looked at him. Then I said, "I promise."

"You should come here on a hot day," called the boy. "This is a good place for swimming."

I ran most of the way home because I didn't feel safe, but I had to stop because I couldn't breathe properly. Perhaps they really were building a tunnel. No wonder the notices said Danger. Perhaps it really was possible to hear the war at night. I wheezed for ages.

August 1916

Dear Mother and Father,

We're still at Hebbal, and we're still going for those terrible route marches which whack us out. It's all exercises of course – please don't think we're actually engaged in any real action. The only enemies in sight are other troops playing the part of tribesmen we have to track and shoot at. For some reason we Londons (I've become quite used to calling myself a London) never get the chance to be the enemy, which is a pity because it's quite good fun to do that.

The locals here are entirely friendly towards us and they work for us for practically nothing. I've had a twisted ankle (it's better now) which prevented me from having to do one of the marches, and while I was resting one of the wallahs washed every item of my clothing for a few annas. These particular natives aren't dirty – but many are.

Quite a few men collapsed because of the heat and exertion, including my friend Sidney. However, yesterday he was well enough to have a pint with me at The White Queen. Did I tell you there were several pubs here? The trick is to cover your beer when you're not actually drinking it, or you get sand or flies in it. Usually both. And I forgot to say that in some places when you are carrying your plate of food from the mess to where you're going to eat it, you have to keep waving your spare hand over the plate to prevent the kite-hawks from swooping down and grabbing it.

Have I thanked you for the papers you sent? It was so good to get those. We all swap what we've got and someone lent me a cycling magazine which made me long to be speeding along to Archie and Ed Welham in Chedburgh, or going into Bury to meet Jack etc. A couple of us borrowed bikes, but the roads are only stony tracks so cycling is hard work, and even if you are lucky enough not to get a puncture you have to keep out of the way of donkeys and oxen and even camels!

I've got two special things to tell you about. The first is that a few days ago we had a big parade to mark the second anniversary of the declaration of war. As well as all those tents I told you about there's a big open space called the Maidan. We use it for drill and parades and sports. Luckily, that day wasn't as hot as it sometimes is, so no -one fainted. We didn't get a holiday, worse luck, but it made a change. Crowds of people came to see us and cheer, and the flag was raised and someone made a speech and the drummers drummed, and we had good food. It wasn't until the end of the day that I really considered the reason for the parade. Sidney and I talked about it a lot, but it would take too long to explain what I mean in this letter. So, although we can't deny we had a good day, celebrating going to war was (as Father would say)"food for thought".

The other interesting thing was a snake charmer. We've already seen quite a few old Indians with long beards charming snakes out of pots and asking for money, but this was something special. This particular man was squatting by the roadside playing his pipe and I got right to the front. Someone was playing a tom-tom which added to the atmosphere. The man started off with a few juggling tricks I'd seen before, and he showed people his snakes.

And then from his bag he produced the dried skin of a smallish snake (about eighteen inches long) which he waved about and shook while he muttered some mumbo-jumbo. Then he put it away in a basket and began to sing in a strange voice, and cast more spells. Then he made marks on the ground and generally built up the tension. By this time he had collected quite a crowd.

Finally, to the beating of the drum and the sound of the pipe, the lid of the basket rose up, pushed by ….

a large, live python!

It was a monster. First the head appeared, and then more and more body. The snake charmer held the head, but invited us to support the body, and at first only Phil dared do it, but in the end there were six of us (including me!) holding it, so it must have been at least ten feet long! We couldn't work out how it had managed to fit into the basket.

Elly, I think you would have loved it, but perhaps you would have been scared stiff. Girls are usually scared of snakes. Anyway, I was scared!

I think I told you we've seen butterflies, but recently we've been finding fireflies. They're amazing little creatures. (When I get the chance I'm going to buy a magnifying glass so I can examine all the flowers and bugs I'm finding). We saw plenty of fireflies when we climbed Bull Mountain (we can see BM from our camp). There are hundreds of steps to the top, and halfway up is a huge stone bull. Watching the sunset from there was marvellous. Is there anything like this in England? I've no idea, but being here makes me want to explore as much of the world as I can.

We sometimes go swimming in a lake near here. The name of the place sounds like Setantpurr but that's not the proper spelling.

It'll soon be harvest time at home and I can get a bit homesick if I think about hay making and reapers and thrashing engines. You'll be in the middle of it in West Stow. I can imagine the reaper starting at the edge of the field and going round in smaller and smaller squares until there's only a tiny bit of the crop left standing in the middle, and the rabbits have to run for their lives. Does Uncle Arthur still shoot the rabbits? I used to hate him for doing that when I was little. There are small fields of arable land here, but I don't know what they're growing. Some sort of cereal, but not wheat or barley. And nothing is green. The whole place is brown – much browner even than the brecks during a hot summer.

We don't know when we're moving from here but it won't be long, because we know from what the officers are saying that we're doing well and will soon be ready for what's ahead. I feel good too. You'd be surprised if you could see how muscle-y I am! Conrad would be astonished at the strength of his younger brother - I'm sure I'd beat him in an arm wrestle!

And right now I'm going to have a game of tennis with Sidney, if we can grab a court.

So, all my love to all of you,

Your loving son,
Lawrence

August 1916

Eric picked up the telegram which, as soon as it had arrived that morning, he had placed leaning against the mantel-piece. It had been there for three hours and he could no longer resist opening it, so he did so.

The words *Conrad P. Bailey* were written by hand across the centre of the paper.

Infantry Record Office

Sir and Madam,

It is my painful duty to forward the enclosed message of sympathy from Their Gracious Majesties the King and Queen. I am at the same time to express the regret of the Army Council at the soldier's death in his country's service.

The report is to the effect that he was Killed in Action in the field in France on July 1st 1916.

I am to add that any information that may be received as to the

soldier's burial will be communicated to you in due course. A
separate booklet dealing more fully with this subject is enclosed.

I am,
Sir,
Your obedient servant

He turned the paper over, and found on the reverse

NOTE

If any articles of private property are found they will be
forwarded to this office but some time will probably elapse
before their receipt, and when received they cannot be disposed
of until authority is received from the war office. Some delay is
therefore inevitable.

Any application …

He stopped reading, sat down, wondered again whether he
should have waited for Hattie to come back from Ampton.
But it was too late now, for now he knew that their eldest
son had been killed on July 1st and Hattie did not. And he
could not undo that knowledge which was spreading
through him like intense heat. He had to hurry to the privy
to relieve himself.

Strangely, although it was so unimportant compared to
the real message of the telegram, he found himself wondering why it had taken six whole weeks for this news to reach
them. Surely such important information could have been
communicated faster than that? He and Hattie had not
voiced their concerns about the recent lack of letters from
Conrad, for neither wanted to make the other anxious. A
similar gap in correspondence had happened the previous

year – they hadn't heard from him for a month, and then they received eight letters at once – so they trusted that an absence of letters might not mean the worst. However, it was unusual. They were also aware that sometimes letters just disappeared. But here, in his hand, was the letter they had hoped never to receive.

Eric read it again, looking at every detail of Army Form B 104-82. He checked Conrad's name, number and regiment. They were all correct. He was able to decipher the name of one of the signatories but not the other. He noticed how a fold in the paper separated, untruthfully and illogically, the place of death from the date of death.

He cursed himself for opening the letter without Hattie. How had he thought that it might be better for him to know first? Could he have been able to break the news to her more gently than this thin piece of paper with its enclosed booklet about burial? Of course not. There was no hope of gentleness. No hope of anything other than grief.

He heard the back door open, Perhaps Hattie was home early? But it was Bridget who came in, complaining about soldiers swimming in the Lark in the nude. Eric put the letter away in his pocket hurriedly. His wife should to be the next to know, not his sister-in-law. He hardly looked at Bridget as he got up and went out, saying, "I need to see Hattie," and he did not heed the expression of surprise and concern on her face.

August 1916

Elly, shocked by Conrad's death and her parents' pain, stayed out of everyone's way. She hid herself in sheds, and did not answer when Aunt Bridget called her.

She thought about her brother a lot. After she heard the news she went up close to his photo on the mantelpiece and studied it. Conrad was wearing uniform and appeared serious. His cap didn't look too secure. He had a small mole on his left cheek, which she'd forgotten. She recalled him sitting on a horse, for he had loved riding – as long as he was on a horse, not a bike. He had never understood Lawrence's passion for cycling at all. And she remembered how, when she was little, she used to beg Conrad to swing her round by her hands, or, even better, by an arm and a leg, until she ended up in a dizzy heap on the grass.

He wouldn't be bringing home any more silver cups for cricket. Nor would he bore the family with details of the brewery and beer, nor go to the Bury Empire and insist on telling the family, before any of them had seen it, the entire story of a film and his opinion of it. Father used to say that Conrad was larger than life, and she'd known what he meant. But now, it suddenly struck her, death had made him small.

Elly was told that he had died in the Somme, in France. She had once seen a dead, half-submerged sheep in the Lark, and now she imagined Conrad's body floating along the river's surface with other Englishmen, all joined together in a sort of raft buoyed up by the air in their uniforms. Would the current push them as far as the sea, or would they sink to the bottom before then?

She dared not ask exactly what had happened to him, but she wanted to know where Conrad himself was. Not his body, but his *self*. Heaven didn't seem likely, because there clearly wasn't room there for the souls of everyone who had ever died, even if lots of people went to hell. Where could he be? And what could he be doing?

Over the following days Elly wondered too how long the sadness would last. Recently her father had told her that every soldier's death announced in the Bury Free Press was put there by a family who was mourning, and that most people took a very long time to recover from their unhappiness. Mother seemed to be the saddest person in the house, but she also said it was no good being like that for ever, and that soon she would go back to Ampton and do what she could to help the men being brought from the front. Father would continue his work too, for convoys continued to come.

But why so many of them? Father and Uncle Arthur said that England had pushed the Germans back weeks ago. Surely that meant that there would be more dead and wounded Germans, not Englishmen? She didn't understand what it said in the paper either, because although it said the English had won a victory, the lists of the dead were getting even longer. Strangely, it turned out that lots of men had been killed on the very same day as Conrad. Elly wondered if it was an unlucky day like Friday the thirteenth, so she checked on her aunt's Beautiful Villages calendar. The picture for July showed Polperro in Cornwall, and when Elly had first seen it, she loved the way the houses gathered round the harbor and how the photographer had made it look as if the gulls were sailing through that odd name, Polperro. But now she saw that July 1st had been a Saturday, which showed that you can't tell whether a day will be lucky or not. Anyway, a day which was unlucky for one army was obviously lucky for its enemy.

Elly was also worried about the tunnel, even though that boy (whose name she now knew was Dan Hunt) had said it was the way to win the war. Yes, it was true that

English soldiers could go through it and surprise the enemy, but what if the Germans found it and sent all *their* troops through it, and they turned up in Elveden? It was hard not to tell her parents about the tunnel, especially now that Conrad's death made the war seem even nearer, but she had promised Dan that she wouldn't. It would be so terrible if she did anything that led to more war. Instead, months ago, in her attic room, she had written on a piece of paper.

The army may be digging a tunnel from Elveden to France. If they do, English soldiers could go into France (a good thing) or German soldiers could come to England (very bad). This may not be true. But it might be. Signed Eleanor Barbara Bailey. May 16th. 1916.

She had hidden this in her box, locked the box, and hidden it and, in a separate place, the key.

When, by chance, she had met Dan again a few weeks later, he had said a German invasion through the tunnel wouldn't happen, but could give no reason as to why it wasn't possible. When Elly had told him about Conrad he had become quieter, and he told his brother Greg to shut up because he was shouting about how, if he was in charge of England, he would make more aeroplanes to bomb all of Germany.

"Can't you see Elly's upset?"

"I'm only trying to make her feel better."

"Talking like that doesn't help."

One evening she heard Father telling Mother that he had had a bad day, because when the convoy arrived at Ingham, one man was already dead. He had died on the journey from London.

Elly wasn't supposed to be listening, but, sitting at the

top of the stairs in her blue nightdress, she could hear everything. Father said they had dealt with the walking wounded first and then the stretcher cases, as usual. Then, when the platform was almost empty, he and another ambulance man had carried the dead man from the train into a van so he could be driven to Ampton. Father thought he would be buried the next day at Ingham church, near the others who had died in hospital.

Her father said he had felt terrible and had found himself thinking of the dead man as Conrad. He said, "I wanted to do all I could for him, so I lifted the handles of the stretcher carefully so we would not jog him. I wanted Conrad to come home, so I thought of this body as him coming back to where he belonged. Hugh, the other ambulance man, had to walk at the front because I was crying and couldn't see where I was going. We moved slowly, taking our time, taking Conrad's time, taking the dead man's time. That's how it was."

When Elly heard Mother and Father crying she cried too, then ran downstairs and hugged them as hard as she could, and they hugged her.

"We've just got to get through it," said Eric. "As best we can."

September 1916

A few weeks later, when Elly was walking a little way along the road with Father, as she sometimes did when he was going to Ingham, Mr Mellis came to speak to them. By now, all the neighbours knew Conrad had been killed, and everyone was polite and friendly and sad, all at once. After

Father and Mr Mellis had had a few words, Mr Mellis turned to Elly and asked with a smile, "And how are you, young lady?"

She didn't answer, so he said, "Are you going to the sports at Elveden next week?"

"Sports? What sports?"

"They're having a sports day on the 15th. I think you'd enjoy it."

Elly hadn't heard anything about it, and nor had Father, so Mr Mellis told them that on Saturday the Royal Defence Corps was organising races and games, and that it wasn't just for the army, but for the public. Elly immediately wanted to go, but she knew she wouldn't be allowed to because of Conrad.

However, her father said he thought it would be a good thing because they needed to get on with their lives in a positive way. Then Mother said, though she cried when she said it, that Conrad used to love sports days and would have wanted Elly to go. But Elly was worried as to whether she was sad enough about her brother. Was it wrong to go the sports? If she wasn't as sad as her parents were, which she didn't think she was, did this mean she was a bad person?

"Of course you're not bad!" said Mother. "And wanting to go to the sports doesn't mean that you didn't love Conrad. Young people are better than older ones at getting on with things, and that's exactly what you're doing," and she hugged Elly hard, and her tears made Elly's collar all wet.

It was arranged that on Saturday Mr and Mrs Mellis would pick Elly up from the farm and take her to Elveden in their car – a rare treat. Their son was coming too, but he was only six, and Elly wished that her friends Libby and Alison could be there instead. On the day the Mellis family found a good place to watch the events from, and laid out a tarpaulin and a rug. Elly forgot all about the tunnel and only thought about Conrad part of the time.

She had a wonderful afternoon. There were funny races like a whistling race, a three-legged race, a beer race, a sack race and a book race. One man, dressed as a clown, tied one of his legs to one man and the other to another for the three-legged race, so they couldn't walk at all. Then there was wrestling on horseback and tilting the bucket. Mrs Mellis brought some sandwiches and biscuits, so they had a picnic too, which was a treat. In fact, it was better than her birthday, but Elly felt bad for thinking that.

While she was sitting on the rug, Mr Mellis was talking to a man and his two boys. The sons were older than Elly but younger than Lawrence. The man had light brown skin, the colour of weak tea, and both boys had hair the colour of the very strong black tea that Uncle Arthur liked to drink without milk but with plenty of sugar – when it was available.

When the man had walked on, Elly asked, "Mrs Mellis, why is that man brown?"

"Which man, Elly?"

"The one Mr Mellis was just talking to," Elly pointed. "The one with the two big boys."

"Don't point, dear," said Mrs Mellis. "Well, we're all different, aren't we? Perhaps they're from another country. Italy, perhaps or Spain."

"Or India," said Elly. "Indians have brown skin."

Then Mr Mellis said that he had been at school with

Reg Bullett, and that his hair had once been like that of his sons. "They're not foreign, he said. "The Bulletts are English through and through. My father knew Reg's father."

September 1916

We were going to have to send the tanks to France before we had finished training men thoroughly. This was not as it should be, and I would rather have waited, but my opinion was overruled in this matter. So I sought and gained permission to use the farmhouse here on Earl Iveagh's land for target practice. It was a substantial building, but elsewhere ammunition ricocheted up to the north and put civilians in danger. So, this was the only place we could use, and I already made it quite clear that I would refuse to send men to France who'd never fired a shot on the move.

Within a few days the tanks did a good job of destroying some of the farmhouse walls and its roof. So far so good. I was very confident that our huge machines would make a great difference to our progress in the war.

Because we were short of training time, I thought it would be useful for the troops to have a list of instructions. I used simple, short instructions in everyday language so that anyone could understand them easily.

TANK TIPS

Remember your orders.
Shoot quick.
Shoot low. A miss which throws dust in the enemy's eyes is better than one which whistles in his ear.

Shoot cunning.
Shoot the enemy while they are rubbing their eyes.
Economise ammunition and don't kill a man three times.
Remember that trenches are curly and dugouts deep – look round the corners.
Watch the progress of the fight and your neighbouring tanks.
Watch your infantry whom you are helping.
Remember the position of your own line.
Smell out the enemy's machine guns and other small guns and kill the first with your 6-prs.

You will not see them for they will be cunningly hidden. You must ferret out where they are, judging by the following signs:

Sound
Dust
Smoke
A shadow in a parapet
A hole in a wall, haystack, rubbish heap, woodstack, pile of bricks
This will usually be placed to fire slantwise across the front and to shoot along wire

One 6-pr shell that hits the loophole of an MG emplacement will do it in.

But at the very end, on the very day when we put our arrangements (necessarily complex) into practice, and at last had them ready to be moved from here by rail on flatbed loaders, Zeppelins appeared at night.

They arrived when men were working under acetylene lights to assemble and pack up and load all the ammunition, sponsons, spare guns and so on which had to be sent on to the tanks which had left. I was sure that the Boche must have learned about what we were up to, and would target us. We extinguished the lights, laid low and held our breath as the closest airship nosed its way above us, humming like some giant poisonous bee. It dropped a bomb on the edge of the estate, but did no real harm, and at last it headed north-east towards Thetford. I breathed with relief when it was confirmed that no tanks had been damaged.

September 1916

Hattie was now as busy at Ampton as she had been before we heard about Conrad, but she had not regained her customary steady self. It was at home that she let out her emotions. She was often in tears, and we both knew we just had to let time pass. September 10th was going to be difficult because it was her birthday.

That morning, Bridget, who had managed to find some dried fruit from somewhere, was going to make a cake. Elly had gone out to seek some small stones and flowers to make a miniature garden on a tray, with a tiny mirror for a pond.

I walked down the road with Hattie, and we noted how the leaves on the horse chestnut were changing colour. I squeezed her hand as we approached another lady who was also a VAD at Ampton. Each morning they waited together at the corner for a lift from one of the doctors. I saw them into the car and waved them off. I felt relieved Hattie was going to be occupied all day and would have little time to think about what she – what we - most wanted but would never have.

I started back up the road, crunching on acorns under the oak. I stretched up to reach a few blackberries from a bush. Hayricks stood in rows and two pairs of horses pulled harrows across dry, brown fields. From the other direction I heard a tractor. It sounded like Percy Horrex's new Ransome. I waited till it came into sight, looking forward to shouting a greeting to whoever was driving it. Ted, maybe, or Cyril. But it was a woman. It was the first time I'd seen a woman drive a tractor, and I waved a wave of encouragement to her. She must be one of the WLA girls employed by George Abley. Good for her.

That morning I had promised to help Arthur mend the chicken shed, and as I came through the gate I saw that he had already taken the tools round to the run. I was thankful that I, as well as Hattie, had some task to focus on. Rex, Arthur's sheepdog, was nosing around happily, pleased to be out of his kennel.

About fifteen minutes later the postman arrived on his bike and handed me several letters. One was a military one and I recognized the handwriting as soon as I took it. I was completely taken aback and my hand was shaking when Arthur appeared carrying a roll of chicken wire over his shoulder.

I held out the letter towards him and said, "It's from Conrad."

He lowered the wire to the ground, resting it on one end. "*Conrad*?"

"Yes." Perhaps he wasn't dead. Perhaps he wasn't dead. "But, how .."

"I don't know." I didn't know what had happened, but immediately I saw the envelope hope surged through me that Conrad was alive and that the notification of his death had been wrong. Such things were not unheard of. I wanted to open the letter there and then but I had so regretted opening the last one without Hattie (though she had never given a hint that I should not have done so) that I made myself save this one until she was home.

"Come on," I said. "Let's do the chicken shed." I put the letter safely in the breast pocket of my shirt.

Rex stayed close as we replaced several rotting fence posts and dug the new ones in well, wedging them in with stones. I held them firm while Arthur fixed netting to them. Then we worked on the shed, shoring up holes and repairing the roof. While my hands were hammering and sawing, my mind was imagining scene after scene: Conrad safe with his fellow Tommies; Conrad captured in a camp; Conrad wounded and being looked after. I also forced myself to consider the possibility that the letter had been written before he was killed, and subsequently delayed. As I veered between hope and despair, I tried to follow Arthur's simple instructions.

As usual when working, he said little apart from "A bit more to the right, Eric," or, "Can you tug that corner tight?"

I asked him not to mention the letter to Elly or Bridget, and when we went in for lunch Elly was there, wanting to show me her garden. She had crunched up dry leaves to look like a path, and stuck twigs of red berries into little balls of mud for bushes. She'd made a shrubbery out of beech mast and a fence of feathers.

"Mother will love it," I said.

Elly smiled. "I hope it makes her happy."

I looked out of the window to where the elderberry bush was heavy with its dark, gleaming fruit.

"She'll love it."

I filled in the two hours before Hattie returned moving barrow-loads of wood closer to the house from where they'd been tipped out of a cart by the roadside. Bridget brought out a pot of tea at about three o'clock, and Arthur left his digging and joined me on the bench, in the sun. Rex sat at his feet. Though it was already September, it was still warm.

When we were alone Arthur asked, "When do you think Conrad wrote that letter?"

I hesitated. "I don't know."

"Do you think he's alive?"

I couldn't speak, but just put my hands over my face.

Elly came with me when I went to meet Hattie that afternoon, so I could say nothing until she had given her mother the miniature garden and run off to lay the table for supper. As soon as we were alone I gave Hattie the letter. On seeing the military issue envelope she gasped. "Oh … not Lawrence too?"

"Look at the handwriting."

Breathing hard she looked more carefully, then sat down. "You open it," I said.

She did, and inside was a letter dated June 23rd.

Dear Mother, Father and Elly,

Well, we're nearly at the push. I can't tell you how good it feels to be surrounded by thousands and thousands of troops who're all determined to wipe Fritz out. The enemy CAN'T *have as many men as we do. Last night we were allowed to light fires, so we did, and we* SANG, *and it was a wonderful experience to be warm and alive and close to so many friends you've shared so much with. It's a sort of love.*

And this morning, when we had decamped and were on the road towards the front, it poured and poured, and now we've just been told we'll be here for at least two days. I'm sheltering under a broken door in a dilapidated house in some deserted village and am writing this in a hurry because someone who's going in the other direction has promised to take the letter to the post for me. I HOPE YOU GET IT SOON.

This week I was told that I'm to be offered a commission. What do you think of your son becoming a Second Lieutenant? I can't wait!

So you can imagine me wet but beginning to STEAM *because it's crowded here, and waiting for a meal and then, I hope, getting a few hours' sleep before tomorrow which will surely be better than today.*

I'm thinking of you in Suffolk, and I'D GIVE ANYTHING TO BE WITH YOU THERE NOW. *It would be good to be doing something like strolling in the Abbey Gardens. But from where I am now, it's hard to think back to Bury. I can hardly remember how to get to the Abbey Gardens. It's a lifetime away.*

ANYWAY, I'M HERE IN FRANCE. *That's the way it is, so I'm going to live this next day and the next one, and more, in the company of good friends. Friends I would never have made if I'd stayed at home.*

Well, Mother and Father and Elly, I think of you often. And of course I think of Lawrence too but I've not written to him because writing's hard in these conditions and I know you'll be telling him about me, so please send him a friendly punch.

Your loving son, Conrad

Underneath he had added,

And all the best to my aunt and uncle.

September 1916

From the Bury Free Press

Caterpillars and Tanks
Britain's New Weapons at the Front
Super Motors
Germans Bewildered and Terrified
Consternation Among the Foe

Our readers will be deeply interested in the revolution which has been brought about in the fighting line in France by the arrival of some weird and wonderful British engines of destruction which are picturesquely described as "Caterpillars" and "Tanks". These are the serious names for these terrible annihilators of the Boche and Hun entanglements and entrenchments.

A war correspondent describing its work says

Our troops sweeping up towards Flers were followed by a new and wonderful type of armoured motor which I had mysteriously heard referred to as "Land Dreadnoughts". We were stalking the enemy with great weird-looking monster shapes of steel which paralysed their defence. The prisoners gasped and protested against our methods of waging war.

October 1916

From Eyewitness, Swinton

By command of the King, I went down to Windsor to report the progress of events in France. Next day, with two officers from the War Office, I made a tour of inspection to find a more suitable training-ground than Elveden for the projected, enlarged Heavy Section. This visit resulted in the establishment of the unit at Bovington in Dorset. Meanwhile, training was to continue at Elveden until a move could be made.

On the 4th October I paid another visit to the Front. Establishments were being framed for what was now to be a corps of nine battalions. So far I had heard the scheme only vaguely outlined. The centre of gravity of the whole thing seemed to have swung over to the GHQ which was assuming control and working out the organisation for the expanded unit. For me it was a puzzling and embarrassing situation. Possibly I was not very discerning, but I did not in fact realise what was happening until I was taken aside by an officer and told in confidence that he had heard that I was to be superseded. In a certain circle the cry - or, as yet, to be more accurate, the whisper - had gone round, "Swinton must go".

I now had to carry on until my successor was appointed. The nature of the work did not change, but with the departure of "B" Company, the extreme strain eased off. As Tanks came to hand, the training of the two companies left at home was continued. The question of stores, spares and equipment generally was very complicated and still demanded a great deal of attention.

Preliminary steps were taken towards the move from Elveden to Bovington. At home there was to be a Training Headquarters, and in France a Fighting Headquarters, each with a full set of regular officers, and measures were set on foot for the raising of five new battalions.

October 1916

Eric accepted the package from the postman and saw at once that it was from Lawrence. Good. He thought it might be another copy of *The Times of India*, because he had asked Lawrence to send him a few. He opened it eagerly but it was not *The Times of India*. It was *The Londoner*, and a short note.

Dear Father and Mother,

We're just off back to Bangalore but I wanted to post you our battalion magazine before I went. Do read it (I think it's ruddy good) but please make sure you keep it. I'm going to collect them if they go on being as good as this one. I hope you like Nancy's Beauty Hints!

Got to go – I'm being shouted at.

Forgot to say thanks for your last letter and the socks. I'll write from Bangalore.

Your loving son, Lawrence

Eric was on his way out to Ingham so he left the magazine on the table for Arthur. When he got back a few hours later, Arthur greeted him enthusiastically.

"This *Londoner* is amazing. There's articles about the orchestra, a ramblers' weekend, the history of the battalion, chess. And advertisements too, for Indian printing, motor repairs, even silverware. I'm astonished. And it's funny too. Here, read this bit."

"Hang on, let me get my boots off." Eric sat down to unlace his boots while Bran sniffed round him, wagging his tail in welcome.

"I'll read it out. It's about the YMCA:

Mr Waldo Hunt, who has lately taken over the YMCA at Hebbal Camp, tells us that we may expect considerable improvements in the appearance and condition of the tents, including the provision of newspaper stands and some new games. He hopes to be able to arrange a programme for the thatched building adjoining the tents covering 5 nights a week and including lantern lectures, impromptu concerts, Bible discussion classes, bioscope shows and a Literary and Debating Society to which latter Indian students would be invited occasionally. If possible, arrangements will be made for trips to places of interest in the neighbourhood, with Indian guides. Mr Waldo Hunt lives at the NE corner of the camp and will be pleased to see anyone who cares to drop in for a chat."

"Who'd have thought it?" said Bridget who had come into the room while Arthur was reading. "Who'd have thought there'd be all those things to do? There's as much going on there as there is in Bury."

Eric, sitting in his socks, remained silent. Arthur passed him the magazine. Turning the pages he was surprised and impressed. How good that Lawrence had the chance to join in such activities.

"And they're at *war*. How can they be doing those things if they're at war?" asked Bridget.

Eric was sure Conrad hadn't had such opportunities. He hadn't had bioscope shows or Bible discussion groups. He had only had mud and lice. And death. Conrad had had death. Eric did not believe that Conrad's last letter meant he was alive. It had just been delayed, that was all, because wars were never neat and tidy and often things did not work as they should. He accepted that now, and Hattie said she did too, but he knew she still held on to a vestige of almost hopeless hope.

"They're not at war out there, Bridget," said Arthur. "At least, they're not fighting yet."

Yet, thought Eric. He's right. They're not fighting *yet*.

"Have you found the bit about Beauty Hints? Here, pass it back and I'll read it to you." Arthur reached across for *The Londoner* and launched into another paragraph.

"The wearing of shorts, though it keeps the knees delightfully cool, has the disadvantage that it tends to a loss of that beauty of complexion that is to a great extent the secret of our English charm. Fortunately we have an easy method of obviating this disaster, for it would be no less. Take a small portion, say a quarter of a pound of the butter ration so liberally distributed every day…"

"Every day? A quarter of a pound every day? For every man? But we only..."

"Shush, Bridget, there's more," said Arthur, laughing and waving his hand at her,

"and smear it thickly over the knees before retiring to rest. On rising, gently wash the skin in warm water with a little oatmeal added.(Never use soap, by the way). After a few weeks of this treatment you will find your knees again fresh and rosy. A slight drawback to this method is that the butter attracts ants and other fauna of the countryside, but surely no-one will grudge the loss of a few nights' sleep for so desirable an object.

"I think the last bit's in French." He passed the paper to Eric.

"Il faut souffrir pour être belle. It's necessary to suffer to be beautiful." Eric stood up.

"It's wonderful how they've managed to put such a magazine together, isn't it?"

"It certainly is," said Eric. "I'm going to get changed."

November 1916

Bury Free Press

Famous film at Bury Empire next week. 4.11.16

On Monday next and during the week the inhabitants of Bury St Edmunds and district will have an opportunity of seeing the most wonderful film ever screened viz. The Battle of the Somme.

Bury Free Press 11.11.16

Some Impressions of the film

During this present week the famous film The Battle of the Somme *has been screened at the Bury Empire before packed audiences. By witnessing the film the ordinary citizen is enabled to obtain an insight of the actualities of war, if only in a modified form which he otherwise could not get, and only for that reason every civilian should make a point of witnessing this wonderful five reeled film.*

From start to finish the interest of the onlooker is sustained. Almost every feature of modern military warfare is depicted. It has been thought advisable to leave certain of the more sombre scenes to the imagination. It is possible to derive a capital idea as to what the term British artillery means. Guns in action of all calibres are to be seen and the manipulation of the wounded trench mortars is especially interesting. The transport of the big howitzers and the handling of them into position and the

*loading and firing operations are revealed to the onlookers in a
remarkable manner.*

*Scenes of the shells bursting over the German trenches in the
distance are also visibly portrayed, although here again the
havoc wrought in the enemy's line is left to the imagination.
Views of the dilapidated trenches of the enemy are, however,
subsequently screened and the bodies of the dead Germans in
considerable numbers bear tribute of the fatal effect of British
gunfire. Throughout the five reels some thousands of German
prisoners are to be seen coming into the British lines. Nearly all
of them, of course, appear thoroughly dejected and crestfallen
but they were, generally speaking, burly fellows, well set up and
of splendid physique and their general appearance did not lend
weight to the idea that they had been existing on restricted
rations. Contrary to general expectations, aircraft operations
were entirely absent from the film. It was impossible to remain
unimpressed by the marked characteristic cheerfulness of the
British troops. This cheerfulness was apparent under all sorts of
conditions which at different times confronted the lads. When
running the greatest risk such as being under fire or having his
wounds dressed behind the lines, Tommy would be coolly
puffing his "Wild Woodbine". There was plenty of evidence
forthcoming that prowess and pluck are still the chief
ingredients constituting the British soldier. The film discloses
only the fringe of the gruesomeness of modern warfare but
sufficient is seen to stir the imagination and the scenes actually
depicted are quite enough to cast a grave aspersion upon the
much vaunted civilization of this so-called "Christian" Europe.*

November 1916

This morning I went with Mother to Ampton Hall. She had got permission for me to help tidying up an outbuilding they were going to use as a storeroom. At first I had felt a bit nervous because she'd told me I would see people who had lost a leg or an eye. I thought it might be hard not to stare at them, but I don't think I was rude.

Ampton Hall is huge, and we went in at the back because that's where the nurses' entrance is and it saved us going all the way round. I saw a lot of nurses and I think some were matrons. They were the ones who were dressed a bit differently, though they all had red crosses sewn onto their aprons and sleeves. Mother's friends welcomed me – I knew a few of them – and my first job was to make neat piles of masses of empty cardboard boxes. Then I had to wash all the dust off the windows and windowsills.

When I'd finished that I was allowed to help get things ready for a special tea. The tea was going to be in the George Arthur Ward, but there were other wards, like Jellicoe ward, Poley Ward and more. One of them – I forget which – was newly built, and someone said it sometimes had French soldiers in it.

When I followed Mother into the George Arthur, there were many more beds than I expected. In each ward every bed had the same colour bedspread, and most had a man sitting on or lying in it, but other men were walking about, as well as nurses, porters and cleaners. Some of the men wore a special blue uniform called Hospital Blues. Most people had bandages on some part of their body. I felt really sorry for the ones whose faces had been hurt, because they would probably never look the same as they used to. And then I thought how bad it would be to only have one leg, or one hand, or an injury to your back so you couldn't stand or walk properly. There were two men who had no legs at all.

All the patients seemed pleased to see me. They asked my name and they told Mother what a lovely little girl I was. In fact, I'm ten, but I thought it would sound rude if I said so. The trouble is that I'm small for my age.

At three o'clock some ladies from Bury came in. They seemed to know some of the patients because they went straight up to them and began talking. I saw Mrs Sturge who recognised me at once and asked when I would have some more flints for her and Dr Sturge. I said I hadn't been able to collect so many since the army stopped people going to the best places to find them. She had paid me two shillings for the very special one I'd found – the most I'd ever had for one flint. Dan Hunt took his finds there too, but he'd never been paid more than one shilling.

I was allowed to carry cups of tea to the men who couldn't get out of bed. Some of them kept asking me to fetch more biscuits or more cake, and then they wanted to share them with me. I didn't like to accept because Mother had told me that the kind people who sent food and papers and cigarettes to Ampton wanted their things to go to the patients, not to anyone else.

The men were very funny and one called George showed me a trick. First he put a coin in my hand to show me it was real, and then he put it in his mouth. Then he put his hands under the sheet and said some magic words. When he opened his mouth it was quite empty, but when he opened his hand - there was the coin!

It was easy to see into his mouth, because he did not have many teeth. He told me they were knocked out when he was in France. He said he had other injuries too, worse ones, but his clothes covered them and they weren't nice to look at. George stopped smiling when he told me that, so I think his injury must have been hurting a lot. He let me keep the coin and said it would always remind me of him. It's French. I'm going to put in it my special box with my English money.

After tea a man came in who seemed to know nearly everyone. He had a camera, and he went round the ward asking people if they would like him to take their photos. Some of the men had pictures taken on their own, and others posed in a group. It was only when he came near me that I heard him speak, and I noticed that he spoke in an unusual way. George (the soldier who did the trick) told me that the man was called Mr Burrell, and that he was deaf. He said Mr Burrell could understand everyone, and everyone could understand him. I had always thought that it would be worse to be blind than deaf, and now I knew I was right, because he was getting on so well.

Then several of the ladies sang a few songs, and one recited some poems. The soldiers clapped loudly, though the ones with bandaged hands cheered and the ones with sticks hit them against their chairs.

Lots of the patients were talking about the film in Bury. My parents hadn't seen it, and nor had my aunt and uncle. Mother said it would make her cry, and she'd done enough crying recently. Father gave her a hug and said he agreed and there was no need to put themselves through something that was bound to upset them. Uncle Arthur said he didn't want to spend good money on something that was made up. Father told him that most of it wasn't made up, and it was almost exactly what had happened, and though some bits had been added, he'd heard it was easy to tell which bits they were. But my uncle didn't believe him, and said that anyway he would rather get on with jobs on the farm than sit and watch a film for a couple of hours.

Later on, when we had tidied up the tea things, Mother had to give out medicines, and I was sent to take some newspapers and books to men in another ward. They were very cheerful even though there was something wrong with every single one of them. They didn't talk about their injuries or the war at all, but how they wanted to get out of hospital and go home. Edgar told me he was a bus conductor, and Philip was a tailor. But once the visitors had gone I wasn't allowed to stay in the wards.

I tried to imagine how the men had been wounded, but it was difficult to think of the Germans trying to hurt men like George and Ernest with guns or bayonets. And it was even more difficult to imagine George and Ernest shooting or stabbing or blowing anyone up. I don't think the English and French are bad people. They just do what they have to do. But it's bad to fight when there is no need to. The war is so complicated it's hard to know what it's *for*. Father and Mother know, and they've explained, but I still don't really understand. And the reason for fighting seems to keep on changing.

Uncle Arthur says it's to make sure that England holds on to its power and importance, and keeps the Germans away because they will hurt us and wreck our country. He thinks that anyone who doesn't want to fight for that should be sent to prison, but Father's told me it's not as simple as that.

And then I thought about Germany. Surely Germany wanted to be important too? Were their soldiers like ours?

Ordinary people who worked in factories and shops but had to go to war? Conrad was, had been, a good person, and an ordinary person, but the Germans can't have known that.

And were there some Germans who didn't want to fight? I hoped there were lots of them.

December 1916

Dear Father and Mother,

Last Monday we all piled onto a train for a long, long journey north. We knew it would be over 2000 miles, but not that it would take six days and nights! Six of us with all our kit and equipment were jammed into a small compartment. We plodded along at around 15 mph, though occasionally the engine managed to get up to a speedy 20. But the slowness was really because of the numerous stops we made for repairs to the line to be carried out, re-fuelling, and to allow other trains to pass. There was time to play cricket or entire football matches during these periods of waiting. But at last we reached a stop called Burhan not far from Rawalpindi. We were d----d glad to stop travelling, I can tell you, even though we were immediately surrounded by dogs and beggars. Meals were provided at certain stops, and we were served stew and rice pudding at every meal!

So, we're in the Punjab. It's flat and boring and little grows here except cacti and other prickly things. But the view is immense because there's no edge to it. At certain times of day the land just merges into the sky. And in the evening, when there is no wind at all, the smoke from fires doesn't go upwards, but stretches out horizontally, as if someone had drawn a line for it.

No home comforts in Burhan, but the place has a few things to recommend it – especially a river, where we swim, and you can fish. Strangely, there's frost on the ground in the morning, but it's at least 100 at midday!

There are villages where some sort of farming is done: a few cows, a few crops. It's peaceful until the dogs start up. But it couldn't be more different than Suffolk. I'd love Uncle Arthur to see it and tell me what he thinks!

We're all going to have a special treat for Christmas. We'll be doing Kitchener's Test, which is reputed to be ghastly – physically and mentally gruelling. Apparently it's not unusual for a few men to collapse. Wish me luck!

I doubt if you'll get any more letters from me before Christmas, even though I'll write some. I know this Christmas will be very difficult for all of us, so I'll be thinking of you often and I know you'll be thinking of me. I'll think of you going to church (do you still go to Hawstead, or do you go to West Stow now?) and then sitting down to a special meal – even though it might not be as special as the Christmas dinners we used to have. Our service here will be in the open air, and I'll be praying for you and especially Conrad. Now I wish so much that I'd sent him more letters and that he'd sent me more. I'm very glad I have a sister, but I wish so much that I still had my brother. You must be missing him terribly. Every time I get a letter from home my heart beats faster, even before I open it. Is that what happens to you too? Of course I'm not the only one with a fallen brother. Many men have lost a friend or relation in France, and mostly it's brothers.

105

Sidney's older brother was killed in action in Gallipoli, and he's still very cut up about it.

> *Your loving son,*
> *Lawrence*

February 1917

Every week in the paper there were more reports of tribunals as more men refused to attest their willingness to serve in the army. Arthur was reading extracts out, and I was wishing he would stop getting angry about it yet again.

"Obviously, someone's got to do the work here at home. Of course they have. But people seem to be trying to get out of going to the front by claiming that they're needed in a factory, or in a business or something. Why won't they go?"

Hattie said, "Someone may be needed in his job, or he may not want to fight. That's what the tribunals are attempting to establish, isn't it? And if we need more forces, where are they going to come from? Unless, of course, you have women at the front?"

Arthur puffed at his pipe in derision. "I'm sure that some men have real reasons of conscience, while some are genuinely needed here. But there are plenty who are too lazy or frightened to fight for their country. Fighting for our country should be the priority. If not, this war'll drag on for years. I doubt if they have so many tribunals in Germany."

Arthur shook the paper and went on reading. Hattie and I exchanged glances.

But within a minute he called out, "Oh God, listen to this: *'Joseph Banks, of Great Livermere, claims he is needed on his father's farm. Two farmhands from the same farm joined up in the summer, and Mr Banks says he cannot spare his last worker. The tribunal advised him to employ a woman to do the work.'*

"A woman! How do they think a woman's going to harness the horses and milk the cows at five in the morning?" Arthur tended to get particularly worked up about the fact that women were stepping into the shoes of men.

"If they were taught, women would be quite as capable of doing farm work as men," said Hattie.

"But women can't milk a herd, can they? Or lift full churns?"

"Not at first, I grant you, and perhaps not on their own. But the work would get done."

"Women should be at home. Look at Bridget. It would be quite *wrong* for Bridget to do the early milking. That's our yard man's job, and she's got more than enough to do in the house."

Hattie sighed in exasperation. "It's not a question of right or wrong. It's a question of getting work done that needs to be done. And women are the obvious under-used resource. How would you manage if your man Lennie had to go?"

I felt a nugget of anxiety as I sensed Hattie getting into her argumentative stride. "Jobs need doing. Work is important, and valuable, and interesting. I tell you, my VAD work is much more interesting than some of the things I was doing before, and I'm already thinking of what I might do when peace comes."

Arthur asked, "You'd work even if you didn't get paid?"

"Of course I'd want to be paid in peacetime. But it isn't peacetime, and in this particular job I don't expect to be paid. I don't even *want* to be paid, because I'm lucky and have enough money for what I need. And anyway, how *could* all the volunteers be paid? Where would the money come from? But this isn't about money, it's about the war. I'm just one amongst many doing something that needs to be done and which wouldn't be done if there were no volunteers."

I glanced at Elly. She was not used to arguments. She was sitting tight with her elbows on the table and her hands round her mug of warm milk, not looking at anyone. No-one answered Hattie as she got up and topped up her cup of tea. Bridget was staring out of the window.

The silence was again broken by Arthur, who suddenly sat up straight, so he could read the paper better.

"Listen to this! I can't believe it! 'The military representative on the tribunal said to someone *"If you can't get women you must get black men. If black men can be trained to fight, they can be utilized in trade."* ' What nonsense! It's totally absurd!"

I tried to calm things down by saying, "Well, it's different in cities, isn't it?"

Arthur stabbed the paper with his finger. "This isn't in a city, this is here in Bury! Read it yourself if you don't believe me!"

Bridget said, "I've only ever seen two black men in my life. There aren't any in Suffolk."

I protested weakly, "There are in the military hospitals. You know that. Anyway, what difference does someone's colour make? And didn't you hear about the film *The Tanks*? I'm told it showed negroes – all fighting for us and with us."

Hattie was glaring at Arthur. "Can you tell me exactly what's wrong with all those soldiers from India, and the negroes from the West Indies? How can you possibly dismiss them? You don't know anything about them. Come and spend a day with me. Then you'll see they're the same as us."

She put her cup and saucer down noisily and made to leave the room, saying, "I'm due at Ampton at eleven. I must go and change." After a moment or two Elly followed her out. I felt bad. I didn't like arguments and was well aware that I often avoided them. I was always worried that the hurt caused by anger wouldn't be healed.

Bridget took the tray out and Arthur turned to the sports pages. I sat there reflecting on the fact that we four adults were probably going to be living in the same house together for many more months - perhaps for more than a year. So far we had managed quite well. We shared the house, the costs, the work, the meals. But here were cracks opening up in our relationship. I was grateful to Arthur and Bridget and I wanted to keep things smooth between us, but it was hard for Hattie to hold back when she was passionate about something. I'd seen her be sharp with her sister and even her mother. Luckily, she had never turned her sights on me.

I'd have to ask her to be careful or things could be very uncomfortable. She had spoken in a really scathing tone to Arthur, and I thought he'd be smarting from it. She's my *guest*, he'd be thinking. How can a guest be so rude?

I took hope from one thing: Hattie's words and attitude were those of an angry woman, not a sad one, and I chose to interpret them as evidence of healing, of getting over Conrad's death, of re-gaining her spirits.

February 1917

I ran out of the house straight away. I ran down the garden, past Rex in his kennel, past the chicken shed Father and Uncle Arthur had mended, and out of the back gate. I pushed the barn door open, ran into the corner and hid in the straw. It made me sneeze so I crossed my fingers and hoped that I wouldn't start wheezing, and I didn't. I hugged my knees and wished things were different.

Christmas hadn't been a proper Christmas, because Conrad and Lawrence weren't with us, and I had had to go to church about four times, which was boring, and people were sad because so many families had lost someone. Lots of people were crying or sniffing. My asthma had been bad for the last three months, and now the grown-ups were arguing. Was my life always going to have bad things in it? It was the middle of February already and nothing good had happened this year.

But it was a lovely clear day and to stop myself being miserable I decided to go for an expedition. I had found out when I was quite little that I could cheer myself up if I made myself do something like dig a hole or skip as many skips as possible with my rope, or climb a tree. Going on an expedition meant I'd have to go back to the house to get my coat and gloves and something to eat. Luckily, Mother, who was leaving for Ampton by the back door, didn't see me go in the front door while the others were still in the kitchen. There was a big pile of ironing on the table in the scullery waiting for me. I had promised Aunt Bridget that I'd iron the pillow cases, but I just slipped indoors, got what I needed and slipped out again.

I marched straight across the stony fields towards the

river, not caring where I went. I was going to have an adventure, and later on, when I told the grown-ups about it they would be surprised, and think me brave, and be sorry that I was upset.

I crossed the Lark by the bridge. The water level was higher than usual and I stopped to look at it. What do fish do in winter? You don't see many people fishing in the winter, so perhaps they hide or go somewhere else. And what do kingfishers do if there are no fish? Last year I saw two of them just up from here, streaking across the river in a very straight, flat line.

I was careful by the weir because Uncle Arthur had told me that when I was little, a man fell through the ice here. He was lucky because someone was passing by and rescued him. I didn't like thinking about that, so I started off along the path which led to a lane full of icy puddles. An old man wobbled past me on his bike and said something I couldn't hear properly, but I thought he was talking about the puddles and how slippery they were. After a while I went back to the field paths. I kept my eyes open for flints, as usual. A bit later I felt hungry, so I ate the bun and one of the two apples I'd taken. I began to feel better. I decided this was going to be the longest expedition I had ever made. I'd stay out till it began to get dark.

Soon I recognised a group of those strange-shaped wind-blown pine trees, but when I got close it wasn't the place I thought it was. And I hadn't expected the path to divide – a lane turned left past the trees but the path went straight on towards the brecks.

I took the lane past the pines so I wouldn't have to be on the frosty fields. It's not easy to walk on hard earth and flints. I hadn't thought of putting on my gumboots and I was wearing my old school shoes that I used indoors. I'd slowed down a bit by now and was noticing more around me. A broken ploughshare. A scarecrow. Rabbits all over the place. Only once did a wagon come past me. It slowed down and the driver asked me where I was going, and did I want a ride? I didn't want to tell him I didn't know where I was going, so I just waved to say thank you, and he set off at a trot again.

I knew West Stow was directly behind me because I'd been going in roughly the same direction all the time, so when I'd gone far enough I'd just turn round and walk home.

I trudged on at a steady pace, stopping once to pick up a small round object. It turned out to be a coin. I couldn't read the words on it, and it was certainly old. Dr Sturge would know about it so I put it in my pocket.

The wind was blowing harder and I wished I had a scarf as well as my gloves and coat. I ate the second apple. What time was it? I must have been walking for a couple of hours by now. Perhaps I should have accepted that lift. Surely it would be getting dark soon? One of my heels was hurting and my right shoe kept slipping off. I wished Libby or Alison was with me.

And then I saw a church much further away, and there was a footpath leading along a ditch towards it. Good. I'd soon find out where I was, and then I'd go home and they would all be pleased to see me, and Aunt Bridget would have done the ironing. I hurried on, almost running, but after only fifty yards or so I was out of breath and wheezing.

I was going to sit on the ground, but it was too cold and wet, so I just squatted uncomfortably. My whole chest was tight and tense, and I could hear as well as feel my lungs trying to pull air in. At the same time I wanted to cough stuff up but I couldn't. I wished I was at home with Mother. I watched a worm make its way between grasses. What was I doing out here on a winter's day?

I made myself keep calm and gradually the asthma settled down, my coughing was not so harsh and it became easier to breathe.

I looked up and along the path. The sky was overcast now and it was about to rain. The way I had come was quite straight and followed the line of the ditch, but ahead of me it went out of view at the field's headland. At first the thought of getting up and continuing was awful, but the sight of the church cheered me up. When I reached it I'd know where I was. In fact, it could even be *our* church. Perhaps I'd come round in a circle? I'd heard that people who're lost sometimes go round in circles. But I wasn't really lost, just not sure of exactly where I was.

Father knew the towers of every local church by their parapets, gargoyles, patterns of flint, porches and by many other things, but now I wasn't even sure if I'd recognise St Mary's which I have seen every day since we moved here. How could I not know my own village church? Gradually I began to hear other sounds as well as my noisy breathing. A cow lowing. An engine. Rooks.

As I felt the first small drops of rain I heard voices coming from ahead of me, and I saw a group of big boys approaching. They were carrying sticks and laughing. I didn't like the look of them at all and I wondered about running back in the direction I'd come from.

And then, as they came nearer, I saw that they were girls not boys, but they were all wearing the same sort of breeches and the same jackets and the same hats. They all had the letters WLA sewn onto their sleeves. And they weren't carrying sticks, but rakes and hoes. I knew that they were talking about me because they slowed down before hurrying towards me.

They grouped round me asking lots of questions: What was my name? Where was I going? Where did I live? Why was I so far from home? Why was I coughing so much?

"Asthma? What bad luck. My cousin has asthma, so I know how horrible it can be."

"Do your parents know where you are?" asked one called Ginnie. "Elly, please tell us the truth. We're trying to help you."

I started to cry, and shook my head.

Someone else asked, "Do you think they'll be cross with you?"

I nodded.

"No, they won't. They'll be pleased you're safe. Come on, we'll get you back to West Stow.

"I ran away once," said Ginnie. "I was angry with my brother. Have you got any brothers or sisters?"

I started to cry again. "My brother Conrad was killed in the war in July."

Ginnie stopped walking for a moment and took my hand. "Was he? I'm so sorry."

"Lawrence, my other brother, he's in the army too, but I don't think he's in the proper war. He's in another war, in India."

"I hope he comes home safely, and I hope my boy-friend does too."

"What's your boyfriend's name?"

"Ernest. Ernest Reed." Ginnie suddenly put her hands up to her face. "Don't ask me about him or I'll start crying too."

Some of the women said goodbye and went off along the path away from us, but Ginnie and Elsie walked with me.

"Come on, we're nearly there. How would you like to be driven home in a Womens' Land Army car? That'll make them sit up, won't it?"

We reached the road and I saw an army car parked near The Greyhound and a church which I now recognised as Flempton church. They sat me right in the front, next to Elsie who was driving, and we set off towards West Stow, which was in exactly the opposite direction to where I thought it was. We saw two boys ahead and they turned to look at us. It was Dan and Greg Hunt! Dan pointed at me and waved, and Greg just stared with his mouth open. I bet they wished they had the chance to ride in an army car! I hadn't seen Dan for weeks, but I hadn't forgotten what he'd told me about the tunnel.

When I got home Uncle Arthur told me it wasn't even lunchtime yet.

May 1917

At about nine in the evening, eight hundred men clambered onto trains at Jullundur. They were heading for Tank, several hundred miles to the west. Their whole reason for being in the North West Frontier of India was to protect the borders from incursions from Waziristan, and the aim of their first action was to punish the tribal Mahsuds whom they had never seen but whom they had been told were *"wild treacherous beings over whom the only power of persuasion was the rifle and the sword."* The punishment was to avenge the recent killings of Major

Hughes of the South Waziristan Militia, and a number of his men.

The journey through monotonous and mountainous country went on and on, until, on the second day, they reached the Indus at Mari, where they got off the train.

On the way, the men from London had been talking about the Thames. Its length, its historic buildings, its port and shipping. They were proud of their river and were taken aback when they saw the Indus.

Though they did not know it, they were to see the Indus and cross it many times over the next two years. In some places it was a solid body of water, in others it spread out into numerous braided channels separated by sandbanks and islands and occasionally joined by insubstantial bridges. The land it flowed through was high, arid and devoid of colour. The sun glared down fiercely, making the Londons long for a dull English day, but they were told that the cool season would not be heralded by calls of returning cranes and geese until September.

In essence the Indus was a huge expanse of fresh water making its way south. A senior officer said that while the Thames was a little over two hundred miles in length, this river was nearly two thousand miles. He also spoke of the blind river dolphins which nosed their way around the delta. While few believed him, others said that by now they accepted that anything was possible in India.

The natives sailed across the Indus in crowded, frail-looking ferries, hauled water out to irrigate their crops, and fished. One day a group of soldiers saw a strange sight on the river. Quite close to a small boat, two weird birds seemed to be hovering about the water. Something seemed to be wrong with them, for they did not fly off when the boat approached. As the Londons got nearer, they realised that the birds were decoys. Fixed to a man's head, their purpose was to attract and encourage herons to come close enough to be caught.

The Londons embarked on a steamer which took ten steady minutes to cross the river, then walked to Kalabagh station to reach the narrow gauge railway. They carried all their equipment with them, and were dog-tired, but the only place to rest was on the railway track so they lay down between the lines. The next day they boarded another train and finally reached Tank where they lived under canvas for a fortnight, subject to flies, mosquitos, dust, stench and intense heat. At that time of year the maximum temperature in the day was about one hundred and thirty degrees, and though cooler in the evening, it was far too hot to sleep. Some men suffered heat stroke and had to be invalided out.

The advance into Waziristan commenced on the night of 6th-7th June. At last, after more than eighteen months of preparation spent in Chiseldon, Bangalore, Hebbal, Burhan, Jullundur, at sea and on trains and on foot, the battalion's time had come. Though debilitated by lack of both sleep and food, they set off after midnight along a track that would take them past a British-held fort at a place named Zam. As they approached Zam before dawn, they became aware of scattered rifle fire ahead and found that a group of Gurkhas, their brothers-in-arms, had been ambushed by the enemy. Fierce fighting had already taken place. They were too late to do much, but it was their first taste of combat.

Gurkhas stumbled towards them, seeking help for the terrible wounds the Mahsuds had inflicted on them with knives and swords. On the rocky ground lay dead Gurkhas and dead Mahsuds. Many had been mutilated, and, even as they watched, the British troops were shocked to see the Gurkhas setting alight the hair and beards of the dead enemy's corpses in a rage of retribution.

After a short halt at Zam the Battalion continued trekking towards Kot Khirgi along the boulder-strewn river. It was only about sixteen miles, but their path kept crossing and re-crossing a river, which meant they had to wade at times, and their feet were continually wet. Frustratingly, they were ordered not to drink the river water, despite the fact that they were dehydrated and nearing exhaustion. So they did what they could to cool themselves: in full uniform, they lay down in the stream and soaked themselves. As the day passed and their boots dried, their feet became more and more painful, and some of the troops had to be carried by pack animals. Several men collapsed and one died.

The next morning, after a meal and a brief sleep, they set off for Jandola, where they were able to rest for three days. Here they were united with the guard which had gone ahead of them.

On June 12th, Major General Benyon decided to conduct a reconnaissance over the hills on the north bank of the Shahur river. The expedition out was undisturbed, but on their return the men were attacked from the bare rock ridges around them. The Londons had to hold the ridge on the north side before retiring rapidly. They succeeded in doing this, and they felt confident enough to stop at the river, unstrap their mugs from their rucksacks and drink their fill, for by then the water had been assessed as fit to drink and they felt invulnerable because they had demoralized the enemy. However, on the south side, the Mahsuds knew that everyone had to cross a narrow plank bridge so they concentrated their fire on that spot, causing two casualties.

The Londons were twenty days into their war. At last they were doing what they had been trained for.

May 1917

Casualties continued to arrive at Ampton, and one Thursday evening Hattie told me that, unusually, she was going to work all weekend. They were going to rearrange one of the wards in order to cope with a particular batch of men who would be arriving in a few days. Some of these men, they had heard, had been blinded. It would be Hattie's third weekend on duty in a row, and meant she would be working for nine consecutive days, then have just one day off, and then a run of eight more.

It was too much. I told her she would wear herself out working so hard. She couldn't deny her fatigue for each evening she was falling asleep after our meal. She'd also been having backache, which she had never had before.

"It's just while Queenie is away. She's had to go to Anne, her sister, because Anne's about to have a baby and she's on her own with two small children. Assuming all goes well, Queenie will be back on Friday."

I pointed out that I too, expecting that she would not be working, had volunteered to work on that same weekend, and I was reluctant to let my colleagues down even though I knew someone could cover for me.

"Elly will be all right here if we're both out the whole day."

"Yes, she will. I don't think she'll go rushing off on her own again, do you?"

We both laughed. Elly's adventure was already becoming a legend, even though I still felt uncomfortable when I recalled the argument between Bridget and Arthur. I was sure they hadn't forgotten it either. But I made an attempt to steer conversations into safe territory, though Arthur still huffed when he read the paper. Neither Hattie nor I could be cross with Elly. After all, she'd been gone for less than two hours, and we couldn't help laughing at her arriving back here in a WLA car. Bridget, however, made it clear that she would have given Elly a strong telling-off if she had been her daughter.

"Elly's good at occupying herself. She'll find herself something to do," said Hattie. Then she added, "In fact, now that I think about it, I suppose she could come with me on Saturday, as long as she keeps out of the wards. She'd probably enjoy that."

So, on Saturday morning, the three of us set out together, with Elly between me and Hattie. I recalled the family going for walks in the past: Hattie and me and three children. Now one was dead, and another in danger. I reached out for the hand of the one who was here, and linked arms with Hattie.

As usual, I was looking forward to meeting the train, but we spent the morning hanging around because it arrived much later than expected. When it came it was only half full, but from one carriage a group of men alighted slowly, one at a time, holding on to each other's jackets and belts. Some held hands with the person in front of or behind them. Some had bandages round their foreheads and others had eye patches. There were also some with no visible injuries, and I discovered that several of these were blind. Could an explosion cause loss of sight as it could cause the loss of hearing or confuse the mind to the point where it no longer functioned as it should? This work was making me reflect on the complexity of the human body. There was so much to go wrong. Not for the first time I found myself feeling relieved that Conrad was dead rather than severely wounded, but I then blamed myself for thinking so. Was life precious even when it was hardly life? Would I prefer to be dead than severely wounded, with no hope of recovery? I did not know.

The men were given tea before being led to the vehicles and driven to Ampton. They were an animated bunch, and while I put that down partly to them having been together for most of their journey and having had the chance to talk, it might have been because many shared the same condition. I was one of the first to get out of the vehicles and therefore went into the hospital to announce our arrival. To my surprise, Elly was just inside the entrance, next to the office of one of the doctors.

"Surely you're not supposed to be here?" I asked.

"I've been coughing a lot, and Dr Dix heard me. He told Mother that he would have a look at me. Mother should be here too by now, but she's late … "

Just then Hattie arrived in a hurry. She smiled and nodded me a brief "I can't talk now" look, then knocked on the doctor's door. A voice called "Come in," and they both went inside.

An hour later I was given a lift back to Ingham, then set off to West Stow on foot. It was a beautiful May evening and I decided to extend my walk by ten or fifteen minutes. When I reached the row of slanting pines, one of my favourite spots, I took off my glasses and shut my eyes for a few moments. I was feeling acute sorrow at the thought of Conrad never again being able to experience such an evening. Then, on opening my eyes and seeing the summer panorama I suddenly thought of the blind men. They would never see this. They would never see this view.

I looked at the ground. Compared to the landscape it seemed dull until I examined it in detail. Then, numerous small flowers seem to present themselves: red sorrel, chickweed, blue speedwell, saxifrage, cranesbill and several I could not name. Ants clambered across leaves and spiders scaled stalks. No blind man would see any of this. I closed my eyes again. But at least they would hear those wheat-ears, that blackbird and the willie-e-reeve call of a stone curlew. And they would feel this soft air and smell the summer growth.

And Lawrence? His last letter said he was in a place called Jullundur, where he was drawing more plants and going for runs. I'd found Jullundur on the map, spelled slightly differently, near Amritsar and Lahore. How strange that Duleep Singh had come from that very region to our part of Suffolk, and Lawrence had gone from here to Duleep Singh's part of India. I had urged him to visit Amritsar for I knew it had exquisite temples, but he wrote saying he hadn't been. We were due a letter from him, and I kept hoping that perhaps he'd say something about it.

There was a droning of bees to my right, and to my left I could hear a cuckoo which, now that it was June, had changed its tune. A game of cricket was underway somewhere, and a plane from Thetford airfield droned above the fields.

How would things turn out over the next few months? I still put in an appearance at Hardwick House every now and then, and I think Mr Cullum welcomed it. But I had no real function there any more, and the place looked and felt very different. Lawns had been turned into hay meadows, and formal flower gardens given over to growing vegetables. Even with soldiers around the place, it felt deserted. I was used to servants, the butler, the ostler, grooms currying horses, gardeners wheeling barrows, maids carrying baskets of washing or chatting in the sunshine outside the kitchen door. But now there were fewer voices, much less movement. And I sensed that Mr Cullum, though by no means old, and certainly doing his best for the war effort, was finding it difficult to adapt to the changes he was being obliged to make.

In respect of the changes to my own life, was helping my brother out when he needed it, and the hospital escort work enough? Though I was well over 50, shouldn't I be doing more? I thanked God that I was healthy at present, for being ill at Arthur and Bridget's would create difficulties. Losing Conrad had knocked me. I can't describe how I felt, other than to say that I felt weaker and older. But Hattie's response, after her initial distress, was the opposite, for she was throwing herself into the VAD work as vigorously as before.

I was thankful that Elly seemed to take things in her stride: a change of home, rarely seeing her best friends or indeed any children, Conrad's death, the absence of Lawrence, not going to school. At least the last would be remedied at the end of the summer. Hattie and I had agreed that she should return to her school in Bury as soon as the autumn term began. It was only about four miles, so she'd be fine cycling. She kept reminding me that the bike she has now, which was passed on from the rector's daughter at Hawstead, was too small. I would have to look out for a bigger one for her.

But her asthma had not improved this year. Was it the dust from the harvest that made it worse? Or the cows? Thank God for Potter's Cure, the only thing we could rely on to relieve it.

I strolled on, heading for home and looking forward to a cup of tea. At about six, when I was sitting on the bench outside reading the paper, with Bran at my feet, Hattie and Elly arrived.

"How have you got on today?" I asked.

Hattie nodded. "Elly, go and see if there's any tea in the pot. I'm dying for a drink."

When Elly was out of earshot she said, "I had quite a talk with Dr Dix about Elly's asthma. I'll tell you in a minute."

I was pleased to hear this. The doctor we took her to in Bury had not been helpful. "She'll grow out of it," he'd said. "No need to worry." But though Hattie and I were no longer alarmed when Elly had a coughing fit, it continued to concern us.

Elly returned with a cup of tea for Hattie and announced, "I'm going upstairs to read."

"Well?" I asked, when we were alone.

"Dr Dix examined her – looked down her throat, sounded her chest and so on – all the usual things. Then he sent her out to walk right round Ampton Hall, and while she was gone he explained to me that he believed asthma was a psychological illness, not a physical one." Hattie took a drink of her tea. "He said it can occur when a child is abandoned by its mother."

"What do you mean?"

"He said that when a child is separated from its mother, he or she can have problems with breathing."

"But Elly's not separated from you."

"Dr Dix said that she is, because I'm away from her for so many hours at Ampton."

I took a moment to digest this. "That's ridiculous! What about Douglas Church's children? They lost their mother several years ago and they don't have asthma."

"He said it's a psychosomatic illness."

"What does he mean by that?"

"That Elly's asthma is 'a suppressed cry for her mother'."

"A suppressed cry for her mother? What does he want you to do? Stop going to Ampton?"

"Not exactly. For a start, he knows I'm needed there."

"Then what's he saying?"

"That I shouldn't spend so much time there."

"But it's nonsense. Elly's had asthma for years." I stood up and gazed out of the window. "And what about all those evacuees? They're away from their mothers, but they haven't got asthma, have they?"

"He asked me if I thought Elly was happy, and I said yes, I thought she was, especially since she knows she's going back to school." Hattie paused to drink her tea. "But then he asked about what she did when alone, and I made the mistake of telling him about how she went off that day and ended up at Flempton."

"What did he say about that?"

"He said, 'Mrs. Bailey, that incident is clear evidence of Elly's need for you. She did it on purpose to worry you, so that you'd pay her more attention.'

"And then Elly came back from her walk round and he listened to her chest again, even though she wasn't wheezing, and of course the only reason he'd sent her out was so that we could talk."

" 'A suppressed cry for her mother.' What rubbish."

"Dr Dix is the most senior doctor at Ampton. He came to us from Cambridge."

Despite my concerns about Hattie spending too much time at Ampton, I said, "That may be the case, but it doesn't mean that he's right or that we have to agree with him."

"Well, he'll be pleased to know that I'm taking a couple of weekends off."

"Are you? I'm pleased too. I'm sure you'll benefit from having a bit more time to yourself."

June 1917

The next Saturday morning, a particularly beautiful morning, Arthur was in the middle of telling Eric about the two Zeppelins which had recently been shot down locally – one over the North Sea and one at Theberton near Saxmundham – when Bridget appeared waving something white.

"Eric! The postman's just been! There's something from Lawrence!"

Eric broke off his conversation and hurried towards her to take the precious package.

"A copy of *The Londoner*! How wonderful!"

Hattie appeared from the garden and they opened it right there, on the garden bench in the sunshine, and read it together.

Dear Mother and Father,

The last few nights have been rotten. The Mahsuds have hardly stopped sniping. We let them carry on, and no-one was hurt, but I couldn't sleep. Yesterday we marched through a steep gorge. Imagine that giants smashed a crevasse in a mountain with giant axes – that's what the ravine was like. It was hundreds of feet deep, so deep that at the bottom it was dark and cold except in a few places where the sun reached it. If the Mahsuds had ambushed us there we wouldn't have had a hope, but we managed all right, and even the bullocks and camels came through without losing their packs. I don't mind admitting that I was very scared. Everyone was. I don't want to die from a bullet fired by one of these wild foreign tribesmen, and I don't want to die here, in this God-forsaken place.

Once safely through, we had to build a perimeter wall, and it had to be done before nightfall. We built it out of boulders because there is no earth to speak of. And then we guarded it by putting picquets all the way round, each man sheltered in a little hollow scraped out of the stony dust only an arm's length away from the next one.

We spent the next few days destroying local villages. We're doing this because their people have done bad things to us. We burn their houses and crops and lob hand grenades to destroy as much as possible. Yesterday we smashed up a water mill. These are not as solid as ours, but they are cleverly made. The river here, the Indus, provides water for everything. The mills are needed to get the water out of it to irrigate their land which is very dry, particularly in summer. The main thing is that the more we make things difficult for them, the less likely they are to trouble us.

Is this war? It's certainly not fighting, because although there's an enemy, they're often out of sight. Whatever you call it, it stops the tribesmen from invading India, and that's what we want.

Recently we've often found ourselves together with Indian troops - Sikhs and Gurkhas. I knew a bit about them, but before this I'd never heard of Dogras or Rajputs, and there's others. Most of them speak good English, but when they are together they speak their own Sikh language, or perhaps it's Mohammadan. We can only understand a few words so you don't know what they could be saying about you. At first I was not sure how reliable they would be, but they are very good indeed. The only problem is that some don't eat meat, and some of those who do won't eat it unless the animal's been killed in a special way. It's because of the different religions. We Christians tuck into anything that's going!

So we're moving from one ghastly place to another searching out the tribesmen and destroying their villages, all the while being shot at. The Mahsuds know the country well which is a big advantage for them, but we have better weapons and more of them. We've caused some real damage, but we've also lost a few Londons. Yesterday we buried one of them. We dug him a grave under the shade of one of the few trees here and when we had covered him with sand and were walking away I felt bad that we were leaving him alone in a place so far from his home and family. He had lived all his life in London until he joined the colours, and he should have been buried in London, close to his people. We said prayers for him, but I don't know how they can help.

Here's another copy of The Londoner. Please hang on to it for me.

But here's a happier story, about Ginger. Ginger is not a man, but a female donkey. Yesterday she was in a train of animals *going along a steep path. She was loaded up with hand grenades, but for some reason (perhaps because she was near camels, which she hates) she went wild. She kicked, twisted, bucked and finally broke her traces. She managed to shed her load and began to jump on the grenades. Everyone ran for shelter, but not even one exploded, and Ginger came to no harm!*

We're told the weather will cool down in a few weeks, and we can't wait for that. Apparently what happens is that the wind gets up, clouds are formed, and then it really pours down – much harder than it ever rains at home. The brown land is covered with new green growth within days, and you can't sleep for the bullfrog noises!

I hope all is well at home. I'm imagining the wheat ripening, the trees at Hardwick covered in young leaves. Are there enough men left to make up decent cricket teams? That reminds me, Father, could you please oil my bat? It's in one of the outhouses but I can't remember which one.

We've no idea when all this will be over.

Your loving son,
Lawrence

Hattie and I hugged each other. Lawrence was in danger and in combat, and he was doing things which we could not believe were right but which we could do nothing about. The important thing was that he was alive. And not only was he alive out there, but two Zeppelins had been shot down here. And the sun was shining. Suddenly, things felt better.

On the spur of the moment I said, "Hattie, let's make the most of your free day and go for a walk. It's a gorgeous morning. Let's go along the Lark. I haven't walked that way for years."

Hattie hesitated. "Yes, I'd love to. But what about Elly?"

"She'll come. It'll be a treat for her."

Within twenty minutes the three of us set off with some sandwiches, some hard-boiled eggs and a flask of tea.

We started at West Stow bridge and headed downstream along the river. It was an exquisite summer's day and we started well, each of us delighted with our unexpected outing and the novelty of walking for the sake of it.

I hadn't been along that towpath for at least ten years, and as a boy I had seen horses being led along here pulling barges laden with coal from King's Lynn and returning with grain or phosphates, and I had grown up calling this river the Coal River, but now it hardly seemed worth the name of river at all, for in places it was much narrower and quite silted up. Occasionally we almost lost sight of the water, so hidden was it by undergrowth. It was hard to imagine it as it used to be when Arthur and I came here. At one point I even had to pull a stick from the hedgerow to knock away the nettles. Elly thought this a good idea, so broke a stick for herself and led the way.

The first lock we reached was Fulling Mill Lock, then Fulling Staunch. The next was the curved Cherry Ground Lock which used to hold up to eight barges at once. When we reached Lackford Bridge we paused for a while. There was little traffic on the road and we sat in silence taking in the quiet movement of the water, turquoise dragonflies, and a pair of wagtails. The remains of brickwork which had edged a lock or supported a metal gate were just visible. The Lark was very different from my memory of the Coal River, and I felt it could never return to how it had been. I found it sad to think that someone walking along here in, say, fifty or sixty years, would never know what had been lost.

We walked on and reached the point where a stream on the other side of the river extended towards Cavenham Mill, and then we were at Marston's Mill at Icklingham, but though Tuddenham's tall chimney was already in sight we decided not to go any further. We had walked far enough, so we had our picnic looking south across the Lark towards the heath. Hattie and I lay in the sun while Elly went off in search for fish. Almost without looking we saw herons, stone curlews and butterflies. In my contentment I reached out for Hattie's hand and squeezed it, but she was less at peace than I was.

"I've been thinking about Lawrence and his troops breaking mills down. It's terrible, isn't it? It feels so, so wrong to deliberately destroy things on which people have spent time and money and effort."

I watched a brown beetle slowly scaling a stem. It was less than two inches from the top. Hattie was right of course. War was wrong.

"I agree, but I'd rather he destroyed mills than men. He seems to have avoided the worst of it so far."

Unlike Conrad, I thought but did not say. Conrad had been in the centre of the worst of it.

"To think he joined up as a cyclist. No-one could have predicted what would happen, no-one could have predicted that he would be fighting people he never even knew existed."

I stroked her arm, warm from the sun. The brown beetle hesitated at the top of its stalk. The river glinted.

Suddenly Elly arrived, full of excitement. "I saw two snakes swimming across the river! They were as long as my arm, and they swam with only their heads above water, like this. Look, like this!" Elly made her head sway from side to side as she imitated the snakes' movement in the water. "Come and see, they might swim back." We stood up and followed Elly to a place she'd found where she could get close to the water. We crouched there for a few minutes but no snakes appeared.

It was while watching the water intently that I remembered ministers used to baptise people in the Lark. Up at Isleham, by the ferry, the river was even known as the Jordan. Elly was astonished at the thought of people wading into the river and immersing themselves.

"Does it happen now?" she asked.

"I honestly don't know. It might do."

"I wouldn't want to do that."

"Well, you've been christened at the font in Hawstead, so unless you decide to become a Baptist you needn't do anything else."

We collected our things and made our way back to West Stow. Elly skipped ahead, singing to herself, while the two of us walked slowly, in comfortable silence. I felt that Hattie, like me, was making an effort not to dwell on the bad things.

All in all, it was a good day.

June 1917

Arthur and Bridget had spent the day in Cambridge, a rare event. They had taken the train and then a bus to All Saints Church where they attended the funeral of Jack Trott, an old friend. The only people they knew were Jack's wife and his daughter. His two sons were at the Front, unable to get leave. They went back to the Trott's house for refreshments, and then walked back to the railway station and so back to Ingham, and a short walk home.

It had been a long, sad day, and Bridget was relieved it was over. Still in her black clothes she settled down on the seat by the window with a cup of tea and the Bury Free Press. Arthur changed his shoes and took off his black jacket. He had bought the Morning Post in Cambridge, and sat down with a comfortable grunt. Bran sat at his feet snuffling in satisfaction.

"Nice to have the place to ourselves, isn't it?" said Bridget. "I don't mean I don't want them, but I'm finding it difficult to live with Hattie. She's feeling so low."

Arthur looked over the top of his paper. "It's nearly a year now, but she's still grieving. They both are. I'm glad they are with us, even if Eric and I, and Hattie, for that matter, don't always see eye to eye. And it's good that they both have something to do other than fret. I know Eric likes working outside. In fact, since I lost our yard man to the colours, he's been quite useful. Much better to be here than at Hardwick House. It must be like a morgue there."

Hattie took a sip of tea and said, "Jack had seventy-eight years of life. I hope we have as much."

Arthur laid his paper on the floor so his hands were free to loosen his tie. "At the funeral, instead of… no, I mean, as well as … thinking about Jack, I found myself thinking of all those young men who won't be coming back."

"And I was thinking of those bombs falling on London. Falling on ordinary men and women. And children, of course." Bridget sighed. "Those poor, poor children in Poplar. Eighteen of them. *Eighteen*. And their families."

"There'll be many more deaths. Jack's sons might be

among them. So might Lawrence. I feel for Hattie and Eric, both because of the danger Lawrence is in, but also because they can see that his experiences are changing him."

"But Lawrence is in a different war with a different enemy. Out there, the farms they've been destroying can't be like ours, can they?"

"I don't know. The farmers will have livestock and crops, just as we do. It's true that India's not like France, and the war there is not like the war in France. But what Lawrence is doing might be just as risky. And unlike in France I'm not sure if they can always tell which tribes are enemies and which are friends. There are no uniforms."

"But if it was very bad there, or very important, the newspapers would be saying something about it, and they're not. Almost all the news is about France. And did you hear about Theberton?"

"Yes. Of course. Everyone was talking about the Zeppelin."

"I mean the women at Garrett Engineering Works."

Arthur looked up. "What about them?"

"They've volunteered to dig graves for the Germans who died when the Zeppelin crashed there."

Arthur closed his eyes, then, hearing voices, raised his head and looked out of the window just as three soldiers went past on bikes, riding with no hands.

The curtain billowed. Bran got up from the rag rug, turned round twice, sighed and settled down again.

"There's yet another of those tribunals in the paper," said Bridget. Do you want to have a look?"

Arthur passed the Morning Post to her and swapped it for the Free Press. He went straight to the meat of the article.

A single man, aged 21, a blacksmith at Rougham who appealed against being sent into the Army, based his appeal on conscientious grounds, which the local tribunal stated was an after thought. The appellant said he did not believe it right according to the Bible for a Christian to take life.

Mr Perry, (a member of the appeals tribunal who has lost two sons in the war): Oh lor!

Appellant: It is not according to our faith to take human life.

Mr Perry exclaiming that he could not sit and hear such a case, left the room and only returned after it was decided.

Answering Capt. Denton (one of the military representatives) the appellant admitted that in his first appeal no mention was made of his conscientious objection.

Capt. Denton: How long have you been a conscientious objector?

Four years.

Before the war started?

Yes.

That was when you were sixteen. Were you ever hit at school?

I cannot say. It is such a long while ago. I daresay so.

If you were stopped by anybody in the darkness on the way home and attacked, would you defend yourself?

I should not take their lives.

Would you protect yourself?

The Lord says Vengeance is mine.

The Chairman: Answer the question. We don't think much of your knowledge of the Testament, and we don't want instruction on that sort of thing. We prefer our own reading of the Testament.

Capt. Denton: If you were attacked on the way home tonight, what would you do?

I should get out of the way as quickly as I could.

Capt. Denton said he held that a man of the appellant's age could not have a real conscience, and in cases he had taken before the Central Appeal Tribunal his views had been upheld.

The appellant said he was prepared to do work of national importance, but he would not take life.

The man's appeal was dismissed, the Chairman emphasising the point that the appellant made no point about his conscientious objection in his original appeal. It appeared to be an after thought.

It was understood that the appellant would be put to work as a blacksmith in the Army. Cap. Denton remarking that he would not be in the firing line.

"He doesn't say he doesn't want to be shot – it's just that he doesn't want to shoot. No logic. Still, I suppose he couldn't shoe horses if he was shot. Is he really a CO? Doesn't sound like it. At least he put his own case to the tribunal and didn't have the benefit of that Mr Bankes Ashton, who seems to spend his whole time representing shirkers. Is that all the man does these days? I suppose it's one way to earn a living."

Bridget, who found *the Morning Post* too dense and rarely made it past the advertisements and announcements, picked up *The Londoner* Lawrence had sent. She read the Roll of Honour carefully, tutting over the names of those who had been killed, and those who had been injured. Six men, she noted, had died of disease.

Turning the pages she found, unexpectedly, a short obituary:

It is with great regret that we have to announce the death of 742052 Private H. Leventhal. H.C. Coy., drowned at Dera Ismail Khan.

On mobilisation he followed the Battalion a fortnight after its departure, but owing to fever was unable to proceed further than Zam Post. On his recovery he was given a light job at Khirgi, where he remained until the Battalion had returned to Jullundur.

While crossing from a barge to the ferry, on his return, he unfortunately slipped from the gangway, fell into the Indus, and weighted by his rifle and equipment was not seen again.

He enlisted in July in 1916 at the age of 19 years and arrived in India in March. He is deeply missed by his friends in the Battalion, on whom his generosity and evenness of temper have made an everlasting impression. This will be a great shock to his parents who have already given up their only other son who was killed at Neuve Chapelle in the early months of the war.

July 1917

I was eleven the Saturday before last. After lunch I sat on the wall and waited for my friends to come to tea. I watched Mrs Cox go past with her new baby, and Mrs Dean with her walking stick, and some of the troops who are billeted up the road cycled past. Everyone said hallo, and I went to look at the baby but he was asleep. You can't see much if they're asleep, but his bonnet had slipped and I saw that he was completely bald.

And then Libby and Alison arrived, a bit out of breath and ready to get off their bikes. They pushed them through the gate and leaned them against the inside of the wall. They've both been here before and they like seeing the animals, especially the horses, but there's only one horse now. They gave me a birthday card and a joint birthday present: an autograph book. In it, Libby had written a short poem and Alison had drawn a picture of a pony. I was very pleased, because autograph books are very popular.

For tea we had egg and cress sandwiches, but not many because the King has said that everyone should eat less bread. My aunt said it will be hard to cut down the amount we eat by a quarter and she wondered how the King manages to do it. Anyway, we had sandwiches and cake and apple juice made out of apples from the big tree in the back garden. Mother came back just in time to sit down with us, but Father and Uncle Arthur were repairing the cow stalls.

Aunt Bridget noticed Alison's new short bob. I thought it was really pretty, but I could tell that Aunt Bridget didn't. She doesn't like very modern things. She asked Alison how old she was – I already knew she was nearly 12, but Libby was only 11, even though she's the tallest of us three. Then my aunt annoyed me by saying, "Elly, you'll have to grow a bit, won't you?"

After tea we went outside. Libby wanted us to climb into the hayloft, so we did, although I knew I'd probably start wheezing. But it was a good place to go because it's private, and I had a secret to tell them. It was more than a secret – it was a *plan*. Now that the Elveden military area was closing down, it was possible to get into the estate again. The Keep Out notices were still up, but some of the canvas curtain had been taken down, and obviously that wouldn't have been taken down if any explosives were still there. Now that it was safe, the promise I'd made to Dan Hunt didn't matter any more. So I told them about the tunnel to France.

Alison understood at once that what I was saying was important. "Really?" she asked, "Are you sure?"

I had to admit that I hadn't seen it, but that a boy I know said it was true.

"Did he swear it was true? Did you make him swear on the Bible?"

"Of course not. We were just talking by the river." I didn't say anything about my promise.

"We could try to find it," said Libby. "Why don't we go there now?"

"What if someone saw us?"

"We can't just set off. We need to get ready for a proper expedition."

My nose was tickling, my eyes itching, so I had to climb down the ladder.

Back on the garden wall at the front we went on discussing this idea of searching for the tunnel. I felt jumpy and a bit scared at the same time. What if they told someone? Perhaps it would be all right now that the estate wasn't closed off any more. A couple of cars went past, causing Bran to bark and chase, and then Father and Uncle Arthur arrived, so we had to talk about something else.

"You look as if you're enjoying your birthday, Elly." I certainly was, but Father didn't know the real reason.

I wanted to fix up a time to explore the area, but that wasn't so easy. We needed at least three hours even to make a start on searching for the tunnel, and my weekends seemed to be getting filled up. Mother had started to encourage me to go to Ampton with her, even though only a month ago she was saying that it was a treat for me to go there and couldn't happen often. I usually liked it, even though I was only allowed in the wards when something special was going on, like a concert. But now I was trying to think up excuses not to go. It wasn't easy for Alison, either, because she has a piano lesson every Saturday morning. And Libby has to go to church twice on Sundays because she's in the choir. We wished it was the holidays already, but there were still three more weeks of term. We decided we'd wait and make our first expedition on September 6th, quite a long time away. Each of us would bring some food and a drink, a note book and paper, and a pocket knife.

"Why a knife?" asked Alison.

I told her that on expeditions they are always useful for cutting sticks, sharpening them. Even digging.

Libby says she knew where her brother kept his, and that he wouldn't miss it for a few hours. Alison said she'd only be able to bring an ordinary table knife. But then we decided that two proper knives were enough.

I'd stopped sneezing by then, and it was good to sit on the wall and talk about our plans. A horse and cart came past, and then three of the soldiers I'd seen earlier appeared again, cycling from the other direction.

"Good evening, young ladies," said one of them, braking so hard that he skidded right in front of us. He spoke in a funny way. "Are you watching world go by, or are you waiting for us?"

Alison and Libby giggled. "Neither. We're talking," said Libby.

"Would you let us talk with you?" asked another, with a big smile. "Please don't tell us to go away. We won't be a nuisance." The way he said "don't" and "won't" was different to the way we say it. It sounded like "doornt" and "woornt". And he said "oos" instead of "us".

They stayed and talked and kicked stones and stroked Bran and leaned on Uncle Arthur's wall. One was called Wilfred, one Edwin and the smallest one who was a bit like Greg Hunt was Jim. They talked mostly to Alison and Libby and I felt rather left out. They said they came from a place called Ull, but I had no idea where it was. Somewhere near Scotland? Or Liverpool?

I was quite pleased when they went. "Goodbye, Alison," they called, "Bye, Libby." We watched them run down the road, and Libby giggled again. None of them said goodbye to me, so perhaps they'd forgotten my name, but Edwin waved to me. And then it was time for Libby and Alison to go, so they went inside to say thank you.

Almost as soon as I had waved them goodbye my asthma started up and I needed help. Father could see bits of hay stuck to my clothes, and he told me off for going into the barn. He got out the Potter's Cure and even though it was my birthday I had to sit with my head covered with a cloth and breathe the balm in. It was the worst attack I had had for some time and Father was worried and cross at the same time. But at last the asthma let go of me. That's what it feels like – something squeezing my chest tight so I can hardly breathe, and then gradually letting it go.

It was only when I was in bed that I remembered about looking for the tunnel. I'd take the others into the military area by my secret route, and we'd draw a plan of where we searched, and keep notes about what we found. I shivered with excitement. It would be so good if we found it. Uncle Arthur had said he thought the place was almost empty now and I was pretty sure that even if someone saw us they wouldn't mind. After all, what harm could three girls do? I went to sleep wondering what food I should take. I'd certainly take more than I did on the day the Women's Land Army found me.

And I decided that the next time I went to Ampton, I'd take the autograph book and ask everyone to write or draw something in it. I could get dozens of autographs. More than anyone else I knew.

July 1917

People were used to wartime by now, but in just a few years our lives had changed. Of course we weren't used to so many deaths, or to the grief those deaths brought, but we accepted that there was nothing we could do to stop the war. It overrode everything and everyone and we had to pick our way through it.

We saw uniforms all the time. Not just soldiers, but VADs, Red Cross and St John's Ambulance workers, patients in and from the various local military hospitals. (As well as Ampton there was one in Bury). And Land Army women, like the ones who brought Elly home, seemed to be everywhere.

We were eating different sorts of food, too, because what we usually had was becoming scarce. So many ships bringing food here from abroad had been sunk. Being on a farm, our family was lucky, and Bridget was doing her best with what she had. We were eating less meat, but still had plenty of greens and potatoes, and even eggs.

To be honest, Bridget's life was much as it had been for the last thirty years, but Hattie's certainly wasn't. Before the war, we had lived quite an uneventful but perfectly pleasant life. Years ago, my brother and I had been lucky enough to share a small inheritance from our father. This had enabled Arthur to put down a sizeable deposit on his farm and pay the loan off over a number of years. For me, the capital meant I did not have to seek a high income. This was fortunate because I had significant spells of illness connect- ed to my digestive system. Moreover, the work I did in Mr Cullum's library and collections of antiquarian objects was interesting and rewarding, not to mention the bonus of his providing me with a very pleasant house at a reasonable rent. We managed to afford what we needed, though I was anxious about what would happen if either of the boys went to university. As it happened, Conrad had no desire to do so, and Lawrence ... well, we'll wait and see.

As for Hattie, her life has certainly changed since we've been here at West Stow, but the work and the people at Ampton have caused her to change her thinking. Indeed, Ampton and Ingham and the patients have changed me too.

When I see so many men with wounds that render them completely unable to work, I cannot imagine how they and their families will survive, and Arthur has a point when he questions how factories and workplaces will function without able-bodied men. Obviously, the solution being discussed most is that women should do work previously done by men, but this idea attracts a huge amount of opposition. It's being said that women are incapable of doing men's jobs, either because they are not strong enough or not intelligent enough. It's feared they will undercut men and prevent them from getting jobs. It will take them away from their families. It will make them ill. They will suffer miscarriages. They will become unwomanly. They will be corrupted by the workplace and fail to instill moral values into their families. Men – and plenty of women – are saying women should be mothers, not workers. That they *want* to be mothers, not workers.

Arthur and Bridget's agreement with such opinions is not surprising, and I have to admit that I have some reservations too. I don't object to women collecting fares or inspecting gas meters, but I'm not so sure about heavy work. And *how* can women be both mothers and workers? You can't drive a bus while holding a baby.

But change is happening, and it's even happening here in Suffolk. I've already seen women chopping down trees and hoeing and harvesting – jobs that they have never done before, or only helped with in a minor way. And in the towns they are working in factories. At T. Nice's engineering works in Bury numerous young women are employed to make munitions. (I bumped into a gaggle of them recently, just after they were on their way home from work. I'd thought the heavy work would have tired them out, but they were laughing and joking together). And while at first it was astonishing to see how many women were behind the wheels of cars and trucks, now it's almost commonplace. Our Red Cross ambulances are usually driven by women.

Before she went to Ampton Hattie had enjoyed the company of various women whom she'd known for years, but I've always thought of her as quite quiet except on those odd occasions when she feels indignant about something. While we enjoy each other's company and often spend time walking and talking, she is also independent and happy to spend time on her own. But that is not the case now. Although she has not learned to drive and is not a munitionette, Ampton has brought her new friends, new experiences and new ideas. She is throwing herself into her work whole-heartedly, and I can see that despite the physical tiredness this causes her, it also nourishes her spirit.

She told me that both the war and being at Ampton had "woken her up", that she had had no idea about the lives lived by people in different places and in different circumstances, that she had never properly appreciated how lucky she was. At times, patients had poured out their stories and their hearts to her. And, in the slow hours of the night, nurses had done the same. She was told about intimate and private fears, disappointments, hopes, longings. She heard about the weight of poverty which affected many more people than she imagined. Learning about these things caused her to work even harder.

As she shared these things with me, I noticed that increasingly she was beginning to quote Anne and Vicky, two VAD newcomers to Ampton who had strong views about votes for women. Listening to them, she said, meant she could not avoid thinking deeply about the role of women. She realised that she had never questioned the fact that almost all women were regarded, by themselves as well as by men, as inferior to men. She had just accepted that that was how things were.

I watched Hattie change. She did not change towards me, but at home I saw her become critical of the way in which Bridget took it for granted that she should run around after Arthur. Though Hattie felt guilty that our arrival at West Stow created more cooking, cleaning and tidying for Bridget, she refused to give up Ampton. She said, "I can't justify staying here to clean things which are already clean when injured men needing attention are only just down the road." She asked questions such as why did Bridget run round Arthur and *serve* him when she'd been just as busy as he had all day, especially on wash day when she was really tired? But when Hattie tried to show solidarity, Bridget interpreted her words as critical and patronizing, claiming that she liked to look after Arthur because he was her husband and he deserved it.

Hattie's conversation centred around the growing numbers of women at work, and the unfairness of women not being allowed the vote. One evening she asked Bridget directly, "Don't you think we should have the vote?"

Bridget shrugged. "If we did, I'd vote the same as Arthur."

"Why?"

"He knows about politics and I don't."

"But you could learn, you could find out."

"I haven't got time to learn. And I don't really want to either. I'm busy enough as it is. Which reminds me, I must do the ironing first thing tomorrow. It piles up now there's five of us."

June and July 1917

In Waziristan, after repeated skirmishes in the mountains, in which the British usually, but not always, came off better, messengers were received from the Mahsuds asking for a peace treaty. This led to a five day truce at Ispana Raghza. Hundreds of Mahsuds flocked in to discuss terms. Amongst other things they agreed to return the rifles they had stolen, guarantee their good behaviour in the future and produce two men to be tried in respect of a British officer they had killed. In return, the British agreed to release the prisoners they held.

It was then a question of waiting for the rifles to be handed in, which only happened bit by bit, requiring the deadline to be extended twice. Finally, when the weapons had been laid out on the ground and counted and re-counted, peace was in sight, and it was planned that a full ceremonial jirga would be held beside the Indus on August 10th.

It was an extraordinary, unique experience for the British troops. For a start, they were astonished to see the numbers of tribesmen arriving. Well over three thousand Mahsuds turned up. They came mostly on foot, but some were on mules, horses or camels, and they brought dogs, goats, fowls, and were followed by ox carts. The shouting, baying and neighing, and the singing roar of camels was accompanied by the stink of human and animal excrement, and by the smell of food being cooked over smoky wood fires. Depending on the time of day and on the way the wind was blowing, one of these smells would take precedence over the others.

Each man was provided with flour, the local type of sugar and grain for his animals, but far from giving satisfaction, the distribution of these supplies sometimes caused arguments, blows and stone-throwing.

The tribesmen were wearing their usual mixture of loose, dirty garments, large turban-like headdresses and bushy beards. Many had bare feet, and the shoes worn by a few lucky ones gave little protection from the rocky terrain. The maliks, or headmen, sat in a circle with British officers to confirm what had been decided. The hundreds of Mahsuds settled themselves in an outer circle some distance away. The Londons had never seen anything like it, and were impressed that any semblance of order at all could be achieved amongst men they considered not just very different to themselves, but half-wild, and driven only by the desire for revenge or immediate advantage.

Finally, after speeches, peace was declared. To end the jirga, the huge assembly of leaders and their men rose as one and repeated aloud the long prayer for peace which asked for Allah's blessing. Every tribesman was familiar with this, and Lawrence suddenly came to understand the meaning of that common phrase "by heart". He reflected that he only knew the short Lord's Prayer, which he often gabbled rather than recited. For a moment, the experience of hearing these united voices in this dry, barren place moved him. It was not that he felt close to God, whom he rarely thought about, but that he felt close to all men, including these rough and alien men.

At night the huge moon eased its slow path through the darkness, and the stars appeared as tiny white dots.

Gradually, over a matter of days, the tribesmen made their way back to their homes along the valleys, across the rivers, over ranges of hills. Most of the Londons were sceptical about the future. Would wild tribesmen stick to the terms of the Treaty?

August 1917

Dear Mother and Father,

Thank you for the letters. So good to hear that everyone's well.

Well, we've finished! At least, that's what we're being told, and although we've been told things before that turned out not to be true, it's certainly the case that our officers seem confident about the Treaty I told you was going to be agreed and has now been agreed. One day I'll tell you about the jirga (meeting). I've never been to anything like it.

So, what next? I'd like to think it was back to Blighty as soon as poss. but don't raise your hopes.

Here's a question for Elly. Have you ever got wet through when you've been on a walk?

I bet you have, but I bet you've never been as wet as we have.

After the jirga we marched to where we were going to spend just one night before getting on a train for Jullunder. We made ourselves as comfortable as we could at the railway station. Though we were feeling pretty pleased with ourselves we could also see, now that we were together but away from those hordes of Mahsuds, how our numbers have been depleted. 800 of us started out, and now there's less than 400. We've got men in hospitals and depots all over the place, and we've lost some.

So, imagine 400 men trying to make themselves comfortable lying along the railway line. We were so tired that we hardly noticed it was beginning to rain when we settled down to sleep. Not just to rain but to rain BUCKETS, to the extent that people began shouting and trying to get out of their tents! The rain caused a dam to burst, and we were in the way of the water flowing from it! It was soon waist high and everyone woke up soaking wet and scrambled to get onto the platform which was raised above ground level. But we couldn't protect our tents and what was in them. I grabbed the nearest item of clothing (a shirt) and my rifle, then tried to collect up my equipment and things, and find a place for them on the platform. Officers were running around wearing only socks, hats and blankets! There were natives all over the place!

The next morning we salvaged what we could and spread it out to dry on the platform. What a mess. Plenty of stuff had to be destroyed completely. We spent four days sorting out our possessions and supplies.

Never mind. We're dry now! We've crossed back over the Indus and are spending tonight at Mari Indus (again). I'm writing this in a YMCA. I've bought a nice cup of cocoa and some decent sandwiches, and there's even a gramophone playing a catchy tune that you probably know all the words of but I've never heard before.

We're expecting to assemble at our HQ at Gharial and stay there until everyone's fit enough to travel to Jullundur. Then I'm hoping that we'll be travelling south to Bangalore. I'm not going to attempt to guess where we'll spend Christmas, but I'm sure it'll be a good one.

I'm thinking of you all.

Your son Lawrence

August 1917

The force had fully accomplished its task, and although the operation had lasted only a short time, it was carried out during the hottest and most enervating season of the year in one of the most unhealthy areas of the Trans-Frontier Province where dysentery, diarrhoea, malaria and sand-fly fever were rife. Of all frontier expeditions there was none in which the troops had undergone more continuous hardship and fatigue.

A unique feature of the campaign was that it was the first occasion on which the Royal Flying Corps, British territorial battalions and regiments of the Nepalese army had participated in operations against the tribesmen of the North-West Frontier.

August 1917

My autograph book was getting full. I had sketches of views, dogs, cats, horses, little verses, several riddles, two portraits of me (everyone said one was very like me) and detailed drawings of cap badges and mottoes. Most of all I liked a sketch of Ampton Hall. Some men had written only their Christian names, while others wrote their surnames too, and their rank and the name of their regiment. I was very pleased.

Today I walked round the gardens, looking for people I hadn't seen recently and I saw Bob sitting alone on a bench, so I hurried over and asked him for his signature. But I'd forgotten he was blind. Obviously, he wouldn't be able to write or draw. I felt terrible. I didn't think of him as blind because we'd talked lots together about all sorts of things like aeroplanes and prehistoric animals and food we hated. I was so glad that no-one else had heard me.

I apologised at once, and Bob nodded slowly. He remained silent for a minute, then said, "Give me the book and open it at the page where you want me to write. Then give me the pen and put it where I should start."

He wrote his name in clear writing, unlike some people who just scribbled their name. Robert Eldon Borthwick.

"There. How does that look?"

"It's fine. Nice and clear."

"Now you won't forget me."

"Thank you. No. I won't. And I hope you'll remember me."

"I've got a good idea of what you look like. Small. Brown eyes. Long hair."

"I'm small and have brown eyes, but my hair is quite short."

"Well, two out of three things right isn't bad for a blind man."

After lunch I made for Laurie because I'd heard he'd written a poem. Some of the patients had told Mother how good it was, and they asked Laurie to read it aloud, so he stood up straight, took a deep breath and did so. He was on a step in front of a statue, and it looked as if he was on a proper stage at the theatre, only out-of-doors. While he was reading some birds flew in front of him, but they didn't put him off. He spoke in a strong voice.

Ampton Hall

When you're battered, beat and broken
  On the sodden fields of France
And you think you're going to glory
  You've got just a fighting chance

When the good ship sails for Blighty
  With a smile on one and all
Then, my lad, if you're lucky
  Just you head for Ampton Hall

Such a lovely spot in Suffolk
  Home of luxury and ease
Now a tiny bit of heaven
  Where all suff'ring they appease

Where the doctors and the nurses
  And the sisters all combine
To make Tommy's stay in Blighty
  Absolutely fine.

Girt around with scenes of splendour
  Such as only England knows
Scenes that make our dear old homeland
  Envied by both friends and foes.

There you soon get fit and ready
  Aye, to go and fight or fall
For the honour of Old England
  And such homes as Ampton Hall.

Everyone clapped loudly.

Mother said, "That's lovely, Laurie. Well done. Thank you so much." Then she asked. "Elly's not bothering you, is she?"

"Not at all, nurse. She's a cheerful little thing, always smiling. One day she'll make some man very happy. Let's hope she won't have to go off to a factory somewhere."

Hugh added, "All the women'll go back to their homes once the war's over. Back to normality, thank God."

I waved at the men and went out with Mother. I was looking forward to showing her all the new entries in my book. She had to go to Bury straight after our quick lunch, so there was no chance, but she allowed me to stay at Ampton without her. She said I could ask people for autographs as long as I stayed out of doors and the Matron knew where I was, in case there was a job I could help with. It was funny how I liked doing jobs here but tried to avoid them in West Stow. I knew I could be useful in the wards, but children were only allowed if they had special permission. Mother said, "Remember, it's not a place for children." So the jobs I was given were things like posting letters, or collecting up plates and cups which had been left outside.

But I wanted a quick look in the kitchen while no-one was around. I was hoping there might be something I could take with me on the tunnel expedition, because that was only a week away. I had seen Alison and Libby once since my birthday, and we had agreed where and when we'd meet. Now would be a good chance to get some food.

There were lots of vegetables and fruit in the store cupboards, and meat and cheese in the cold store. I needed something that I could carry home easily, without being seen, and it had to be something that wouldn't go bad. Something nice. I thought of some biscuits which had been sent to the patients. No-one would notice if I took some of those. I looked round the shelves and guessed where the tins were kept, and I was right.

Suddenly I heard someone coming, so I grabbed a small tin, pushed it under my apron and walked towards the kitchen door. I nearly bumped into Nurse Sayle, and we both apologised. "Are you all right?" she asked. I told her I had just gone in there for a drink of water.

That evening, up in my attic, I opened the tin. It was full of ginger biscuits. I tried one. Delicious.

The next day the postman brought a letter for me, which had hardly ever happened in my life. It was from Alison, and she wrote,

Dear Elly,

I'm sorry but I won't be able to come with you as we arranged.

I hope you have got some good things in your autograph book now. You're lucky to be able to go into the hospital. I'm going to Cambridge next week to see my grandparents, so I'll ask them and my cousins for their autographs.

Good luck!

Love from Alison

I was very disappointed. I wanted Alison to be there as well as me and Libby. I'd feel braver if she was with us. I felt upset and cross. Why had she changed her mind? And why had she left it till now? She could have told me weeks ago.

Still, Libby and I would do it on our own. As planned, we would meet at eleven o'clock at West Stow church on September 6th. We'd leave our bikes by the church, and start walking towards Elveden. I would just have to cross my fingers and hope that no-one asked where I was going, but if they did, I'd tell them I was going to the Sturges with some flints.

Only five days to wait.

I tore up Alison's letter and burned it in the kitchen stove to make sure no-one else read it.

September 1917

It was the day of the Fete. The special fete in the Abbey Gardens to raise money for the Suffolk Prisoners of War Fund. I'd promised to take Elly and she'd been excited for days. She had insisted on my buying our tickets in advance because doing so gave us the chance of winning a prize. I had been in Bury the day before and seen the displays and stalls in the streets, and on Saturday we were lucky enough to get a lift into town and be at the front of the queue. People were not particularly smartly dressed, for good clothes were rare these days. Also, rain was expected, and everyone knew there were plenty of unruly activities to get involved in. The occasion reminded me, a little sadly, of the wonderful annual fetes at Hardwick, when Mr Cullum opened his gardens to hundreds and hundreds of visitors, and people dressed up in their very best clothes and walked or came in carriages from the town laughing and looking forward to their day out.

The war stopped all that, of course, but here we were, about to enjoy a Fete. The band from the 1st Suffolks set the scene, and before long everyone was streaming into the Park. I regretted that Hattie couldn't be with us, but, as usual, she was at Ampton.

Elly hardly knew where to go first. She loved the organ grinder and gave handfuls of grass to his horse. We sat and listened to a group of musicians from London, and I remembered the piano lessons I'd had as a boy in Thetford. Hattie and I would have struggled to provide our children with music lessons, but as I listened to the instruments I suddenly felt that I should have more music in my life than hymns at church.

Every now and again I saw people I knew, and they all asked after Conrad and Lawrence. Many did not know of Conrad's death. I greeted them with enquiries after their families, and of course I heard about more lost sons, husbands and brothers. We were at a fete, a typical market town fete, I supposed, where games and entertainments displaced grief for just a few hours or perhaps only a few minutes. Money was being raised to help those Suffolk men who were held in captivity. I could not stop myself from thinking that though they might be subjected to appalling treatment and be living in terrible conditions, they were alive, and at least some of them would come home.

When the little concert was over, Elly pulled me across the grass to see some dancing. Several of her friends went to Miss Tinkler's School of Dancing, and she was hoping to see some of them in the performance. And yes, Gertie Field was taking part. She was wearing a long dress, and her hair was piled up on her head. Elly thought it would be difficult for her to dance like that but Gertie managed well in her role as a nobleman's wife, and smiled at us when we clapped enthusiastically at the end.

We listened to children reciting poems for a while, and then we called in to the Peter Pan tent to see Peter and Wendy and Captain Hook. But Elly decided against the Mystery tent.

I was on the look-out for the Fortune Teller, and I found her sitting at a table with a crystal ball. This, I impressed on Elly, was a real crystal ball. The paper confirmed later that "It was lent to the Mayor by Mr Milner-Gibson-Cullum, of whose priceless collection of antiquities it forms part."

Elly begged me to have my fortune told, but I said that I'd prefer to accept things as they came. Of course I don't believe in crystal balls and I don't want Elly to, but she pleaded with me so I gave in. I watched her stare at the ball in anxious silence, and lean forward to catch every word of what she was told. The teller spoke softly to create a mysterious atmosphere, and in doing so ensured that what she said was private.

Elly came bouncing back. "I'm not going to be very rich, but I don't mind, and I don't know who I'll marry, but I'm going to travel and I'm going to have many friends and one day soon I'm going to have a *dog*." She was delighted.

I had heard that a Bury man, a Mr Fiddaman, had written a play called "The Last Zeppelin", set locally, and I was keen to see this. It only had two characters, both Royal Flying Corps officers, one a Lieutenant, one a Captain. These were both played excellently by women, one being a member of the Fiddaman family. The action took place in Suffolk, and the lieutenant brought the Zeppelin crashing down, and the spectators cheered as the Boche perished. Finally, the lieutenant was rewarded with promotion. People enjoyed the play partly because it was full of local references and used contemporary expressions, but mostly because the evil Germans, like the ones who had dropped bombs on Bury, were defeated.

Bombs and their impact were never far away. Recently, in the Bury Free Press, I'd read

East End Tots and the Huns

Last Sunday's "Weekly Despatch" contained an interesting article entitled The Village of Air Raid Babes. It deals with the work being carried on in the village of Bletchingly, where Mr Sneezum, son of the late Mr Geo. Sneezum of Bury St Edmunds, and his wife, are in charge of a home where the little victims of the Poplar bomb raid have been sent to find a rest cure to restore the shattered nerves of the little mites so cruelly shaken in mind and body by the exponents of German kultur.

We were three years into the war, and there seemed no end to it.

I had a go at the coconut shy, but I won nothing, and Elly commented cheerfully that Conrad and Lawrence would have knocked all the coconuts down. We sheltered from the rain under the trees before looking at the garden produce entries for the competitions. I wished Arthur had entered his vegetables for his were certainly equal to these perfect cabbages and beans and radishes.

And then it was time for the races. We were intrigued by the idea of a Garden of Eden race. Whatever could that be? When Elly met another girl from her school they ran off to watch the Musical Chairs on Horses race, and the Tilting Bucket. We agreed on a time to meet back at the Fortune Teller's tent.

I wandered down past the ruins to where the Lark flows slowly under the Abbot's Bridge. The usual assembly of ducks was nowhere to be seen, their territory having been invaded. I sat down on a dryish bench for a rest, and my thoughts returned to the play with its popular message: kill the Germans. I was mulling over what Mr Cullum had recently told me about a speech he had heard.

It was given by the President of the London Society of East Anglians. Apparently he'd said that what the Germans were trying to do was to break the nerve of our nation. They thought that if they inflicted pain on innocent people they would create panic, but panic was foreign altogether to our nature. If they laid a few houses in East London desolate they presumed we would despair and become a nation in dismay. But we wouldn't! Nothing of the kind!

The speaker went on to say that if there were not enough aeroplanes at present to go round, it was General Haig who must have them. The country would rather go short on aeroplanes for defensive purposes than that Sir Douglas Haig should have insufficient. He ended up by saying that in a few months time we would have enough to protect London and East Anglia and give Haig all he wanted into the bargain.

Mr Hayes Fisher, the speaker, was warmly applauded and Sir Courtney Warner said there was no fear of the County of Suffolk being frightened of air raids. We should know how to stand shoulder to shoulder till we had crushed Germany or driven her to an honourable peace.

Crushing Germany. That seemed to be what most people wanted. But not everyone, for more than a few conscientious objectors were refusing not just to crush and kill but to play any part in the war effort. Were they right?

As I made my way back to our meeting place Elly and her friend raced up to me. It turned out that the Garden of Eden race was one where a rope, stretched between two posts at above head height, had apples suspended from it on lengths of string. Competitors had to eat an apple without using their hands, a tricky task much enjoyed by spectators. Elly and her friend had been given boxes to stand on because they were not tall enough. This had the result of making things even more difficult, but they had loved it.

"And now it's dancing, Father! Let's go and see the dancing!" And so we walked towards the music, and I sat down while Elly skipped around with a new friend she had made. Hattie and I had never danced together. We had never talked about this, and I supposed that there were plenty of men who had never danced with their wives. I had danced a few times when I was a student, and there may have been a few opportunities later on, but I'd never taken them.

Looking out across the grass, which had by now become rather roughed up, people were swaying to the band's melodies. I noticed that many couples consisted of two women rather than of a man and a woman, and that many of those watching were women. All over Europe, I thought, numerous women were without partners. Elly, hand in hand with her friend, was making up steps to the music, and I found myself hoping that one day she would find a good man and dance with him. I seemed to remember that Conrad had attended one or two evening events at Greene King, but I had no idea if these had included dancing.

He would never dance again. That was all there was to it. Conrad would never dance again.

And who could tell about Lawrence? I tried but failed to imagine him dancing.

"Father, what's the matter? Are you all right?"

"Yes." I stood up. "Come on, we need to get good places for the Tattoo."

Along with everyone else we admired the marching, the drill, the drummers, the precision, the brass, the uniforms, all contributing to music that somehow raised everyone's spirits. The audience's pleasure and pride were almost tangible, and when the time came to sing God Save the King, we roared it out. Later, people said that our voices had threatened to wake the long-dead monks of the Abbey.

September 1917

From *The Londoner*, The Chapatti, by O H Bond

In the minds of the happily uninitiated the word chapatti may, very probably, conjure up nightmarish versions of some prehistoric mammoth whose skeleton has been disinterred in Siberia or other such delectable region. Before proceeding further in this malodorous subject, I will interpret, for the benefit of these ignorant beings. In the first place, permit me to utter a word of warning. He who values his life, an idiosyncrasy by no means uncommon, should abstain carefully from mentioning this sinister name to anyone whom he even suspects of having had acquaintance of the North West Frontier of India. It is a remarkably sore point with such people and allusions to a chapatti should, in all circumstances, be absolutely shunned.

The process of manufacture of this delectable article of diet may possibly be a source of entertainment to any who are interested in cookery or any of the other occult sciences. It would doubtless appear simple if set down in cold blood in one of Mrs Beeton's manuals for busy housewives, when the possession of rolling pins, pastry boards, cake cutters and all other modern culinary equipment is taken for granted: but in central Asia the trade in these articles is most disgustingly slack and antiquated methods prevail in consequence.

The predominating motion in the construction or rather in the finishing of the chapatti closely resembles that used by a conjuror when dissolving eggs or tame rabbits into thin air. The detail is as follows:

Holding the chapatti limply in the palm of the left hand, palm uppermost, grasp the edge at any convenient point on the circumference firmly between the thumb and forefinger of the right hand, thumb uppermost. With a firm pressure vertically between the thumb and the forefinger of the right hand, and at the same time maintaining a steady anti-clockwise motion, pass the ... but no. Only a very king among drill instructors would ever succeed in enunciating clearly this complicated movement. I will desist. It may be stated without fear of contradiction that in Northern India wars are won and lost and chapattis are made and eaten with the most alarming regularity – in fact one might almost say daily, but still the British Army in India lives and laughs.

September 1917

Grand Football Carnival in Bury

Lady Munition Workers Victorious

"Well played, Celeste," piped the light soprano of a pretty, well-made munitionette as with strong brown hands she gripped the rope in front of her and with glowing eyes and heightened colour watched a finely proportioned girl artistically dribbling the football towards the opponents' goal, and followed by four or five other young ladies, all equally intent in putting the leather spheroid between the two wooden be-netted uprights guarded by men. And they would have realized their ambition had a couple of the fair ones following energetically behind anticipated events and led, instead of followed the chum who was pedally propelling the ball onward. But never mind, the ultimate result was the same. In the case of each match played the ladies won, by a brave margin, so what more do you want? And the same success attended their efforts in subsequent tugs of war with the masculine footballers. Thus it was quite a ladies' day.

Ladies had been invited to play or help at these Novelty Football Matches against men whose right arms were to be secured behind their backs.

Miss Manning's eleven wore light and dark blue striped jerseys and grey skirts with blue caps with black bands, while Miss Shorter's eleven wore yellow and black striped jerseys, crimson skirts, and yellow caps with black bands.

Prior to the kick off it was quite pleasant to stroll about the field in the genial sunshine watching the public and the players and listening to the strains of the excellent band of the 1st Suffolks. The colourful costumes of the lady players lent a bright and picturesque air to the scene, and their savoir faire was equally attractive. Standing about in groups talking, or walking about with arms linked, humming snatches of catchy airs they looked the personification of insouciance. But were they? Ah, there's the rub! You never know a woman's mind or thoughts. When you do, life will have lost its savour, for there will be nothing more to solve in humanity. Mayhap these demure looking munition workers were fully aware of the concentrated gaze of hundreds of eyes upon them, and of the open admiration expressed therein, but they were as apparently as unconscious of it all as the Sphinx, and absolutely as unresponsive. And so we have to leave the eternal question where we found it.

So far as the actual games were concerned, it may be briefly said that the first contest was between the Bury St Edmunds X1 and Miss Manning's X1. During the first half Miss Hogg registered for the active and sprightly feminine players. After change of ends, Miss Ely added two more goals, and Miss Manning's X1 thus registered three goals to nil.

In the second contest between the Bury St Edmunds X1 and Miss Shorter's X1, Miss Shorter's team scored seven goals to their opponents' four.

But the importance and interest of the exceptional occasion demand something more than this terse description. Those who were not present will want to know how the ladies shaped, what was the demeanour of the onlookers, and other points. And quite right too. Otherwise, how are they to know that the lady goalies played an intelligent game, each displaying a keen eye, a quick pair of hands and clean kicking capabilities; that the backs used shapely limbs with effect in getting the football away, and that the halves and forwards raced about here, there and everywhere with the vigour and ease of athletes and the daintiness of fairies.

September 1917

Eric decided to see the prisoners-of-war for himself. For the last week or so a lorry full of them had been brought to Lackford Bridge from their camp each morning. At the end of the day it returned to pick them up. They were repairing the staunch and crumbling banks of the Lark, shoring them up so the river could not flood into the fields in winter and spring as it usually did. For the last few years Cecil Pickup and George Abley, whose fields stretched along each side of the Lark, had not been able to grow anything there other than brown mustard, and even that had produced only poor harvests.

As Eric got nearer he could see several men wielding long-handled drainage shovels. Others were measuring with rules and ropes, others pounding posts into the wet black earth, and some were working on drainage culverts. It was an industrious scene, quiet except for the thudding hammers and a few calls between the prisoners. There were about a dozen of them. There was nothing about them that indicated they were anything other than ordinary, healthy young men getting on with their work.

Eric approached to the point where he would sink into mud if he went further. The workers all wore wellington boots, but as it was a mild day they had taken their jackets off and put them on a wire fence where they hung like hunched vultures.

Eric tried to guess the circumstances in which they had been captured. Could their paths have crossed with Conrad's in France? Could one of them have killed him?

And here they were now, in Suffolk, within a mile of his home.

On the other side of the Lark a rowing boat was tied to a metal stake, ready to ferry men and tools backwards and forwards.

How sad that we kill each other. Eric gazed across the river to the north as a slow heron launched itself into the air. How stupid we are. How stupid and how sad.

"Good morning."

When he realised he was being spoken to he turned

round and returned the greeting.

A prisoner holding a mallet said, "Not cold. October, but not cold."

"No, it's quite warm."

The man gave the wooden post in front of him another blow. "But winter soon. Schnee. Snow."

Two men approached with a pile of poles on their shoulders, and lowered them onto the bank. They nodded at Eric who was wondering where their camp was, for he was sure there wasn't one locally.

"Where are you from?"

"Munich. In south Germany." He pronounced the word south "souse".

"No, I mean here, in England. Where are you living?"

The man named a place which he indicated was quite a distance away, but Eric did not recognise it.

On the other side of the river a man was getting into the boat. He was clearly in charge of the prisoners, though his manner with them was no different to that of any supervisor with any group of workers. He rowed himself across in just a few minutes, then tied the boat up to a tree trunk.

Eric introduced himself as an interested local observer, and asked where the prisoners came from.

"Kenninghall, in Norfolk."

"On the other side of Garboldisham? Right out by East Harling?"

"That's it."

"It's a very long way to bring them."

The supervisor explained that while everyone wanted prisoners to be usefully employed, and had agricultural and building work for them to do, finding accommodation for them was difficult. He laughed. "People are happy for them to work in their village, but not to live there. But then someone thought of Guiltcross in Kenninghall. Do you know it?"

Eric shook his head.

"It's a very big building. Rather, I should say, a collection of buildings. From the eighteen-fifties, I suppose? It used to be a workhouse until, not many years ago, they improved it greatly by building new blocks, and it was used for mentally deficient people and inebriates. And now prisoners-of-war." He scratched the back of his head. "I tell you, it's good accommodation."

"Will these men stay there until the end of the war?"

"I don't know, but if I was one of them I'd hope so. I'd lie low and do as I was told. These ones are the lucky ones. They've escaped injury and death; they're being fed and watered; they sleep in dry beds. They've nothing to complain about."

The supervisor called out to the men and beckoned them as it was time for a meal break. Each put his tools in one barrow and collected a bag from another. They sat on benches improvised from barrels and planks. As Eric walked away and they began to eat, several acknowledged him by raising their hand.

Everyone he knew whose work was connected to the land needed more labour. It was shortsighted for villages not to accept groups of prisoners-of-war living amongst them. There was so much they could contribute. In West Stow it was the river which needed, and was now receiving, urgent attention, thankfully. But there had not been enough men for the recent harvest, nor for ploughing, nor for rat catching or rabbit trapping. Surely these prisoners were blessings in disguise?

September 1917

No-one stopped me. No-one even saw me, except Rex, and he took no notice. I walked out of the house with a bag containing

Pencil and notebook
Trowel
Knife
Small tin of biscuits
2 slices of bread
2 apples
2 carrots
small piece of cheese

I meant to pick up a few flints with me in case I had to say that I was going to the Sturges, but they would make my bag too heavy, so I decided not to.

I remembered to put on my strong shoes.

I got to West Stow church in plenty of time. In fact, by the clock on the tower I was five minutes early, so I wandered round the churchyard. I'd never realised before how many graves there were. Among them was one new grave with the earth still loose on top. It didn't have a headstone yet but there was a wreath on it. It must be Mrs Porty, who had lived in the cottage on the corner. Uncle Arthur said she had had a good innings.

I knew Conrad wouldn't be buried here, because Father said that men who were killed abroad were not brought back to England or to Scotland or wherever they had come from. This seemed sad to me, but I could understand because there were too many of them, and anyway, how could they know exactly who was who on a battlefield? They might take the wrong man to the wrong place.

Mother said that Hawstead, not West Stow, would be the best place for Conrad's headstone, because that's where he lived for almost all his life.

I sat in the porch where I couldn't be seen from the road, in case someone asked what I was doing there, but this meant I had to keep walking down to where the path goes through the wall to the lane so I didn't miss Libby who'd be arriving any minute.

The graves reminded me of a poem we'd been learning at school. I'd had to stand up in front of the class and recite it.

My heart leaps up when I behold
A rainbow in the sky
So was it when my life began
So is it now I am a man
So be it when I shall grow old
Or let me die.
The child is father of the man
And I could wish my days to be
Bound each to each in natural piety.

Libby still didn't come, not even when I went out into the road and looked for her.

I became so tired of waiting that I decided to go and search for the tunnel on my own.

I set off away from the village and out into the breckland. I was heading for the middle of the Elveden estate because I thought no-one would ever dig a tunnel at the edge of the area near where the canvas curtain had been. I tried to go in a straight line towards a group of trees, but had to go round the outside of patches of bracken because they were too tall and strong to push through. I was looking out for piles of earth. I didn't expect to come across the entrance to the tunnel by accident, but the more I thought about it the more I expected to find it. Dan had said that huge machines made it, and if that was true the entrance would have to be huge too, like an entrance to a cave. Surely I wouldn't miss something as big as that?

I kept looking all around for people, but I saw no sign of anyone. No soldiers, no-one working, no-one picking blackberries, even though there were plenty of bushes with lots of fruit (which I kept on eating). There was just me and birds and rabbits in this big heath, and it was strange to think that not so long ago it was full of troops getting ready for war.

There were hundreds of rabbit holes. Aunt Bridget had a rabbit fur coat and I wondered if the particular rabbits it was made out of had lived here. After an hour I began to feel hungry, so I found a heathery place to sit and eat an apple. The brecks spread out round me, almost flat, but there was much more sky than land. The clouds were puffy today and I lay on my back to look at them properly. Some ringed plovers flew directly into my view, and then rabbits came up really close and I could even see their faces. I had a pet rabbit once, but it died. I wouldn't want a coat like Aunt Bridget's.

Then I saw a bird I'd never seen before. Its shape and size were like a pheasant, but its colours were very different. What I noticed first was its bright yellow head, and a sort of stripey collar. It had blue feathers too, and red, and even more colourful tail feathers than an ordinary pheasant. It was pecking at the ground by some bushes. In order to see it better I stood up slowly and carefully but it flew off, making that loud hoarse sound that pheasants make. Father would know what it was.

I was very cross with Libby and Alison. I had never told them I'd do something with them, and then not done it, so why did they? But I'd find the tunnel myself if I kept looking, even if it took several days of exploring and even though I was the youngest. I closed my bag, put it over my shoulder, and went on walking away from the sun towards a little wood. I didn't think the tunnel would be there because of the tree roots, but it was worth a look. Mother used to say that sometimes, when you're looking for something important or interesting, it turns out that you find something else which is just as important and interesting in a different way. And that's exactly what happened to me!

I walked in amongst the trees, and there, right in front of me, a bit above eye-level, were marks cut into the smooth bark of a tree-trunk. Someone had carved their initials with a knife, like Lawrence did once at Hardwick, years ago, and Mr Cullum was furious. Did this say RJ or BJ? It could have been either. I looked round for more carvings, and instead of letters, on one tree there was the outline of a woman's face, and on another was a man's. I copied them and the initials into my notebook. I walked on, wondering about who had done the carvings, and when, and why, and if anybody else had seen them.

I came to a belt of pines and made myself look carefully in every direction so as not to miss anything else special. It was sunny and I could see a long way. There was no sign of the tunnel but I knew it must be lunchtime so I ate some of the bread which had got crumbled up but still tasted good, and a carrot and two ginger biscuits. I wished I'd brought a drink.

On the ground there was a plant with small pink flowers. I didn't know its name, but I picked it and put it in between the pages of my notebook. Then I walked on further, singing one of the hymns we sang in church.

Breathe on me breath of God,
Fill me with life anew
That I may love what
Thou dost love
And do what Thou woulds't do

Breathe on me breath of God
Until my heart is p

A sudden sound shook me. Gunshot.

I froze. Nothing else happened, so I crouched down on the ground. Was someone shooting at *me*? Did they think I was a deer?

What could I do? I was out in the middle of someone else's land, and I had no excuse. I started to run towards a big stand of bracken, but my foot caught in a rabbit hole and I wrenched my ankle.

"Hey! You!"

I turned towards the voice and saw a man walking out from the copse of trees I was heading for. He was carrying a gun.

My ankle hurt badly when I tried to walk, so I curled up in a ball on the ground.

The man was getting a little nearer but was still some distance away. I was looking at him, and he was looking at me. He was angry. He was a gamekeeper. An angry gamekeeper. He came right up close to me, stood his gun on the ground and leant the stock against his leg. Then he pulled his pipe out of his pocket, filled it, and lit it. He did all this without saying a word, and that made me even more frightened.

"What are you doing here? This is private land. You know you're not allowed here, don't you?"

I nodded.

"So why are you here?"

I didn't answer.

"What have you got in your bag?" He puffed on his pipe. "Show me."

I held the bag up to him and he looked inside.

"A knife? Why? Girls don't have knives. And a trowel. What's that for?"

"I dig up flints. I take them to Dr Sturge. In Icklingham."

"Is that where you live?"

"No. I live in West Stow."

"And where are your flints?"

"I haven't been looking for them today."

"Then why bring a trowel?"

I looked at the ground.

"What's your name?"

"Elly."

"Elly who?"

"Bailey."

He gave me the bag back, then said, "Up you get. I'm taking you home. Come on."

I tried to stand but couldn't. "I've hurt my ankle. I twisted it in a rabbit hole."

"Try to stand. Go on."

I couldn't do it, so he took hold of my arm and the back of my jacket quite roughly and lifted me on to my feet, but as soon as I put my weight on my left ankle, it hurt.

He was very cross. "You'll have to stay here until I fetch my horse. Don't move an inch. If you do you'll be in worse trouble. Much worse. Do you understand?"

"I *can't* move. It hurts too much." I felt myself beginning to cry.

"Crying won't help. You're in serious trouble and crying won't help."

And he walked off, his gun under his arm. There was nothing I could do except wait.

October 1917

Dear Mother and Father,

You'll be pleased to know that things have improved a lot since I last wrote. For a start, now we're at Jullundur we're gradually getting back together again. For the last few months we've been spread out but last week almost all of the Londons came back here. Some of the others had been taken up into the Simla hills where they found snow (lucky blighters), while others have been in convalescent depots at Dagshai and elsewhere. Father, I'm not surprised you can't find the all the places I mention in the atlas, because some are little more than forts, and in some cases I'm sure I've got the wrong spellings. All I can say is that we're in the best place we could be (in India, that is) for Christmas, especially as most of those who were injured or ill are gradually arriving here so we'll be together for Christmas. Imagine – we're living in proper bungalows.

But there's one very sad thing. My friend Sidney died. He was wounded at Tank, and never recovered. He was a good man, and I miss him. I've written to his mother. He's the second of her sons to be killed.

Father, we are only 30 miles from Amritsar and I knew you wanted me to go, so I took the opportunity just a few days ago. I went on the train with two friends. The journey took about 2 hours, and cost 15 rupees (which isn't much). I'd heard a bit about the Sikhs' Golden Temple, but it was far more exotic than I expected. I know you've seen pictures, but this is what I saw. ...

A huge, elegant golden building standing in a huge man-made lake. This lake is known as a tank, but I think that's the wrong word, because it's quite lovely and is full of exquisite reflections. It's supposed to have healing powers. Even the clouds were perfect. The palace has delicate minarets. Golden onion-shaped domes. Ivory. Pinnacles. Doves and parrots flying around. Golden pheasants. More gold. Delicate arches and carvings on the building itself and at its four entrance gates. These gates face in different directions and are to show that the Sikh temple is open to all people of all religions, because there are Hindus and Mohammedans here as well as Christians. A sort of elegant promenade reaches across the lake. Before anyone goes inside they have to take off their shoes and gaiters, and leave any sticks, luggage and tobacco. We weren't sure if we'd see ours again, but we were wrong to mistrust the man who said he would look after them for us, because all was well. Then we put on rope-soled slippers, and once we got inside the gate, flowers were showered on us, as if we were being married! It felt like a sort of blessing.

There were crowds and crowds there. Many were praying, singing or listening to readings from what must be a special religious book, some were giving money to the poor, others sight-seeing, some asking us for more rupees when we wanted to go up to the next level. A temple has been here for hundreds of years, but it's changed and been rebuilt. We read that significant restoration was done in the early 1800s by Maharajah Ranjit Singh. I've discovered that all Sikhs seem to be called Singh, but I wondered if this one was related to our Elveden Duleep Singh? Wouldn't it be strange if he was? From the top we could see that men and women were allowed to bathe in the lake, which seemed rather odd, until we learned that it was connected to their religion. Rather like we have baptism, I suppose.

When we came out we came across a statue of Queen Victoria, and a church like an English cathedral. It's even called St Paul's! The bells started to ring and we suddenly all felt very homesick. I recalled that when you took me to Icklingham (or was it Culford?) to watch the bellringers, I thought one old man was going to be swung off his feet! And hearing the bells inside the church was so different to hearing them outside.

The Golden Temple is the most beautiful building I've ever seen. It made me think of what you told me and Conrad about Elveden Hall, but on a bigger scale – a combination of richness, decoration, marble. Apparently it is lit up at night and I wished we could have seen that, for the buildings and their reflection would be quite lovely. Before we took the train back we wandered along the bazaars, and I bought a little ivory horse for Elly.

So you see, this time at Jullundur hasn't been all sports and relaxation. I'm broadening my mind, too.

Christmas will be here shortly, and we've decided that our decorations will be the best in the battalion. If you could see us cutting, sewing, measuring, painting, rigging up lights and curtains, you'd be astonished. Even I'm astonished! Can you imagine me practising carols, and dressing up as Father Christmas's wife?

I'll send you more letters before Christmas, but in case they don't reach you in time, I'm sending

A VERY HAPPY CHRISTMAS
to all of you

Mother, Father, Elly, Uncle Arthur and Aunt Bridget, and to Grandmother in Bury and to Uncle Stan and Aunt Kitty in Downham Market

I'll think of you and drink to you, and I'm hoping so much that I will be with you this time next year.

October 1917

Elly hasn't been able to go to school for a week because of her asthma. She's been up in her room reading. And she's still feeling embarrassed in the wake of her Elveden adventure, as we are. It's hard to understand it.

That afternoon, a few weeks ago now, she limped in to the kitchen just as we'd all started to wonder where she had got to. She was in tears as she threw herself into Hattie's arms. Behind her, hovering at the back door, we were astonished to see Mr Gage the gamekeeper, (who, it turned out, knew Arthur) telling us how he'd found her out on the Elevden estate, all alone, with a sprained ankle. He had thought it best to bring her home on his horse.

But what he had not been able to find out was *why* she was where she was, even though she had admitted that she shouldn't be there. When we asked her, she just shrugged and said that she wanted to go into the estate as she used to, now that the soldiers had gone. Harold Gage said she had been near animal traps which could have hurt her badly, and she could have got lost and that the army was still using big areas of the estate. We thanked him for bringing her home and he left. Straight away, Hattie strapped Elly's foot up, and I was thankful that she knew how to do it properly.

It wasn't until Hattie went upstairs to tuck Elly in that she heard the whole story. It was quite simple. A boy in the village, Dan Hunt, had sworn to Elly that a tunnel was being dug from Elveden to France, and she had decided to try to find it with Libby and Alison. Even though Alison had written to say she couldn't come, and Libby hadn't turned up, she decided to set off on her own.

But a call made on a neighbour's phone to Alison's mother proved that this account wasn't true: Alison completely denied it, and Mrs Gawdy insisted that her daughter was far too sensible to do anything like that.

"But Alison sent me a letter saying she couldn't come! We had arranged to go together. Ask her about the letter!" But Alison denied writing a letter. When we asked Elly to show us the letter she cried again, because she said she had burnt it.

Two days later a visit to Libby's parents shed no more light, for her mother said that on that morning Libby had been at her grandmother's as usual. No such expedition had been mentioned, and she did not allow her daughter to just go off on her own as Elly seemed to be able to do.

That afternoon I asked Elly, "So you're telling me that both Libby and Alison are lying?"

"Yes! But *I'm* telling the truth."

"Elly, you should never accuse someo .."

"But I've told you! I'm telling the truth!"

And the tin of biscuits? Hattie had recognized them at once as being the same as the ones in Ampton pantry. Had Elly taken them?

In tears again, Elly nodded. Hattie and I exchanged glances. Why would Elly steal biscuits which she knew full well had been given to Ampton to make life a little more pleasant for injured soldiers? Surely our daughter knew that was wrong?

"I didn't want to be hungry like I was before. There were lots of tins there. And the soldiers often give me biscuits."

"But the biscuits weren't yours. You knew that. So it was stealing, wasn't it? "

Elly's sobs were now changing to coughs, and the third evening in a row ended up with her coming downstairs to breathe in Potter's Cure.

When Elly was settled in bed and we were sitting by the fire, Bridget, without looking up from her knitting, said, "Well. It's clear that something's wrong, isn't it? Something's very wrong. What are you going to do?"

Hattie was staring into the fire, and I poured myself and Arthur each a small whiskey.

Hattie said, "Probably nothing."

"But what if she makes up more stories and goes off again by herself?"

"I don't think she will."

"But she did before, didn't she?" Bridget's knitting needles were clacking fast. "She's twice just walked off without a by-your-leave. It's very lucky that on both occasions she's been found, and found by decent people. With that ankle she might have been there all night, with you not knowing where she was, and her and us all scared out of our wits."

Hattie went on staring into the fire.

I put another log on. Was Dr Dix right after all? Was this adventure of Elly's 'a suppressed cry for the mother'? Her asthma had certainly got worse recently, but what was the connection between her physical health and her mind?

Bridget's needles were getting on my nerves, but other than the kitchen this was the only room with a fire and enough light to read by, so I stayed put till it was time for bed, my mind going round in circles while I attempted to read the paper. After a while Hattie went upstairs, and half an hour after that Bridget followed her. I sat by the fire as it turned to ash, feeling unsettled. Finally, I stood up, let Bran out for his last run of the day and checked that the doors were locked. In the kitchen I paused to look at the calendar. October would soon be over. And what then? Christmas. Another Christmas without our sons. There was little to look forward to.

It was when lying in bed sleeplessly, thinking about Lawrence's description of Amritsar, that I suddenly remembered that October was the anniversary of Duleep Singh's death, although I had forgotten the exact date. I had attended his funeral in 1893, and I still remembered it clearly. There and then I made up my mind to check the exact date and make a visit to Elveden church in his memory. There were not many people who cared about him, given his slide into anonymity in France, but he remained for me a legendary, imposing figure.

The next day I rummaged through a box of my papers and found the now fragile newspaper cutting about his funeral. It had taken place on October 26th 1893. I gave it to Hattie to read, and left it out for Bridget and Arthur, but I don't think they were interested.

Bury Free Press, October 28 1893

Death of Maharajah Dhuleep Singh

The Daily News comments as follows upon the death of His Highness. "The Maharajah Dhuleep Singh has succumbed to a stroke of apoplexy at Paris. He dies a disappointed and it is feared a miserable man. His career was a mistake from the first. He was a child of misfortune. His father, Old Ranjeet Singh, the Lion of Lahore, aimed at something like universal dominion in India, but his death cut short his project of ambition. His empire crumbled to pieces and the British finally stepped in to make Dhuleep a mediatized ruler and a Prince without a vocation. Ranjeet Singh was a character whole and compact. The son, under British upbringing, was a patchwork of the English country gentleman, member of Quarter Sessions and convert to Christianity on a background of the Sikh warrior King. He came here to live and married a Protestant lady. But he was without a part. He was not such a good squire as one to the manner born, though his preserves at Thetford were among the best in the country. He was no more than a sort of exotic ornament to the throne. His turban made a great impression at state ceremonies, and the dark face and glowing eyes beneath it looked well by contrast among a group of courtiers, as a symbol of the Queen's worldwide dominion. But the part left much to be desired by the man whose circumstances had forced him to play it. Dhuleep had extravagant notions of his race, and his traditions, and he was not to be tied down to a balance of income and expenditure, or even forty thousand a year. He pestered the Indian Office for more and more money and he seems to have been goaded to madness by the studied calm of the official replies. He began to ask himself and others how much money he might have had to play with, but for the fortunes of war and the annexation of his kingdoms. One of the great jewels of his house, the Koh-i-Nor, which had become lawful prize of the conqueror would have given him a free hand in pocket money for many a year. Perhaps he had evil counsellors; he certainly had bitter thoughts. One fine day he blossomed as a rebel or at least as a malcontent. He talked of resuming his hereditary leadership of the Sikhs, and seemed quite ready to renounce the faith of his conversion, which perhaps had never been much more than skin deep. But the Sikhs knew him not, and the land of his adoption began to fear that he was, after all, not thoroughly respectable. He was too much of an Englishman for his own people, and too much of a "native" for ours. Then he was ill advised enough to coquet with treason at foreign courts. He sounded Russia ostentatiously, as though to frighten the India Office. Russia took no notice of him, nor did any other Power and the poor Prince soon learned to see himself in his true proportions. There was nothing left but to beg pardon, and this he did, by a formal submission to the Throne, by which he finally obtained forgiveness. He was henceforth without any honour in this country, or any other, and he became but a second-rate King in exile, a passing wonder at continental spas. He was an unfortunate, without being precisely an injured, man, and all his misfortune came from his having been, from infancy, cast for an impossible part."

On Sunday 26th, which was a beautiful day, we all went together to the early service at West Stow church as usual. In the afternoon Hattie decided to stay at home but encouraged Elly to come with me to Elveden. We borrowed a pony and trap from George Abley and reached the church by three o'clock. I tied the pony to a railing and was pleased to see we had the place to ourselves.

Elly asked, "Was the Maharajah old when he died?"

"No. He died when he was about the age I am now. Exactly twenty-four years ago. Nearly a quarter of a century."

I told her that at the funeral the Maharajah's coffin had been brought from France by ship and then by train, arriving at Thetford station. I showed her where the dark coffin had been placed in the chancel.

"Where did you sit?"

"I waited outside with my parents, with many others who had come to pay their respects. We just managed to squeeze in."

"Was Uncle Arthur there?"

I reflected a moment. "No. He wasn't. But I can't recall why not."

"And another train arrived from London with members of the Maharajah's family, and they were all brought here to the church by carriage. There were lots of policemen, too.

"There was quite a crowd in the churchyard, and as the time of the funeral approached the people moved inside. Victor and Frederick were there of course (I hadn't seen them since we had played cricket together at Cambridge), and the daughters, and lots of important people from London. The Queen didn't come herself, but someone was there representing her. They took up all the seats so there wasn't any room for us to sit down. We stood at the back, and many people even had to remain outside."

"Did you sing hymns?"

"No. We didn't. In fact, there was no music at all, which my parents thought was very odd. After the service some men from the estate (a keeper, I think, and a gardener, and a woodman) lifted up the coffin and took it outside to the grave which was lined with moss and ferns. There was an enormous number of bouquets. I particularly remember exotic yellow flowers, black mourning clothes and a bright blue sky."

Father and I went outside and made our way to the three graves we knew so well. One for the Maharajah, one for his second wife Maharani Bamba, and one for the couple's youngest son Albert.

"Albert was about my age when he died. That's very young to die, isn't it?"

I nodded.

A few kilted soldiers walked past the church, and some rooks flew up from the trees. We went around the back to see the cloisters and the bell tower before taking a last look at the grave. I felt sad.

I said, "When Duleep Singh was born in India he was a Sikh, but he became a Christian later on."

"What do Sikhs do?"

"They believe in Sikhism, which is another sort of religion. Like us, they believe in God, and they have a holy book, though of course it's different from the Bible."

"Do Sikhs come here to visit the grave, like we visit Grandfather's grave at St Peter's in Brandon?"

"I don't think so. Nearly all of them live in India."

"But the Maharajah was a Sikh first of all, wasn't he? So it would be good if they came."

"Yes. It would be. Perhaps they will come one day, but I rather think he may be forgotten."

Elly began searching in the grass, and I leant against the wall. What sort of a headstone or memorial would Conrad have? Would *he* be forgotten? No. Surely not. Could any one of those hundreds of thousands of soldiers killed in this war ever be forgotten?

It was getting cold. "Come on, Elly."

"I'm looking for flowers."

"You won't find much at this time of year."

But in a hedgerow she found some red rosehips. She took a few minutes to break twigs off the wild rose plants, then laid a few on each of the three graves.

January 1918

Dear Mother and Father, Happy New Year!

I'm happy today and one of the reasons for this, apart from being relaxed and cool under an awning, is because I'm confident that this time next year I'll be at home in Suffolk with you.

Apart from training, which never stops, we haven't really got much to do now except play football, wait for our post (you are wonderful correspondents – not everyone is so lucky), and read. There's a library here consisting entirely of books donated by people at home and it's a godsend. Surprisingly, I've come across several books about wild flowers, and I've been enjoying Walter Scott's Ivanhoe.

We can't imagine what else we'll be needed for here. We feel we've done our bit. We just have to hope that the Mahsuds go on keeping to the treaty. So far so good, as far as we know.

Some of the men have been away from home for three Christmases in a row.

Anyway, at least we should all now be safe from disease, because we've been dosed/inoculated against malaria and cholera.

We're the only white battalion in the 45th Brigade. All the others are Gurkhas or Sikhs. I have a Sikh friend named Pal. Well, his real name is Deenpal, but we all call him Pal because it's what we know. Until now our lives could not have been more different, but we get on fine. When I told him that Duleep Singh had lived near us, he could hardly believe it. Then he told me everything he knew about the Maharajah, and how unfair and bad the English had been to him, and strangely we've become good friends because of all this.

He's five years older than me, and he already has a wife and two children. I've heard all about them, and his brothers and sisters, and his parents and I've told him about all of you. He hopes to return to his home in the Punjab and his job with the Indian Railways.

He wears a turban for most of the time, but sometimes needs to take it off. His dress turban is 15 or 20 feet long, and you should see how long his hair is! Sandy told me Sikhs don't cut their hair as a sign that they recognise God's perfection, though I'm not quite sure how to understand that. They all wear a special bracelet too. Pal is extremely slim. I've lost weight since being out here, but he and many of the Indians are naturally *really thin. He speaks pretty good English for someone who's never been to England. He told me that a relation of his was fighting in France, wounded, and is now in a hospital on the south coast of England. Apparently it's not an ordinary hospital, or even an ordinary military one, because it's in a Royal Palace! And he said every one of the patients is a Sikh. Can all this be true? I can't imagine what palace he means, but he's going to try to find out. Do let me know if you ever hear anything about such a hospital.*

One thing which has been good fun recently was a series of firing tests. You'll be pleased to know that I did well – much better than I (or anyone else) expected. Also, the Colonel is keen on cross-country running competitions. Each is about three miles. Our platoon has done well on one of them, middling on another and not well at all on the third. Personally, I didn't do too badly, but I don't enjoy it one bit.

Did you like the drawing I sent you of our bungalow at Christmas? I hope so.

Your loving son,
Lawrence

January 1918

The Prime Minister, on January 5, issued the following New Year message to the nation.

At the beginning of a New Year the message I should like to send to all at home is an appeal to do their utmost in these latter trying days for the cause for which the democracies of the world are now leagued together.

The sacrifices which the men, and the women also, are making at the front we all know. Despite all they have gone through they are still facing frost and mud, privation and suffering, wounds and death with undaunted courage, that mankind may be freed from the tyranny of militarism and rejoice in lasting freedom and peace.

Every man, woman and child ought to make it a point of honour to increase his holding of National War Bonds as the year goes by. Bonds which have behind them the whole strength and resources of Britain itself.

The road of duty and patriotism is clear before you. Follow it and it will lead ere long to safety for your people and victory for your cause.

D. Lloyd George

January 1918

I got up early on Sunday morning because lots of snow had fallen in the night. Before Christmas the Lark overflowed its banks so some of the Abbey Gardens was a huge smooth pond. When Father went to Hardwick he found that the Cullum Road was flooded, and footpaths had turned into streams.

Anyway, on Sunday I went out and looked for animal tracks. When I saw some strange marks I didn't recognise I followed them and found two pigeons. They were in the stable, by the door. They must have gone in there to get out of the snow, dragging their wings. They looked weak, and when I picked them up they hardly struggled. One tried to peck me but it didn't hurt. I gave them grain to eat and one of them gobbled it up. Then I made them a sort of nest in straw, even though I thought that perhaps they needed to roost like hens.

An hour later one still looked very tired, but the other was poking about in the straw. I poured some water into a dish, and the strong one drank it. And then I saw he had something attached to his leg. It was little thing like a box, or tube, made out of metal. When I tried to hold him still to see it properly, he wouldn't let me. I thought the other one must be ill because it had hardly moved, and it kept shutting its eyes. I decided to go and tell someone, and the first person I found was Uncle Arthur.

He came to the stable with me. "They're carrier pigeons. Look, this is a canister. There's a message inside that."

"What sort of message?" I asked.

"A message from someone in the army."

"Who's it for?"

"I don't know, but we should report it. It might be important."

"But why's it come to us?"

Uncle told me how carrier pigeons fly home from the front and thought these ones must have got lost or injured in the bad weather. He didn't know why only one of them was carrying a canister.

"Tomorrow, Monday, we'll take this pigeon with the canister to the police."

"What about the other one? Can we keep it?"

"I'm not sure it'll survive, looking at the condition it's in."

"Don't say that! I'll look after it and make it better."

"Well, why not? You can certainly try."

Uncle stood up and dusted the straw from his trousers. "Come on. It's time for church."

Half an hour later we tramped to West Stow church through the snow. It was wonderful! Father promised to get the sledge out after dinner.

We had to kick the snow off our boots in the porch, but even so the flagstones were soaking.

The vicar read some prayers and we sang *Father hear the prayer we offer* and Dr Sturge read the lesson. He always reads very slowly, unlike Mr Newton. Then the vicar climbed up to the pulpit and looked at us all and waited until we had stopped coughing and shuffling. Then the boring part began.

This morning I want to talk about a subject we often forget, tied up as we are with despair and destruction. I want to talk about healing.

Healing, we pray, will follow this war. Each person, each family, each nation hopes to be healed. Is it possible that we could help God bring this about?

In simple physical terms, no-one would deny that bombed buildings need to be reconstructed or replaced. In human terms many of us have healed a child with comfort, or a bandage. Some of us need to be healed from the hurts that others do not see. And there are those who have suffered and are suffering the grief brought about by the death of those they love, whether because of war or age or illness.

The essence of healing is to make whole.

The word "heal" shares its derivation with words such as "health" and "whole", and if we are to help God to heal the destruction caused by war, we have to think of making

I was trying to think of good names for the pigeons. Should I give them proper names, like Lucy or Richard? Or should I give them names like Jet, or Swifty?

… . to take a minute or two to think about something you believe has been broken by war. This is probably something which you already do a great deal. Please hold that thought in your mind, painful though it is.

Then, if you will, try to imagine any single thing, word or deed, which would lessen the pain caused by the damage. I am suggesting that although we may not lessen the damage itself, we do

I settled on Peter for the one with the canister, and Poppy for the other one. I don't know why. I didn't even know if they were male or female, and I didn't know how people could tell whether they were male or female.

Uncle said that when we handed Peter to the Police they would keep him and take him away so someone could read the message he was carrying, but no-one would mind if I kept Poppy. She would be my pet, and I'd train her to sit on my wrist.

… . are irreplaceable, for each person is unique. Naturally, those who love them want them back, and they mourn. Do not underestimate the value of mourning. It plays a big part in healing.

People often say that time heals. Is this true? Certainly many would agree. Others find that work and activity heal. Still others are healed by the love of their families and friends. The adoption of new enterprises can help too. For some, giving or receiving apologies may be the route to an unexpected

If I looked after her well, her feathers would soon be clean and shiny, and her eyes bright. Perhaps she would fly to meet me when I called her.

…. not forgotten prayer. In church and at home or abroad our prayers seek solace and peace of mind, and God may help us find these. But I would suggest that rather than seeking to return to or replicate what used to be, we try to envisage what might be

One of the lines of Psalm 34 is The Lord is near to those who have a broken heart.

When we think of broken hearts we tend to think of young lovers, or perhaps of older people whose lives have been blighted by misfortune or loss in love as well as by death. But God will help us to

Suddenly, everyone was kneeling on the hassocks and saying the Lord's Prayer. I said an extra prayer for Peter and Poppy. And then we had another hymn, *Teach me my God and King,* which has the bit about a servant sweeping a room.

I'd forgotten about the snow and when we came out it was snowing again and all the children were running and laughing in the churchyard, and no-one told us not to.

When we got home I went straight to the stable to see Peter and Poppy, but Peter wasn't there. I looked carefully for his footprints, but the new snow had covered everything up. I went on looking until Aunt Bridget called me in for dinner. When I told Uncle he said I shouldn't be unhappy, because the food I had given him must have made him strong enough to fly home, even if his loft was hundreds of miles away.

January 1918

When the thaw came I couldn't go to school because there were more floods. Uncle Arthur took me on the tractor to show me how water was rushing down the roads and why I mustn't go in it. Some sheep had been swept away. They would drown if their coats were soaked through, and we were glad when we found all but one of them huddled up against a fence. They were frightened but, with help from another farmer, Uncle and Lennie managed to haul them up into a trailer. Father doesn't do heavy work because quite often he used to be ill.

We went home and changed and warmed up, but I felt sorry for the missing sheep.

Someone had brought us the paper, and the front of it was all about Barclays Bank which didn't interest me one bit. So I turned straight to the third page. This was always the saddest page, but I could never not read it. Every week, the whole page was about soldiers and officers, and nearly all of the news about them was bad news. A few people had been decorated because they had done something brave but most of them had been killed, or wounded or taken prisoner or were in hospital or missing. There were lots of photos. Sometimes there was a row of three or four men, and they were all brothers and had all been killed. Once I found Mother crying as she looked at these photos. I didn't know what to say, so I just cuddled up against her. Another thing I wondered about was that if so many men were killed in England and France and Germany, there wouldn't be many left after the war which would not be a good thing because surely the world needed as many men as women?

And I didn't know if the names of all the dead or hurt or missing people were printed, or if there were even more names which couldn't fit on the page. Uncle Arthur said that each local paper like ours had a similar page. He said that there were lists and photos of soldiers and officers in every part of the country, and the papers tried to print all their names because their families wanted them to be remembered, and that sometimes meant going over onto another page.

Another thing I find strange is that the government still needs more soldiers. It seems that every week there's another notice about a recruiting drive. They keep sending new ones to take the places of the ones who've been killed or wounded, but they might be killed too, and then they'll have to send even more. And the Germans must be doing that too. Surely they've got to stop, or England and Germany won't have any young men left?

That evening, after I'd finished with the paper I passed it to Aunt Bridget. I knew she read the sad page, just as Mother and Father did, but she was also interested in the Hints for Allotment Holders. This column told you how to grow certain vegetables, and when to plant seeds, and what tools to use. Every week she'd look at the article and say, "You could have written this, Arthur." Father and Mother agreed, because it's true that my uncle is a very good fruit and vegetable grower. He always reads the Hints, and sometimes he criticizes them, but he never bothers to enter the weekly competition for the best new idea for allotment holders, which is a shame because he has invented clever things like special seed sowers, and bird scarers. The most important things for him in the paper are the prices of sheep and feed, poultry and pigs. In the evenings he makes notes in his little red book and sucks on his pipe. Sometimes he keeps his pipe in his mouth for too long, and the smoke comes out of his mouth and into his eyes which makes him screw his face into a funny shape. He even does this when he is pleased with the prices and knows he will make money.

These days Mother usually only glanced at the paper. She said she'd decided to stop reading the lists of who had been killed and who was missing because it made her sad and angry. But today, while Arthur and Father smoked and Bridget got on with her knitting, she read it almost from cover to cover, except for the advertisements. She said she was looking for an important piece of news, but couldn't find it. I could tell she was getting annoyed by the way she turned over the pages.

"It's not in there. I can't believe it. It's just not there. Or if it's there, they've only written a sentence about it and I've missed it."

"What isn't there?" asked Bridget.

"The news about votes for women. Women over thirty (not all of them, but many of them), or those who own property, or are graduates, are now eligible to vote. The Act was passed on January 11th – over a week ago."

"Perhaps there wasn't room for it," said Hattie. "The reporters have a lot of things to write about. What about that poor child who was found filthy and neglected?"

"But this is one of the most important pieces of news I can think of. There ought to be something about it."

"Tomorrow I'll try and get you copies of the Morning Post for the last week," said Father. "It's bound to be in that."

"I'm going to write to the editor. I can't believe they've ignored something as important as The Representation of the People Act. It will bring about so much change."

Hattie counted the stitches on one needle, changed her needles round, and started on a row of purl. "This'll be my sixteenth pair of socks. I'm going to make mittens next, for a change."

March 1918

Everyone is longing for the fighting to finish, but there were more attacks on London this week, this time from Giants rather than Gothas. A wing of Chelsea Hospital was hit, and so was St Pancras station. It just goes on and on. And although we are out of reach of bombardments from the sea, and bombs are unlikely here, things don't feel completely safe. At least Lawrence, at present, is well out of the way of danger. I don't care if he's bored or doing something he doesn't like. I just want him to stay alive.

There's an election coming up in Suffolk but I can't say I'm particularly interested, although it will be a shame if Bury St Edmunds loses its own MP, as seems likely. I'm planning to read about one of the candidates, a Mr Howard, later this evening. Also in the paper there's an advertisement for a play called Damaged Goods, and I think I'll get tickets. I had heard about it from one of the ambulance men who strongly recommended it. When I asked what it was about he wouldn't tell me. Of course I asked why not, but all he would say was that it would have more impact if I knew nothing before I went. He said, "Keep an open mind and be prepared for a play such as you've never seen." It's supposed to be "the play of the moment".

This seemed distinctly odd and I read again, "This play is an education in itself and drives home with great force the evils resulting from ignorance".

"I wouldn't touch it with a bargepole," said Arthur.

"Do you know what it's about?" asked Hattie.

"Enough to make me decide not to see it."

Hattie and I decided to have a rare evening out, and managed to arrange a lift to the Theatre Royal.

"Can I come?" asked Elly.

"I'm sorry," I replied. "But it's only for adults. Children aren't allowed."

"Why not?"

"I'm not sure. But I'll tell you tomorrow."

Hattie had already heard from some VAD friends that it was about syphilis, and I couldn't for the life of me think how anyone could make a play about that.

But we watched the story of George, a young man who contracts syphilis. This is confirmed by a specialist doctor who advises him against getting married for three or four years because until he is properly treated he is likely to pass the disease on. But he is engaged and soon to be married and delaying the wedding would compromise him financially. He seeks a second opinion and, for a fee, is told he can be cured within months. George marries, and all is well until his baby daughter is diagnosed with syphilis. Gradually, the first doctor's predictions come true with implications for the baby, the wet nurse, and George's wife's parents. There are angry arguments. Bribes, law suits and divorce are considered. The couple separate. Blame is laid. The central theme opens out to include how lack of money forces women to become prostitutes. Most of the characters end up feeling embarrassed or ashamed, though there was little discussion of why men, especially married men, use prostitutes. It was only the doctor whose eyes were fully open and who was not driven by self-interest.

When the doctor is asked how syphilis can be avoided he says that a man should love but one woman, a virgin, marry her and love her so much she will never deceive him. He also believes that couples planning to marry should be required to produce a certificate guaranteeing their good health.

It was sombre drama, hardly entertainment, but it certainly held everyone's attention.

"But how prevalent is syphilis?" I asked Hattie, as we walked out of the theatre. "As much as that doctor suggested?"

"I only know about patients at Ampton – a small sample. It's true that many of them have some kind of venereal disease."

I reflected on this. "But they're not typical. They're in the army."

Hattie turned towards me, and looked at me with an expression I could not at first interpret. Then I understood. "No," I said slowly. "Not our son. I know Lawrence is in the army, but..."

"Every one of the Ampton patients is somebody's son. But I agree that Lawrence is less likely than them to be having sexual adventures." She took my arm reassuringly. "After all, we haven't been promiscuous, have we?"

Hattie and I had met when we were in our early twenties. I had never been intimate with anyone else, and nor had she.

I smiled at her. "No, we haven't. We're just country mice!"

Then I thought about Arthur, and about the ambulance staff, and all the men I knew. Surely they had not taken risks like those taken by the character George? I concluded that the play exaggerated the situation. Recently there had been a small article in the paper stating that there was very little venereal disease in Suffolk. After all, there were no unhygienic and crowded tenements here, and I had never, ever seen any woman I thought might be a prostitute. Indeed, would I recognise one if I saw one?

But there are poor people here, and how are they supposed to manage? The usual wage for farm labourers is five pence an hour, with more for overtime, though it's up to nine pence an hour during harvest. I began a rough calculation in my head to work out whether that was enough to keep a family above the breadline. It was not. So perhaps, though I had never seen it, there was and still is prostitution here.

April 1918

Dear Mother and Father,

Happy Easter!

Thanks very much for the papers, mags and chocolate. Well, I'm sorry, but there's not much to tell you about. Very little has happened since I last wrote, other than doing plenty of sport and digging trenches. We don't need trenches, of course, but the powers that be seem to think that we might forget how to dig them, and that should not be allowed to happen.

But we (or some of us at least) are expecting to move to Simla, which should be much better than this place. It'll be quite a trek, but at least it's a change and we think it will be better in every way. You'll see there's an article about it in this copy of *The Londoner*. It makes it sound a lovely place.

Also, a few weeks ago we got a new Brigadier-General. His name is Dyer, and I can report so far so good. He's unusual in that he speaks several Indian languages, which means that he is particularly liked by all the native officers and troops. Apparently he makes it his business to know exactly what's going on, which is more than some commanders do.

Today is April Fool's Day. My accomplice and I have got hold of a bag of flour, a bucket of water and a couple of sheets. With luck, we will succeed in covering several people with flour or embarrassment or both!

I'm sending my love to you all. I hope that spring is arriving as the days lengthen. Have you heard a cuckoo yet?

Your loving son, Lawrence

Article from The Londoner

Simla

The Railway to Simla, which is of the narrow gauge variety, starts at Kalka, a village at the foot of the Simla Hills. On leaving this place, the train quickly ascends into the hills, skirting the khuds in a fashion calculated to try the nerves even of a tight rope artiste. The tonga road, which can be seen for the most part of the journey, is 58 miles in length but owing to the way in which it winds, loops, "S"s round and through the hills, the "toy" railway, strangely reminiscent of the Scenic Railway at the White City, is much longer. It is indeed a marvellous engineering feat, there being over 100 tunnels in the journey, while in other places the train, like some gigantic centipede, seems almost to hang on the cliffs themselves.

The train goes on, over ravines where babbling mountain streams flash down to the valley beneath round the edge of cliffs where the river conveys an impression of a vast garden laid out with terraces of green carpet, one above the other. Little white houses nestle among a curious mixture of palms, waving grasses and fir trees. Still the train goes up, sometimes at a tremendous gradient while the little engine puffs and shrieks and skids as it negotiates a bend at a tremendous angle. After going through the longest tunnel on the route, a halt of some twenty minutes is made at flowery pine-clad Barogh, from where, after crossing a four-tier bridge at Kanogh, Tara Davi is reached. All passports are examined here, and the state of the health of the passengers enquired into by a native official, who also makes many other vital investigations.

As one leaves the station a glorious panorama is unfolded. Nature's beauty is at its best, resplendent in flowers of red, blue and white and stately lines with their vivid hues of green brown and yellow, the whole set off against a background of cloudless blue sky. It is a blaze of colour that would have made Turner long for palette and canvas.

Below, and on the right of the long road into the town, are the Government

Offices, lower still is the bazaar which stretches up to the Mall on the ridge above. Further along is a huge red building – the Secretariat – and everywhere are the rickshaw wallahs with their rickshaws. On the left of the Mall, pure white against a blue sky, is the Post Office; a few yards further the road divides, one branch leading up to the church, the other continuing along the Mall, down round the foot of Jakko. On the left again is the Town Hall and Library, next to it the Gaiety Theatre, a small but cosy house filled with possibly the best stage accessories in India. On the right, past a row of shops of all descriptions, many of them under European management, one notices the Fire Station, which is hardly of the type familiar to a Londoner, neither does the lethargic fireman on duty bear much resemblance to the navy blue, brass-helmeted product of the metropolis. On the right too, at intervals, are steep steps which lead to the native bazaar below; narrow alleyways, barely six feet across, reminiscent of the Scores at Lowestoft.

The best time to appreciate the mountain Jakko and his surroundings is at sunset. There is then a solemn hush over everything, and even the monkeys are still. One looks over Elysium Hill, and in the distance the snows on the Himalayas, that gigantic "Roof of the World" glisten in the last rays of the setting sun, a sight to impress for all time. In the valley wreaths of blue smoke from the natives' quarters curl slowly upwards, the conches in the temples scream and bray for the faithful to come to prayer, the lights from the hotels gleam through the shadows and distances become undefined and mystic. Through the mist now creeping along the valley, comes the musical "chink-chink-chink" of the pack-mules' bells, and the plaintive piping of a herdsman. Above the sky-line, the moon rises with a sickly pallor, later it will be bright and clear. Altogether it is a wonderful experience to stand on Jakko at this time and the pen of a Gray or Tennyson is necessary adequately to paint the hushed and solemn beauty of the scene.

P C Chisnall

May 1918

The summer was full of fetes. The first of the year was at Hengrave Hall on Whit Monday. I walked there with Maggie, the daughter of a VAD who worked with Mother. She was nearly two years older than me, and she went to school in Thetford. As we got near the Hall we could hear the band, and that made us hurry along with everyone else. Just as we reached the entrance gateway one of the Red Cross ambulances arrived from Ampton, and some patients I knew were taken out of it in their wheelchairs. Maggie hadn't met any of them so I introduced her to George and Nat and William and a few others. She was rather embarrassed to meet men with bad injuries and said I was "wonderful" to be so comfortable with them, but I said that anyone who talked to them soon found out that they were just ordinary, nice people.

The Military sports were not until the afternoon, so we wandered around, spent our money on ice creams and sweets and played clock golf.

Later we thought we'd go and talk to the Ampton men again but we found them sitting in the shade of a tree having tea with a group of young ladies. They waved at us but didn't talk to me or tease me like they usually do. Maggie said I shouldn't be disappointed, because it wasn't surprising, was it, with those elegant girls standing around smiling? We didn't go home for several hours.

Then there was a fete in the Abbey Gardens for Empire Day, which had dozens of stalls and sideshows, and then there was a Red Cross Fete. But by the time they advertised the one at Culford Hall I wasn't very interested in going. Maggie wasn't either, and she suggested we went swimming in the river at Icklingham instead. It was just after my 12th birthday. After that time when the gamekeeper brought me home I'd promised my parents I wouldn't go on any more expeditions on my own, so I asked permission to go with Maggie. Father came down to the Lark with us in the morning, to make sure we were going to a safe place. He had swum there when he was a boy, and he stayed and watched us, and he made rules about where we were and weren't allowed to swim.

After that we went two or three times a week. It was a hot summer and I loved that moment when you jump into the water and it's cold for a second, and then it's not so bad, and then it's even warm. Sometimes we floated and just watched dragonflies and water beetles and bugs. At other times we opened our eyes under the brownish water and ran our arms through thin green reeds. Mostly, the water was not deep, and we could stand, but I didn't like my feet touching the soft mud of the river bed, so once I was in I kept swimming. One day we swam in the pouring rain. It was lovely!

Usually we had the staunch to ourselves, but one day we came down to the river and found the Hunt brothers there. They hardly talked to us. They showed off and kept jumping from the bridge. When Dan was sure we were watching, he jumped off backwards. Another time we arrived as some soldiers were leaving. "Careful," called one of them. "There's a hungry pike in there!" But we knew it was quite safe.

On another day we found some bikes and clothes and towels on the grass, and three girls and two boys already in the water. I didn't know them, but Maggie did because they all went to her school. They were older than us, and two of the girls were sisters. The younger one could hardly swim, and one of the boys was teaching her. He kept shouting things at her, like "Relax!" and "Kick!" and "You're all right!" but she didn't get the hang of it. The other boy liked diving, and the other sisters just splashed about. They said hallo to us and we said hallo back, but then we went on duck diving and seeing how long we could hold our breath underwater.

One hot afternoon there was a cricket match, Elveden v. Barnham. Maggie's father was playing (for Elveden) and we went with him. Some of it was a bit boring because nothing seemed to happen, or, if it did, I missed it. But I saw one man catch a ball that a man hit high into the air, just like Conrad used to do. And I felt sorry for a schoolboy who waited for nearly an hour to go in for his innings. He was all padded up, and when, at last, one of his team was bowled, he walked out onto the pitch and took up his stand by the wicket. And then, on the very first ball he was out lbw. Everyone said "Bad luck" when he walked back off the field again. He kept his head down and poked his bat into the grass fiercely as he walked. He must have been really fed up.

But Maggie's father scored twenty-eight, and he took a wicket, so he was quite pleased. And then it was time for tea, and we sat on the grass and ate some scones, and fetched second cups of tea for the cricketers. I liked seeing all the men in their white trousers and shirts, though some had grass stains on their knees and one man, who had done much of the bowling, had a red stain by his pocket, because that was where he polished the ball. It was a good thing that Uncle Arthur didn't play cricket, because Aunt Bridget would have complained a lot about how difficult it was to keep whites white.

Later, Maggie and I walked right round the pitch, but when we passed behind or in front of the wickets we had to check that we were not getting in the line of the bowler or batsmen when a ball was being bowled, because that could put them off.

Maggie's parents had seen *Damaged Goods*. Maggie said it was about how a frightening illness could be spread easily and that people needed to know how to stop it. It was a sort of epidemic, like the flu epidemic only it didn't kill everyone who got it.

"Did they tell you the name of the illness?"

"No."

"My parents saw it too. They said it was about a disease that you can get when you try to make a baby."

Maggie stared at me. "When you try to make a baby?"

"Yes. You know. When a man .. you know what I mean."

"I know about that. My cousin told me. But I don't understand why everyone who makes babies doesn't get the disease."

"I don't either."

Maggie said, "I want to have children when I'm grown up and married. I hope I don't get the disease."

"I'm sure you won't."

"How can you say that?"

"I think it's mostly in cities, or in unhealthy places."

Suddenly there was a loud shout of "Howzzat?" and everyone looked at the umpire. Slowly, he lifted his finger and signalled to the scorers that one of the batsmen was out. Some people groaned, while others clapped.

In the end Elveden won. Maggie doesn't understand cricket scores. On the way home she said, "Sometimes I've heard people say "So-and-so won by two wickets" but I've also heard, "Our team lost by fifty-four runs." Maggie's father said that it was only girls and women who found it complicated. But I know how it works, and so does Mother. It's true that Aunt Bridget doesn't, but I wouldn't expect her to.

August 1918

Dear Mother and Father,

I tell you, dear parents, that my career as a ballroom dancer is almost established. I can do the walk forward and the walk backward faultlessly, and the natural turn and the reverse turn passably well. Now I'm working on the chasses. You should see us all paired up and listening carefully to the groan box as we practice our steps in our newly acquired dancing shoes. Some of us make fine ladies. Indeed, we all take our turn at being ladies, and very graceful we are too. Who would have thought I'd learn to dance here in Jutogh? I look forward to gasps of surprise and admiration when I take to the floor at balls in the Athenaeum in Bury, sweeping both my partner and on-lookers off their feet.

But, in between our dancing lessons and concerts we have been in just one incident (I'm not counting the minor things we have to deal with, such as cattle raiding and the odd kidnapping of a child). About 100 miles to the west is a fort called Phillour which is used for Police training, and one night news came that there was trouble at the Police Barracks. There was some argument between the two lots of police stationed there, Sikhs and Mohammedans. One lot had even attacked the other. (It's impossible to imagine that happening in England, isn't it?) About 50 of us had to go there in the middle of the night and occupy the

Barracks while the Brigadier-General sat down with the leaders. We were very impressed because he sorted it out without even one shot being fired. It could easily have flared up into something more serious, but it didn't. Then we went straight back to Jutogh. After all, we didn't want to miss any dancing lessons.

As you can see from the sketch book I've enclosed, I'm continuing to draw flowers and plants. Am I improving? Let me know if the book survives its journey without being bent or spoiled. The cardboard should help keep it flat. I'd like to send you a whole batch, because I don't usually have anywhere to keep them. Other lads have accumulated stuff which they cart around with them. One man collects little brass objects (heavy), and several have paint boxes, palettes and brushes, let alone the paintings they've done. And just imagine what it's like for our regimental orchestra!

There's one bit of bad news. A few days ago a man became ill from what might be cholera. My friend Pal says there's no need to worry, and he knows a lot about cholera because his father worked in a hospital. But of course we are very worried about Ian.

No news of any move, but we're not complaining.

So what's happening at home? I hope Uncle's farm continues to produce good things for you. What's the rationing situation now?

Next, it's the zigzag, and then I'll attempt the natural spin turn. Meanwhile, it's slow, slow, quick quick slow. ... ..

Your loving son
Lawrence

September 1918

Bury's Mayor speaks at the Great Meeting in Trafalgar Square

Fellow countrymen and fellow countrywomen, there is no misunderstanding my attitude. I am a whole hogger against the accursed race we are fighting. I shall not call the Germans Huns. My reading of history has taught me that the Hun was a beastly, bad lot, but he was a gentleman compared to the German we are fighting at the present time. When we remember the foul actions of which they have been guilty – the bombing of defenceless towns and Red Cross hospitals, the crucifixion of our men, the mutilation of women and children, the murder of Edith Cavell and Captain Fryett, and other things too numerable and vile to mention – I trust that the name "Hun" will be discontinued and that they will be handed down to posterity as Germans! Germans! Germans! so that the name German will be for all future times associated with everything that is bestial, damnable and abominable.

"Have you read this, Eric? It's sterling stuff!" said Arthur. "Listen to this: 'everything that is bestial, damnable and abominable'. Well spoken, Mr Mayor!"

I decided against commenting, and merely nodded. Instead, I said I was interested in the plans for the new flax factory they want to build at Almoners Barn in Southgate Street. I've only just found out that we need flax urgently because linen is used in building aircraft. It would make good sense to have a factory in town, but some of the bigwigs don't want smells or industry. And wouldn't the money be better spent on new houses? There are many poor people who need homes locally.

Bridget changed the subject. "And did you see this bit, about women and prisoners-of-war? They're not to work together, by order of Melford War Agricultural Committee." She was both shocked and amused. "Would anyone even consider letting them do so? Letting silly little girls from the Women's Land Army near the Hun prisoners? Just imagine what might happen."

Again, I decided to say nothing. I hoped Arthur had not read the small paragraph in which someone was stating that women were completely unsuited to being railway signalmen, and that if they were allowed to do so they would put themselves and the public in danger. But he was already head down into the farming section, checking on prices and sales, and pleased as punch about his sheep which had been doing well all year.

I walked over to the window and thought about my visit to Hardwick House that morning. Mr Cullum had seemed well, but it was sad to see how run down the place had become. It was full of troops and some of them were behaving as if they owned the place – shouting and not respecting where they were. I went to look at our house and found it being used as an office. The gate was hanging on one hinge, and the roses Hattie loved had been cut right back from where she had carefully trained them over the years.

I won't tell Hattie about it. Of course it's right that big houses should be utilised by the military but I could not forget the house's history. I wanted to ask whoever was in charge, Do you realise this is Mr Milner-Gibson-Cullum's home, and it's been his family's home since 1656? Do you have any idea of what has gone on in this place? I wanted them to know that there were once doctors and writers and ministers and botanists and scientists here, and that learned visitors came to see Mr Milner-Gibson-Cullum's antiquities and paintings, his libraries and gardens. But of course I said nothing. There was no point. I just pray that after the war the gardens will flourish again, the house be put in good repair, and something of its old life re-established.

But there will never again be more than a few horses in the stables. Even though it's hard to obtain petrol now (I even saw an advertisement recently for dog carts and governess carts because of the shortage of fuel) people will want motorcars, not gigs and carriages.

Mr Cullum came into the library while I was there, and greeted me warmly. He gestured to the window to draw my attention to a group of soldiers wheeling in barrows of timber, and indicated with a small sigh that he had little control over things going on around him. This saddened me. He had been so fortunate since birth, but how happy had he been? How happy was he now? He was often alone. All he had now were his meetings of the Suffolk Archeological Society, and other learned societies, and infrequent visits from members of his family. He still had several staff, but I doubt if they were much company.

Arthur had quizzed me about Mr Cullum's relations. Who would inherit Hardwick House? I had no idea. So, if there was no heir, what would happen to the estate? I couldn't answer, because I didn't know.

At least Mr Cullum was surviving. In June I had read a notice reporting the death of Victor Duleep Singh. Apparently he had been ill for some time, and had died in Monte Carlo. He had been a captain in the Royal Dragoons, and the notice mentioned that he enjoyed performing on some of Suffolk's concert platforms, and that he had been interested in fellow antiquarians of the district. I wondered where he'd be buried. Not at Elveden, I was sure.

Mr Cullum, Victor Duleep Singh and I had been born at roughly the same time and had, at least for some years, lived within ten miles of each other in roughly the same place, close to the Suffolk-Norfolk border. Our lives had been very different, but now only two of us were alive. I wondered who would be the next to die.

September 1918

September 27th 1918

Elly was bored. It was true that things were going well at school in that all the teachers were pleased with her work. In fact, she liked school and was top of her class in most subjects. The headmistress, Miss Pitcher, was very impressed and told us it was a pleasure to have pupils like Eleanor.

She had a group of friends, including Libby and Alison, though they rarely met up at weekends. There was no point in going to Ampton Hall in winter because most patients were confined to their wards. It was far too cold for them to stand and talk outside, and there were complaints when they brought mud in on their shoes and wheelchairs. Someone told Elly that she'd be able to help in the wards when she was sixteen. *Sixteen?* she had repeated. Would the war still be going on when she was *sixteen*?

But there was one new, good thing in her life: her asthma had all but gone and so hardly troubled her. How or why this had happened she had no idea and nor did we, but that did not matter. The improvement in her health enhanced her well-being, increased her confidence, and made that awful business of having to hang her head over a steaming bowl of Potter's Cure a mere memory.

But what could she do at home, other than jobs? She spent a lot of time reading.
but she couldn't read all the time, and one day when it was pouring with rain, Aunt Bridget said that it was a good time for her to learn to knit . Elly had witnessed her aunt making scarves, hats and socks for the troops and it was suggested that she should make a scarf first. She didn't feel like doing it just then, at the very moment of being asked, but, having managed to put it off for many months, she supposed she must.

So she chose some red wool, tried to copy Aunt Bridget and got the hang of it more easily than either of them expected. She was slow, of course, but before long had created two inches of a scarf that would be about ten inches wide. Those two inches had taken her quite a while, and if it was to be a proper scarf it would have to be at least four feet long.

"Please don't watch," she begged me. "It's harder if you watch."

So I left them to it, just as Elly was beginning to enjoy the feel of the wool, and the regular winding movement and, every now and then, the pleasure of holding it up to see how it was growing. By the time I came back she had done another inch and was asking Bridget if she had any other colours, as she wanted her scarf to have stripes.

October 1918

Dear Mother,

I just wanted to write and say that I'm so sorry that you are not well. I can't remember you ever being ill for more than a day or two, so I'm sure you'll be up and about soon. I do hope you stop having those sore throats and headaches. Why don't you take a rest from your VAD work? I know Father thinks you do too much.

I'm pleased to say that the man who was thought to have cholera turned out not to have it at all. That shows what some military doctors are like, but luckily others are fine! My advice is to take what doctors say with a pinch of salt.

Please thank Father for sending me the amusing cutting from Hints for Allotment Holders. Pal couldn't believe that someone had invented a trap for earwigs! He says he'd love to visit England to see Buckingham Palace and Westminster Abbey and the Thames, and it would be so good if he managed to do so. I could even take the train from Bury and meet him there. It's strange how I used to think that going to London was like going to another country – miles away, and hours of travelling. But it's nothing compared to the journeys I've made here!

I have to get ready for an inspection. Dyer is a stickler for detail, but nearly everyone likes him. Because he knows that at present we are bored for much of the time, he has made it possible for those who wish to, to have a ride. I can't tell you how wonderful it is just to sit on a horse, let alone to trot across a hillside. The last horse I rode must have been Busker, on Uncle's farm. Uncle will remember Busker.

Recently the Brig General gave us a talk about how, just a year or so ago, he gained some territory by making the enemy believe than he had a much bigger force that he actually had. Clever man. I need to sign off now because he likes us Londons, and we want to keep on the right side of him.

So, much love, dearest Mother. I know Father will be looking after you well, so do get better soon.

With extra love,
Your son Lawrence

October 1918

That year, Arthur was particularly proud of his sheep. All the ewes except two had had one or two lambs, and the prices had remained high. He was well thought of and people were pleased to do business with him. At the livestock markets on Wednesdays he was often to be found in a group of men talking about shearlings and hoggets. If he took Elly with him, as he sometimes did, she'd go off on her own to see whatever the market had that day. It might be bullocks, cattle, pigs, goats, poultry and even horses sometimes. She loved the noises, the smells, the onlookers, the auctioneers shouting out numbers and incomprehensible words in a sort of song, the occasional escaped calf being cornered and caught, its eyes bright with fright. After exploring the market, Elly would make her way back to their meeting place at the Round House which she had loved since she was a little girl, though no-one had been able to tell her why it had that name when it was octagonal. When Uncle Arthur arrived he sometimes bought her an ice cream, and she would eat it while walking round the Round House and counting its sides.

From time to time Arthur sent bacon pigs to Elmswell, making sure they were there for Tuesdays and Thursdays, the killing days, and when he had a surplus he sold chickens and ducks to a butcher in Abbeygate Street. Bridget cooked the vegetables he grew, sometimes exchanging them with neighbours for groceries she was short of. There was something to be had from the garden all year round. In winter there were potatoes (Arthur had planted more since the announcement of a national shortage), cabbages, leeks, carrots, swedes, turnips, parsnips. In summer: lettuce, tomatoes in the greenhouse, cucumbers, radishes, new potatoes. Then there were the eggs, soft fruit and, if they were lucky, plenty of plums. Arthur had a strong sense of satisfaction about what he produced, and this had increased since Eric, Hattie and Elly had come to stay with them. He had always believed that Eric looked down on him slightly because he had decided against studying for a profession. But he had come to realise that that was not true. It was clear that Eric recognised the work and skill required to ensure that animals and plants thrived. He admired what Arthur did, and often praised him.

November 1918

Here was the letter I had been simultaneously waiting for and dreading. I was relieved that I was alone in the house, and, with Bran stretched out at my feet, I sat at the kitchen table to open it.

My dear Father,

I have just received your letter with its terrible news. I am so shocked and saddened. I had no idea at all that Mother was dangerously ill, and I have not stopped thinking about her for one moment since you wrote. I can't believe how quickly it happened – just three days from when she first felt ill at Ampton and came home early. Whenever I'm alone I start crying. I'm feeling terrible, as you must be.

When I read what you wrote about her condition, I realised that perhaps it was a good thing that the flu did not last long. It would have been worse if you had had to watch her in even more pain and discomfort.

You must be feeling so bad, and I wish I was there together with you and Elly. Poor, poor Elly. To have lost Mother while she is still a child. And such a caring mother, who did so much for us three children. I cannot believe she will not be there when I come home.

And Conrad too. It's so hard to think that two of our family are gone.

Our battalion has had flu deaths too – seven men have died from it. Everyone took a turn at looking after them, but they couldn't be saved.

The only good thing is that there is more and more talk about peace, and as soon as there is peace I will come home. It may take up to a couple of months, but it won't be long until we are together.

I hope that Uncle Arthur and Aunt Bridget are looking after you well. I'm sure they are. I'm sure it's much better to be on their farm with them, than alone with Elly in our house at

Hardwick, even though it'll be good to go back there after the war when things return to normal.

Father, I'm thinking of you, and wishing I could hug you and Elly. It feels so awful and so sad that I am here and cannot be at Mother's funeral. I can't stop these tears. They keep on coming and I just can't stop them.

Please write to me soon.

Your loving son,
Lawrence

As I folded the letter and put it back in my pocket I was weeping too. Great sobs were shaking me, and I had no power to stop them. Bran stood up, disconcerted and whining softly, and I stroked him till I calmed down and he settled on the floor again. Illogically, I found myself saying, "It's all right, Bran. It's all right."

By far the majority of those dying from flu are young, so Hattie's illness and death had completely surprised us all. Arthur wondered whether the fact that she was in contact with so much disease at Ampton Hall might have put her at greater risk. It's certainly possible, but we shall never know. News of Spanish flu is everywhere, and the authorities in Bury are seeking more accommodation for those suffering from it. Many have died already. Even a nurse has died. The doctor advised us to give Hattie brandy and port wine and other medicine, but her breathing became worse, and on Tuesday Bridget noticed a bluish tinge on Hattie's skin – a sure sign that she had flu. I sat with her that night and heard her struggle to breathe at about one in the morning. Then I heard nothing more.

I do not know how to help Elly other than to comfort her. She is devastated. She has not been back to school, and anyway I want her here with me. This morning Bridget suggested to her that they went out for a walk together as it is a mild, clear day. I was pleased when Elly agreed, for she has not been out for a week, and I am grateful to Bridget for her attention. Elly is often in tears, and her asthma has returned. I can hear her progress round the farmhouse, wheezing and crying as she goes. Oh God, may she stay safe. Please let her stay safe.

They say thousands and thousands of people have died from this epidemic. It is sweeping through the world. As if war was not enough.

I cannot help fearing for Lawrence too, for now I know there is flu where he is. Until now I have managed to find a way of pushing aside the thought of him too dying abroad. That thought is unbearable to contemplate, and as soon as I notice my mind going in that direction I jump on it and send it off on another tack by doing bizarre things such as saying the alphabet backwards or listing as many Old Testament books as I can recall. Strangely, this helps me, even if only briefly. But when Elly asked me directly, "Could Lawrence die from flu?" I found it difficult to answer, and today I heard that flu is rife in India. Thank God all our units have doctors. Some of them must be good.

November 1918

On the night of the great news of the Armistice neither Eric nor Arthur, nor Elly nor Bridget had any inclination to go into Bury to be amongst processions, flags, bands, singing in the streets, speeches, three, six and nine cheers, and God Save the King (probably several times) at full volume. Church bells would be rung, the Cornhill packed body-to-body and children shouting and running because the schools were closed. Although the bereaved would continue to grieve, Bury would see an explosion of excited and genuine joy, a sea of people expressing their relief, their thanks to God, their new hopes, their shared delight.

That evening, in the West Stow farmhouse, the family sat quietly in the kitchen. Bridget said there was no point in leaving a pair of socks half-made, so she carried on knitting. Arthur gazed ahead of him, tapping his pipe, filling it, lighting it and occasionally smoking it. Eric had his eyes closed. He was thinking about Hattie's mother, who had been brought to the funeral by her other daughter and son-in-law with whom, since the Zeppelin raid which had damaged her house, she had lived in Downham Market. It was a long journey, but a friend had volunteered to drive them. Eric was recalling her great distress, and was realising to his shame that it was not until after the funeral that he appreciated that her grief at losing Hattie was as great as his at losing Conrad. He had been thinking of Hattie as his wife and the mother of their children, and it was only now that he took account of the fact that she was also her mother's daughter. It was against the natural order of things for a daughter to die before her mother, and he resolved to write to his mother-in-law the next day.

Elly sat on the rug with Bran, caressing his soft, tawny-coloured ears. The sounds in the room were small ones: coals settling in the fire; the tap of a pipe on an ashtray, the click of knitting needles. From time to time they heard a dull thud. "Fireworks," said Arthur. A few moments after each thud they heard pheasants making their raucous alarm call.

They went on sitting together for another half hour, until Arthur got up and went into the kitchen. He came back with a glass of water and took a long draft. "Lawrence will be home before long, Eric. That's what you must keep in the front of your mind. He'll be home before many weeks are up."

Eric opened his eyes and nodded at him. "Yes. He will. You're right."

November 1918

On November 11th, everyone at Jutogh knew that the war was over. The next morning the Londons travelled by train to Simla to provide the Guard of Honour to the Viceroy when he read out the terms of the Armistice in public. Afterwards, Lawrence's battalion were treated by officers to unlimited alcoholic drinks: a completely unheard-of event. Still feeling raw and upset about his mother's death, Lawrence declined the first beer he was offered. It felt wrong to drink while he was grieving. His friends tried to cheer him up, and someone managed to persuade him to at least raise a glass to Victory and to the battalion. And so, passing through stages of warm friendliness (brief), belligerence (even briefer) and being maudlin (too long) he ended up on the floor in less control of himself than he had ever been in his life.

Within a few hours he was hauled to his feet by someone he thought he knew but whom he could not place. It was the company sergeant major. Lawrence swore at him and shouted hoarsely, "Let go! Let me sleep! Go away!" But he was made to stand and to walk unsteadily towards a file of others in the same inebriated state. None of them cared about the opinions of the public who watched them. What did it matter if they were unsteady, in disarray and not properly dressed? The war was over! They'd be going home! Slowly, they stumbled to the railway station, climbed on a train and fell asleep leaning on each other's shoulders and laps.

A good twenty-four hours later, when he was sober, Lawrence felt ashamed. Yes, he could excuse himself for celebrating the end of war drinking with his fellow Londons, but he felt guilty that by abandoning himself to alcohol he temporarily forgot his grief for his mother. He felt even worse when he recalled her disapproval of people who drank too much. The fact that everyone else was as drunk as or worse than he had been, and that on this unique and extraordinary occasion their drunkenness was condoned if not encouraged by officers, was irrelevant. It was also irrelevant that his mother did not know what he had done. What he could not live with was the knowledge that, if she had known it, she would have been saddened by him indulging in such behaviour at all, let alone within a week or two of her death.

When he woke the next day he felt better. He swore that he would not be so stupid ever again. As he splashed his face with water and looked into a mirror, he told himself: The war is over. I shall soon be home. I am now the eldest son, and I shall look after my sister and my father. That is what I want to do, and what I shall do.

December 1918

Lawrence had been sent by his father the edition of the Bury Free Press which described the peace celebrations. Sitting in India he read the column headed

The Procession and the Mayor's Speech

The torch-light procession started from the Abbey Gardens, the fine old gate of which was partially illuminated. Most of the torches were carried by men in khaki and it was a fine sight as viewed from the Angel Hotel windows as the men emerged onto the hill to the accompaniment of lively music of the Suffolk Band. The procession, which traversed Northgate Street, Brackland, St John's Street, Cornhill and back to Angel Hill was led by the Mayor and the Messrs Wilson in a motor car, and on its return the Mayor, speaking from the steps of the hotel made famous by Dickens, addressed an immense throng, his marvellous voice carrying finely, and even carrying over the annoyance of a persistent trumpet.

The Mayor described the victory which had been gained as the greatest occurrence in the history of the world. "We have been engaged for the last four years in a fight for Right against Might, for Christianity against the greatest barbarism that ever existed (Cheers). We have had a good fight, thank God we have had a clean fight on our side (Applause), and more than that we have had a victorious issue (Applause). The enemy that threatened to invade our shores, to destroy our populations, men, women and children, have, by the valour of our Navy, Army and our Airmen been beaten to their knees, and we have every cause to rejoice, therefore, and to be proud of what our men have done for us. (Applause) But in this hour of our joyfulness, our just rejoicing, do not let us forget those who have sacrificed their lives that we might live (Hear, Hear). This is a day of gladness throughout the whole Empire, but it is tinged with that sorrow and with sympathy for those who have lost their dearest and their best.

There was more, much more to read, but Lawrence could not stomach it. Not while his thoughts were still focused on his mother, at least. He would read more of the paper later on, after another night's sleep.

December 1918

It is nearly 1919. I believe this will be a better year, even though Mother is dead. I cannot wait for Lawrence to come home. He has promised us that he will be here by Easter at the latest. I don't know why they can't come now, but it seems they can't. Father is already talking about what Lawrence will do. Perhaps he will go to university? Perhaps he will find a job? Father is determined that he should not hang around in West Stow, because there is nothing at all for him here. I'm not sure if we'll go back to Hardwick. It's changed a great deal and we would feel sad there. Anyway, I'm not sure whether Mr Cullum wants to employ my father again. Father is not ill, but he is not as well as he was.

Uncle Arthur is being very kind to us, and Aunt Bridget has stopped bossing me about. I quite like helping her now. Even though the epidemic is still here, I've stopped worrying about it. After Mother died I was terrified that either I or Father or my uncle or aunt would get it too. Or all of us, perhaps at the same time or perhaps one after another – I didn't know which would be worst. In Bury they had to leave the doors open in the churches and cinemas and schools, to air them. But none of us got flu. I sometimes think that God realises we've suffered enough, but that can't be right, because some families have lost more than two people during the war.

It's holidays for a few more days, and then I'll be back at school. Last term I came top in most subjects. About ten days ago Miss Pitcher asked if I had ever thought about a career. I said I hadn't. Talk to your father about it, she said.

So I did. Father was very surprised. He said it was unusual for a girl to have a career, and that he was not sure if it would be the right thing for me. He said it was likely that I'd get married and have a family, so fitting a career in before that would be difficult. But he said he would mull it over.

Last week they brought two big German guns and stood them in the Abbey gardens. Uncle Arthur took me to see them. People were crowding round them, but I didn't like them, because it might have been one of them which killed Conrad. So we did not stay long.

The strange thing is that though the war is over, men are still dying. In the Free Press there is still a page full of notices about soldiers, with their photos. Above each photo is a heading of a few words, like this: *Ixworth Man Dies of Wounds, Barton Lad Still Missing, Young Fornham Man Killed.*

But some are coming home from hospitals and camps where they have been kept prisoner. And some, like Lawrence, seem to be enjoying themselves. A regiment on the Rhine is even asking for ice skates!

I want my mother. I want Mother so, so much. As soon as I begin to think about her, my asthma comes on. Once I start crying, I keep wheezing and sneezing. I have no idea where all the tears come from. It's a horrible feeling because my chest feels tight and I think I'm not going to be able to breathe.

"Elly?"

Aunt Bridget is calling me, but I want to stay up here in my room, on my own.

"Elly? Are you up there?"

I need the Potter's Cure, so I go downstairs.

"My poor love. My poor, poor love. Come here."

I let Aunt Bridget hold me. I let her lead me to the steaming balm. If only it could cure unhappiness.

March 1919

I'm missing Ampton and Ingham. I'm missing the soldiers and officers we helped, the nurses and matrons, the other volunteers, even the smell and steam at the station. The military hospital has closed and the last men removed to other places. Of course this is a good thing, for no-one wants more war, but the closure has saddened me. I need Ampton, for it gave me a reason to live. I know my loss is certainly no greater than that of many other people. I've lost one of my sons and a wife. I keep telling myself that I still have a daughter, a son, reasonable health, and a home. But I need purpose, too.

So I try to interest myself in Elly, in the farm, in the news.

Gandhi was a name we were hearing more and more. Even Arthur had mentioned it. Gandhi, a Hindu, studied law in London, practised for about twenty years as a barrister in South Africa, and is now leader of the Indian National Congress. He is revered by Mohammedans and Sikhs as well as by Hindus.

Last June, when invited by the British Viceroy to a War Conference in Delhi, he agreed to recruit Indians to fight for Britain. The papers published extracts from his Appeal for Enlistment. He says he is a pacifist, but he wrote, *"If we want to bring about such a state of things* (he was referring to an increased war effort) *we should have the ability to defend ourselves, that is, the ability to bear arms and use them. If we want to learn the use of arms with the greatest possible dispatch, it is our duty to enlist ourselves in the army."* This led people to believe that he was a true friend of Britain.

But now, only a few months since the Declaration of Peace, things have changed and he seems to be working India up into a ferment against the Raj. He has enormous influence and it is known that hundreds of thousands of Indians are hungry for Home Rule and ready to grasp it. But can he control those men? Is it possible that the British could be overthrown? Despite the vast size of the country, it's said that his propaganda is almost everywhere. It is difficult to believe that the Raj is in real danger. Surely a man as intelligent as Gandhi would not put it at risk? The whole world knows how much the British have done for India.

But then I think of Duleep Singh and the way in which he was exiled and deprived of his inheritance, status and culture while still a boy. Yes, he was able to become an English gentleman with wealth and privilege, and his fall from grace might have been due to his own faults, but the British did not treat him well, and Indians, especially Sikhs, must be very resentful of that. No-one knows the whole story, but no-one could deny that the British dispossessed him.

There is discussion too about the methods Gandhi might use to further his aims. While he is supposed to want to find peaceful solutions to create a better India, many British people do not trust him. There is also fear about flare-ups amongst those who are not prepared to wait for his slow way of making progress, such as his policy of non-violent resistance.

Lawrence has only mentioned him a couple of times, so perhaps things are calm, at least where he is, near Amritsar. Dear God, how I want Lawrence here. May he come home safely.

April 1919

Dear Father,

So much has happened since I last wrote. We've been involved in a whirlwind of events. I'm going to take the time to tell you what's been going on even though this letter may be censored or destroyed.

It's hard to explain exactly how it started, but just over two weeks ago we heard there was some unrest in Amritsar. Apparently two doctors had been stirring people up, and they were arrested. (By the way, I wasn't in Amritsar when this happened – none of us were, and I only heard about this from other people). The authorities feared these doctors because one was a Hindu and the other a Mohammedan and they were united in their aim for Indian Home Rule. This unity creates a very dangerous situation.

These arrests upset the natives in Amritsar, and they showed their feelings by shutting down their shops and businesses and walking to the Deputy Commissioner's house to demand the release of the doctors. Then the army and the police heard what was going on, and angry crowds began to assemble. The trouble spread quickly. Stones were thrown and buildings burned. Several white people were killed. Even the hospital was attacked.

At that point I had no idea what was going on and it was a shock when, on the evening of April 10*th*, we were told to muster on the guardroom veranda. We marched to Jullundur Railway Station and boarded a train for Amritsar. Parts of the line had been torn up by rioters so sometimes we had to stop while repairs were done. It was on this journey that we realised how serious things were getting.

At dawn we were sent to cover the various city gates and our job was to prevent any more rioting. There were no white people to be seen – by now they were either sheltering in the railway station, or in the Fort. The women and children must have been terrified. We stayed there all day, feeling rather vulnerable because we were spread out thinly, but that night General Dyer arrived and the next morning we made a proper camp in some public gardens. This felt much better. Then we went to another city gate where an illegal meeting was going on. We broke this up before marching on the centre of the town, where we could see wrecked buildings. Dyer took some of the trouble-makers prisoner.

While all this was going on we heard there might be similar trouble at Lahore, so Dyer decided to make a proclamation. To get everyone's attention, he had a drummer sound a drum before he spoke. He announced that no-one could leave

Amritsar unless they had permission from one of a certain group of people, such as a magistrate or the Superintendent of Police, and when he'd finished saying that, he stopped, and had a translator say it all in Urdu, an Indian language. Then he continued his speech. No-one was to leave their house after 8pm, or they would be liable to be shot. Nor were any processions or parades to take place, and any gathering of four or more men would be considered an unlawful assembly, and might be broken up by force of arms. All this was translated, so there could be no excuse for the General not being understood. And it was done at different places right round the city. We all thought he had given an extremely fair warning.

Some of the people did not believe that they would be fired at, even if they did something they'd been told not to do, which just shows how ignorant and stupid some Indians are.

Despite this proclamation, it became known that there was going to be a big meeting that afternoon, at the Julliwallah Bag (that may not be spelled right), a big, open and scruffy sort of garden area surrounded by high walls. This was clearly in deliberate defiance of what had been announced. True to what he had stated, Dyer ordered about 100 troops into the place where the meeting was assembling, and positioned them exactly where he wanted them – round the edge of one side of the Bag garden, blocking off the exits to the garden. I wasn't present, but I'm telling you what my Sikh friend Pal told me, because he was there. In fact, all the troops Dyer took were either Gurkhas or Sikhs or the Frontier Force. (No white troops at all, except for Dyer's personal bodyguards, one of whom is a London and must have had a clear view of everything that happened, but I've not had a chance to talk to him). Some of the Gurkhas had kukri knives but no guns.

The General had to get out of his car because it was too wide to pass through the entrance gate, and he followed his men into the Bag garden. Pal said someone was giving a speech on a platform, and there was a huge crowd. Thousands and thousands of Indians, mostly men, but women too. He looked to see if any one was carrying weapons, but no-one had any, not even sticks. Some were paying attention to the speeches, other just sitting and chatting.

Pal said that very soon after they arrived Dyer gave them the order to fire. Although he had thought that Dyer might well do that, he was by no means certain it would happen. Pal said he was shaking as he fired into the crowd in front of the platform. A cry of alarm went up and people panicked immediately. Some fell while running away from the soldiers. Others tried to hide, but there was nowhere to go. Men rushed towards the narrow exits but were shot before they reached them. Others couldn't get out because the gateways were either blocked up or crammed with people. White clothes turned red. There was screaming and wailing and shouting. Pal watched a mother trying to protect her son, but both were dead in seconds. As the bodies mounted up he expected to be ordered to stop firing, but the order to fire was repeated, and repeated again. He shot men and women, young and old. He saw a buffalo keel over and crush an old couple. He said they were ordered to shoot at people who were still moving, and he did. They fired for ten minutes, until, just as they were about to run out of ammunition, they were ordered to cease fire.

When it was over, he said that apart from cries of grief and pain from the people, the place was almost still. The soldiers did not look at each other. They wiped their faces on their sleeves and checked their rifles. They stared at the bloody scene they had created, and they looked at the General. Someone overheard an officer say to him, "You've taught them a lesson they won't forget, sir." The troops were ordered to stand up, and they then marched out of the garden.

While all this was going on we were in another part of Amritsar. When I saw Pal he said they must have killed hundreds of people. He was shocked by the events, but most of us Londons were not. The Indians had been getting too sure of themselves, getting above themselves, and if Dyer had not done what he did, who knows what might have happened? Probably a real, violent rebellion. If so, that might have led to a terrible slaughter of European women and children who had taken refuge in the railway station and the Fort, or violence could even have spread to other parts of India.

The next day, April 14th, a delegation came to the General asking permission to collect the dead from the Julliwallah Bag, and bury or burn them. We went out into the city on patrol, and I saw carts filled with bodies being taken out and heard people weeping and wailing. I have never seen anything like it and I hope I won't ever again, but that's what happens in war. This shooting may not seem like real war to you, but this had to be done so that things did not get worse.

Once things had settled down, some of the existing laws were made much stricter, and new laws were passed. A strict curfew was imposed. People had to salaam to any European they passed. Owners of any vehicles, even tongas, had to lend them to the military. No-one was allowed to travel third class on the train, and natives had to get permission to travel. Anything that could be used as a weapon had to be handed in. The police tried to get the names of trouble makers. Some of those who broke the laws were beaten. Water was cut off from the homes of Indians, and the electricity was disconnected.

So, the Indians are having a hard time under martial law, but I'm glad to tell you that we Londons are having a good time. Dyer was pleased with us and has made sure that we're comfortable and looked after. We even have electric fans! We think we deserve it, though I'm the first to say that Pal and men like him deserve it much more than I do.

But I have one particular duty this week that I hate and feel bad about. Just before the riots in the Bag garden a white woman, a missionary teacher, was attacked in the street by a group of native thugs. Fortunately, although she was badly injured she managed to escape, thanks to some Indians she knew who protected her. Dyer was so angry about this assault, that when things had calmed down, he ordered that any native who wanted to go along the street where she was attacked had to do so crawling on their stomach. My job was to supervise people doing that, and I had to stand over them with my rifle. The punishment for disobeying any of these laws was a whipping on a whipping triangle which had been put up specially. It was Dyer's version of Field Punishment Number One, and it put the fear of God into people.

I did not think this order was fair. The natives who had to crawl may have had nothing at all to do with the attack on the teacher. And the streets here are so filthy that men had to crawl through cow dung and all sorts of rubbish. Some had to go along that street to buy food, and then return with it, and it was impossible for the food not to get dirty. Some of our lads said it served them right, but I didn't agree.

I tried to talk to Pal about it, but since the shooting – which some people are calling a massacre, which it was - he doesn't want to talk or join in with whatever we're doing. He just sits somewhere quiet with a cup of chai on his own, or he prays, or he stays with other Sikhs.

My hand is tired from writing. But I'm like many of the men here. We feel that although we've been away from Blighty for several years, it's not until now that we've been involved with much that's important, so I wanted to tell you about it. Of course, compared to what Conrad did in the Somme, we've not done much. Most of those we've lost did not fall in battle, but died from disease. That must be a terrible end. But now the British have done something important: we've helped save India, or at least the Punjab, from rebellion, and that's something to be proud of, isn't it? I expect the papers are full of it, or they will be. Please keep any cuttings, and keep this letter too.

Today I changed duties and I've been checking passes at the railway station. It's not easy because many natives are ignorant and can't read and have to have everything explained before they make their thumb print for a signature. There are plenty of complaints, but, thanks to General Dyer, things feel under control, especially as plenty of reinforcements are arriving now.

I don't think we'll be staying in Amritsar for long, and as soon as we move I'll let you know.

Your loving son,
Lawrence

April 1919

My brother wanted me to read Lawrence's last letter, and I did so yesterday evening. Usually he would just tell me something of what Lawrence was doing, and read out a few bits, and pass on good wishes, but he wanted – he needed – to share every word of this particular letter.

I was silent when I'd finished it. It was easy to imagine the scene, given Lawrence's description. What was there to say? I didn't know much about India and the Raj and Gandhi. It was so far away, and now that the war was over everyone's attention was on making a new start here in England. That Wednesday my head was full of plans for flax.

It was a terrible shooting. Such a thing could never happen in Europe, even when a war was on. British soldiers would never be ordered to kill hundreds of peaceful and unarmed men, women and children. And surely even Germans would not be ordered to massacre English people in cold blood? But there was no getting away from the fact that a British General had done it in India.

"I don't know what to say."

Eric sighed. "At least Lawrence is safe."

"At least Lawrence is safe."

"Since he went to India I've been worrying about the action he might be part of. But he's survived battles with tribesmen and lack of water and too much heat and insects and accidents and diseases. None of those things have killed him, and it's true that he hasn't been in a "proper" war. I've no idea whether what he's done out there is important. I suppose it is if it's made India safer from outsiders trying to get in and cause trouble.

"He says this putting down of a possible internal rebellion was important, but unless I've misunderstood him he was not personally involved in it. So why does he claim he was part of it? Is it that he *wished* he was part of it? That might be the reason. But why? Why would he want to be part of such a terrible event?"

I listened to Eric trying to make sense of it. He went on, "I don't agree at all with Lawrence's opinion that this killing was a good thing. India is one of our colonies. How could a British General fire on his own government's subjects? I don't know how anyone could consider that right. At least he disapproved of Dyer's petty revenge of making men crawl."

No wonder Eric is unhappy. He's struggling both with the account of the incident itself and with the thought that, probably for the first time, he and his son hold different views about important things. It's hardly surprising that Lawrence's years in the army have changed him. He will have been influenced by all that has happened.

And though he's never mentioned it or even hinted at it, I think Eric is disappointed that Lawrence was not offered a commission. We'll never know why, but my feeling is that he has always shied away from responsibility, even though he must be, what, twenty-one or twenty-two by now. And he can be a clown when he wants to.

I understand now why Eric has been so quiet since he read the letter. Bridget and I had noticed that he has been even more withdrawn recently. Having lost his wife and his elder son, and now being made aware of big differences of opinion with his younger son, he is on the edge. Are our lives down to luck, or to God. Who knows?

It was rare for Eric to be in a low mood. I had grown up following a brother who succeeded as much because of his positive attitude as his ability, and who, unlike me, had been to university, was well read and was held in high esteem by Mr Cullum and other gentlemen renowned for their intelligence and knowledge.

I looked at him as he leant against the warm range. He was facing into the kitchen with his eyes closed. I studied his gaunt neck, his receding hairline, the small scar on his temple. I suddenly saw a strong resemblance between him and our father who had died when we were in our thirties. All this made me feel as if I was the elder brother.

I got up from my chair, went up to him and put my hand on his shoulder. He opened his eyes, straightened himself up and said, "I'm going out."

"Come back soon."

I watched him go out of the back door and turn left towards the cow byre. Now that he no longer went to Ingham and Ampton, he took plenty of walks, usually on his own. He also spent quite a bit of time reading, and had taught Elly to play chess.

I moved to stand exactly where he had stood, held on to the warm rail, and shut my eyes as he had done.

My thoughts turned to Elly. She was getting on as well as she could. She kept up her schoolwork, sometimes saw her friends, helped me with small tasks and did things with Bridget which, in the past, she would have tried to avoid.

Bridget was softening. Recently her voice had become a little lower, her movements less sharp. She even left for the next day jobs which she would not have left previously: extra dusting, taking out the compost bucket, weeding the herb patch near the back door. Only a few months ago she would have insisted on completing every single thing she had planned to do on a particular day.

All this was something to do with Elly, and it had begun at the funeral. Elly had not wanted to go close to the grave, and as the procession moved forward I watched her turn away from her father and the vicar towards the main group of mourners, searching for someone to hold on to. She looked at neighbours, at Mr Cullum, at her uncle. She made as if to move to her grandmother, but she was bent in grief and leaning heavily on her daughter's arm. Suddenly Elly went to Bridget, and Bridget held her.

When I was a young man and got married, I had looked forward to having a family, but Bridget did not become pregnant. We went on hoping for years, but gradually accepted the situation. We were both sad, but I felt more for Bridget than myself. Children mean more to women, I think, and I could imagine her disappointment.

Other people were curious. No-one, thank God, asked outright when we were going to have children, and I think that most people assumed that we did not want them. While Bridget longed to contradict this and tell them the truth, it was acknowledgement that she wanted, rather than sympathy. So we threw ourselves into the farm and, I like to think, have made and are still making the most of our lives.

But now Bridget has a child. Quite a big child, of course, for Elly is twelve. Nevertheless, twelve-year-olds need their mothers. This one certainly does. The war had led to many children losing their fathers, and some their mothers too, but it was the epidemic rather than the war which brought Bridget and Elly together. Hattie's death allowed Bridget to express tenderness, and simultaneously Elly, who was so bereft, reached out for it.

I knew that Bridget too was regretting that she had, on occasion, been sharp with Hattie. She said nothing about this to me, but I guessed that at least part of the reason for her extra care of Elly was because she had some regrets.

Last week, I had come in from the farm through the garden when Bridget and Elly were holding out the newly washed and bleached sheets by the corners. The fabric was being blown about and they were laughing as they tried to fold it. And then Elly dropped her end, and the corner fell onto the mud. That was the sort of thing that used to annoy Bridget, but now she laughed and said, "Never mind. We'll tuck that corner out of sight."

It gladdened me to see them becoming companions. Strangely, Elly was now spending more time with Bridget than she had done with her mother. Hattie had always had something on the go. Mostly it had been Ampton, of course, but there had been earlier charitable projects which took her out and away from home, often without Elly who, when Eric was with Mr Cullum, was entrusted to Conrad and Lawrence – an entirely happy arrangement for everyone.

I was worried that Eric would drown in depression. It was hard for Elly to be with him for long, for he gave little. It was easier for her to be with someone who chatted and did things with her, mundane though many of them were.

As I turned to leave the room I saw the letter from Lawrence lying on the table. I picked it up and stood it up on the shelf by the window. I was glad that Eric had not taken it with him, for he needed space before he read it yet again.

May 1919

Aunt Bridget has got hold of a book for me that she liked when she was young. It's called *Little Women*. I read the first few chapters yesterday. It's a bit odd because the book starts when it's Christmas time in America, but I'm reading it here in England in the middle of May! The story is about four sisters called Jo, Amy, Beth and Meg. They seem to be quite rich although they say they are poor. I looked at some pages in the middle and there's a boy in it called Laurie which is what my mother sometimes used to call Lawrence. The girls' father is away at a war, not fighting, but being a chaplain. And their mother helps at a hospital for wounded soldiers, which obviously made me think about my mother all over again. I'm skipping some bits because some of it's boring, so I might have missed something important.

I specially like Jo, because she's a tomboy, and that's what I am. She likes boys' games and boys' manners. She can whistle too, and I'm quite good at that, even though Aunt Bridget says, *"A whistling maid and a crowing hen are neither good for God nor men."* I tried to think what it would be like to be in their family with a mother and father (even though the father's away) and three sisters rather than just a father and two brothers. Well, only one brother, really, now. But I don't feel as if I don't have a mother. It feels as if I have one, but she's not here at present.

In the book, Jo says she would like to fight with her father (although he was chaplain, not a soldier), which I thought was very strange, because if she did that she might be killed. I don't think she knew what war was like, because in his letters their father doesn't write about the war itself, and I don't think they had newspapers like ours with lists of all the men who die and are injured. I would never want to go to war, even though I'm a tomboy.

And I must ask Aunt Bridget who the war in *Little Women* is between, because the writer doesn't say. It's definitely not the Germans. There's a poor German family in the book, the Hummel family, and Marmee, the mother of the four girls, feels sorry for them and helps them, so they can't be the enemy. The Americans must be fighting against a different country. Perhaps another country has invaded them, like Germany invaded France? But that still doesn't explain why the German family are living in America. I'll ask Aunt Bridget about that too.

I'll read a bit more this evening, but Father and I are going to play chess after supper. Chess is a very good game. I love setting the board out with all the pieces in their proper places. I love the way the bishops slide diagonally, and how the knights can jump over other pieces. It's simple, but it's complicated at the same time, and I wonder who invented it and how they decided which moves each piece could make.

Sometimes you have to defend, but you also have to attack, and if you're clever you can do both at once. Uncle Arthur says it's like war. You have to think about lots of things at the same time, and things keep changing. Father is very good at chess, but while I'm still learning, he's deliberately not trying his hardest. I don't think he was concentrating last time we played, because he lost one of his bishops and a castle very carelessly. Even I could see they were in danger. He says that one day I'll beat him when he's trying his hardest, because I'm cleverer than him. He says that because he wants to cheer me up, but it's not true. He's by far the cleverest person I know. He's read so many books and knows so, so much! Uncle Arthur sometimes whispers to me that Father knows *too* much. But I don't think it's possible to know too much.

I don't need cheering up. I'm all right. It's Father who needs cheering up. At mealtimes he hardly says anything, and he used to talk a lot. You can see he just wants to eat his dinner and go out for a stroll and be at peace. I sometimes go with him, but we don't say much. We look at Uncle Arthur's crops, and we scratch a few pigs, and then we go along the field path towards Icklingham, and occasionally down to the Lark. While we're walking I think about lots of things, like Mother, school, what I've done that day, but I've no idea what Father's thinking about. He used to talk about what Lawrence might be doing, but now he doesn't. Sometimes he'll stop walking, put his hand on my arm and say, "Listen. A thrush." Or, "Look. Buzzards. A pair of them." And after about twenty minutes he says, "Let's turn round, shall we? Let's go back to the farm." And so we do.

Lawrence will come home soon because the war against Germany is over, and so is the war he was fighting in, up in the North-West Frontier of India. The real, main war has been over for months now – about six months. We keep expecting to hear when he's coming. It can't be long now.

May 1919

Montagu, Secretary of State for India to Lord Chelmsford, Viceroy of India

I am shortly going to telegraph you suggesting that it will be necessary to have an enquiry into the causes of and the treatment of the riots that have occurred in India. I do not mean by that that there is any reason to suppose that any Government did not handle the question as it should have been handled. But it always seems to me that one ought to investigate allegations of needless brutality in dealing with an emeute.

. . . .

Dyer's judgement and temper have in my opinion proved so unreliable that I am of the opinion that he cannot be fit to retain command. I consider in fact it very undesirable that he should continue in the army of India. Unless the military authority has something to urge on his behalf beyond his previous excellent record of which I am not aware, I think you should relieve him of his command and send him to England.

June 1919

Dear Father,

Thanks for your letters. When I get home we can have a proper talk about what's been going on here. I'll be able to explain it better than any newspaper reporter, because I'm seeing it all directly.

Things calmed down under martial law, but we've just heard that, once again, the Afghans are up to something, and we're being mobilized for service on the Frontier. Why us? Because we're useful. Also, because no units are up to strength (we Londons now consist of only 270 men and 20 officers), we have to join up with other battalions. My first thought when I heard about this was, Oh no, I want to go home. But I soon realised that I wanted to be part of it – we all do, even the men *who are ill - so here I am on my way back to Waziristan. We crossed the Indus yet again en route to Peshawar where we set up camp on the race-course. After a few days there we were told to get ready for another move. For transport, we were provided with 50 mules, 81 camels, and 8 ox-drawn carts. We had to load these up in the dark, with only a few hurricane lamps. Chaos! At last we got to the station and unloaded and re-loaded everything onto a train. Still, that's what we were doing last time we were in Waziristan, so we're good at it now.*

At first we relieved the picquets in the city, but then the Afghan tribesmen crossed the frontier into India. No-one thought they would be able to do so on the route they chose, but they did. Mind you, it didn't occur to anyone that they'd use elephants to pull the artillery! And then other tribes joined in, and things got bad, so the unprotected British troops based in the area headed for safety to the fort at Thal, and shut themselves in. Then the decision was made that we Londons would form the Thal Relief Column. We were a real mixture. There were Lancers, Mountain Battery, Dogras, Rifles and more. General Dyer was given overall responsibility and the night before we left for Thal he addressed us all. What he said made us determined and proud.

Our march to Thal took us hours and hours, in appalling hot temperatures. The whole thing was a difficult business (though we had some help from aeroplanes) and I can't tell you all the details. Many Londons got heatstroke and had to be carried.

After all that we had to cross a river by a ford so fierce we had to join up in parties of 12 or more linking arms and hoping that together we could resist the current. At the same time we had to carry all our rifles and Lewis guns above the water which was up to our waists.

At one point we were longing for fresh water, and although there was a stream, there were dead camels in it. Instead, we had to make do with something that the natives called water but which looked and felt like thick tea. Foul. And then Dyer thanked us and told us an Armistice had been signed.

Even better, how about this telegram? I've copied it down exactly, capitals and all.

ORDER OF THE DAY

The force commander congratulates General Dyer and all ranks which formed the THAL RELIEF COLUMN under his command on the success of their operations.

The march of the Column to Thal was carried out with the greatest celerity and under the most trying conditions, and its success redounds to the credit of the Column.

The General Officer commanding the late THAL RELIEF COLUMN wishes this message to be conveyed to every man in the late THAL RELIEF COLUMN.

Thal

8/6/19

We're feeling very pleased about this, and of course General Dyer must be, too.

We are sure that this is our last campaign, and we'll soon be going to Nowshera by train. And so to England and to Suffolk. Not long now! Perhaps September, if we're lucky.

Your loving son,
Lawrence

July 1919

Memorandum of Lord Chelmsford's Executive Council

We can arrive at no other conclusion than that at Jallianwala Bagh General Dyer acted beyond the necessity of the case, beyond what any reasonable man could have thought to be necessary, and that he did not act with as much humanity as the case permitted. It is with pain that we arrive at this conclusion for we are not forgetful of the General's distinguished record as a soldier and of his gallant relief of the garrison at Thal during the recent Afghan war. We must, however, direct the judgement above pronounced, be communicated to His Excellency the Commander-in-Chief with the request that he take the appropriate action.

Sir Rabindrath Tagore to Viceroy, Lord Chelmsford

The enormity of the measures taken by the Government in the Punjab for quelling some local disturbances has, with acute shock, revealed to our minds the helplessness of our position as British subjects in India.

The accounts of insults and sufferings undergone by our brothers in the Punjab have trickled through the gagged silence, reaching every corner of India, and the universal agony of indignation roused in the hearts of our people has been ignored by our rulers - possibly congratulating themselves for what they imagine as salutary lessons.

Gandhi, in Young India

His (Dyer's) brutality is unmistakable. His abject and unsoldier-like cowardice is apparent in every line of amazing defence before the Army Council... Such a man is unworthy of being considered a soldier... no doubt the shooting was 'frightful', the loss of innocent life deplorable. But the slow torture, degradation and emasculation that follows was much worse, more calculated, malicious and soul killing, and the actors who perform the deeds deserve greater condemnation than General Dyer for the Jallianwalla Bagh massacre. The latter only destroyed a few bodies but the others tried to kill the soul of a nation.

July 1919

Bury held its Peace Celebrations last weekend. There was a huge crowd on Angel Hill for the Thanksgiving Service. It was all flowers and music and speeches and smart hats. Everyone went. People wanted to pay tribute to and welcome the returning soldiers, even though many had also lost a man from their family. Some had lost two or three, or even more, so there was a mixed feel to the day of joy and sorrow. Of course Eric and Elly were thinking of Conrad, and I felt for them. Conrad was a very pleasant young man. A bit bumptious occasionally, but friendly and warm, and, we were told by someone who worked with him at Greene King, good at his job.

My vegetable garden is still full of produce (lettuce, potatoes, carrots, beans), and the sheep, pigs and poultry are healthy, so all is well, thank God. The Border Leicesters have done very well this year, as have the Wessex, but the Large Whites, for some reason, have not been as good as usual.

I keep changing my mind about flax. It's tempting because there's a ready market, and several farmers I respect have decided to plant it. We've been told that the new factory at Almoners Barn, just north-east of Hardwick, will take all the flax we can send.

Bridget is all for it, which surprises me. Usually she's more cautious than I am. She thinks it likely the flax business will thrive, and that even if it doesn't, we can use any new land for something else. She said, "Why not plant soft fruit? People always want soft fruit." But I'm not so keen on having women picking on my land, with all their children traipsing after them. I'd rather keep a proper farm with my own men.

But she's right about one thing, which is that I can afford to buy some acres. I've done well, and the money is there, even for more machinery. There's no point in buying land close to the Lark because of the flooding, and few crops have been grown there successfully. But if I buy elsewhere, the cost per acre will be higher.

It's no good asking Eric's opinion. He's really not at all well in his spirit. He does the odd job around the farm, but I can't see him getting more involved than he is now, even though he has plenty of time. He goes back to Hardwick once a week, but from what he says Mr Cullum is not in the best of health either, and he comes home in much the same mood as he went, whereas in the past, he'd be talking about some new book or acquisition.

My relationship with him is changing. It's true that, when we were young, I rather resented him and his scholarship, and I've always felt that he thought me of only average intelligence and too judgmental. Perhaps there's some truth in that. This has meant that things have not always been comfortable between us. But recently I've been thinking that there's no getting away from the fact that he's my brother. I have never had and will never have another brother. I have known Eric for longer than I have known any other living person. We may not see eye to eye, but we should at least stand shoulder to shoulder. I've been thinking too about Lawrence. It is so sad that he and Conrad will not have the chance to be men together. It makes me think that Eric and I must make the most of each other.

I've thought of our parents, too. About our childhood, about growing up. Our parents would want us to be brotherly as we got older. Of course they would. Eric is the one who needs help now. He doesn't know how to ask for it, but I can give it.

August 1919

From Dyer's report to General Beynon

It will be necessary for me to mention certain events which occurred prior to 11ᵗʰ April, the date on which I reached Amritsar, to show why I considered it my bounden duty to disperse by rifle fire the unlawful and mutinous assembly in the Jallianwalla Bagh on the 13ᵗʰ April 1919.

… I fired and I continued to fire until the crowd dispersed and I considered this is the least amount of firing which would produce the necessary moral and widespread effect it was my duty to produce if it was to justify my action … It was no longer

just a question of dispersing the crowd but one of producing a sufficient moral effect, from a military point of view, not only on those who were present but more specially throughout the Punjab. There could be no question of undue severity. The mutineers had thrown out the challenge and the punishment, if administered at all, must be complete, unhesitating and immediate.

September 1919

Lawrence still isn't home. Other people's brothers and cousins came back months ago, but Lawrence and his unit had to go and rescue some British men from a fort in the mountains. Father says he'll be back any day now.

Little Women turned out to be boring. It was about four girls and parties and clothes and a boy and an old man. I didn't finish it, but I looked at the last pages and it seemed to end happily. I'm not sure why books are supposed to end happily, because lots of people's lives end badly, like Mother's and Conrad's, and all those soldiers.

The pictures are good. The best one is of Amy being rescued when she'd fallen through the ice. It looked very lifelike, and Amy looked really frightened. But Aunt Bridget said she had loved *Little Women* when she was my age!

I'm still knitting, and now I'm making a scarf for Lawrence, because it's hot where he is, and he'll find it cold here in winter.

I'm doing well at chess. Father's taught me some different ways of opening, and I'm beginning to be able to hold more ideas in my head both about moves I might make, and about moves he might make. Aunt Bridget doesn't know how to play, but when I offered to teach her, she said it looked far too complicated, and that she'd rather do some baking.

Much earlier this year, in the spring, we heard that Dr Sturge was very ill. And then we heard he had died. I'm sorry, because I liked him, but the good thing is that his flint collection is going to be put in the British Museum, which means that some of the flints I found will be in London for everyone to look at!

September 1919

We marched from Pathankot to Dalhousie (hill station), taking five days, and then waited to hear when we would be returning to England. We had bets on the date, and I was over-optimistic. But luckily for me, in the excitement of signing our demob papers and being given a firm date, the debt got forgotten. Everyone was talking about England, wives, children, women, parents, work, football, beer, girls, money, jobs! It was wonderful! We Londons all swore to stay in touch and to meet up.

At last we moved through Delhi and so south to Deo-lali – a place I hope never to see again. For ten whole days we had nothing to do except carry out guard duties and attend parades. It was like being in prison. But some poor fellows had been there for months, waiting for the sailing season to begin. We soon realised how lucky we were to have arrived at just the right time.

Some of the men in Deolali were in a very sorry state. They were ill in their heads. The things that had happened to them in India had affected them. Some could not speak properly, some shouted, others sat rocking themselves backwards and forwards. Obviously we've seen Indian natives like that almost everywhere we've been, but I hadn't expected to see British soldiers crying and making strange movements. There's one poor fellow who keeps hitting his head on a wall, and another who repeatedly tells everyone to be careful of the grass. We did not have to share quarters with them, thank God, but they made me feel guilty. Here was I, in reasonable condition, less than one month away from a new life at home, but what was the future for these men? I asked an officer if they would be given treatment and his answer was, "Perhaps, when they reach England, they will be looked after and will come through. But perhaps they won't. Who knows?" I thought that if I were as ill as they were I would want to die.

Finally, we underwent a thorough medical examination, did some last minute shopping and gathered up our possessions.

At last we went up the gangway of SS Lancashire in pairs, and soon we headed out to sea. As we entered open water we were paraded on deck, and, at a given signal we raised our topees and – without permission - flung them into the sea! We had left India!

On the journey some men stared at the horizon, willing England to appear. Others tried to claim a space amidst the chaos below, for nothing had been allocated or prepared. Our journey took three weeks, and five men caught influenza. They died within days. After all we had been through, they fell at the last hurdle. Poor devils.

It was during the service held for the first of these that I began to feel queasy. Was it seasickness, or something worse? I reported sick and was immediately confined to a bunk in an isolation cabin. I vomited over a period of several hours. A rash I'd had on my neck on and off for months spread over my left shoulder. But despite the recent deaths from the epidemic I did not feel alarmed. The doctor did not give my illness a name. I was given medicine, and I slept, and during the last few days of the journey I recovered. I shut off all thoughts about India and what we'd done there and filled my head with home and hope. I lay in bed thinking of my parents, my brother and sister, our house in Hardwick, my school, Bury St Edmunds, cricket, Uncle Arthur's farm, cycling.

I was extremely jealous that I could not be with my friends when they had a night of celebration in Devonport on November 11th – a year to the day after the signing of the Armistice. I was ordered to remain on board. But I made up for it after our reception at Crystal Palace. A group of us decided to enjoy a few hours in London before taking trains back to our homes. We were free men, and knew that such an occasion and opportunity would never occur again.

November 1919

When we went to the station at Bury St Edmunds I was not even sure that I would recognize Lawrence, but of course I did. There he was, much taller than before, hauling his bag off the train. My heart was thumping as I went to meet him. We threw our arms round each other and I wept into his rough khaki jacket. At last we pulled apart and I looked into his face. There he was. Lawrence. My youngest son, now a man. Back from India, back from danger. Six feet tall and in tears.

Elly was standing beside me, shyly. When Lawrence saw her he exclaimed, "Elly! It's Elly!" and lifted her off her feet. And so we made our way down the steps from the platform and out into the yard where Arthur was waiting with a borrowed car. He held out his hand to Lawrence, welcomed him and put the kitbag in the boot.

As we drove to West Stow Lawrence hardly spoke, but looked out of the window drinking everything in. He must have been astonished at the change of scenery. When we reached the farm Bridget came out to the car and hugged him. Then he caught sight of Bran.

"Bran! I'd forgotten you! Oh, Bran, how could I have forgotten you?" We stood in a circle round Lawrence, watching his delight at the small dog which he was cuddling. "Do you remember me, Bran? Yes, of course you do."

Somehow we made our way into the house. I was smiling, crying, talking and feeling emotions I didn't know come surging up, fighting for air.

December 1919

My journey to Suffolk was a blur. One of the Londons made sure I got on the right train at Liverpool Street, and asked some kind passenger if they would keep an eye on me. Confused, exhausted and hung over, I slept most of the way, waking only when I was helped to change trains at Haughley. All I remember was that the train travelled very fast, compared to Indian trains, and, absurdly, each time I woke from my doze, I was surprised that none of the landscape we passed was hilly, let alone mountainous.

Father and Elly were there to meet me, and on seeing and greeting them I cried. We all did. Once we were in the car – my first ride ever in a private car – I found I could not speak. Uncle Arthur was driving, and I sat in the front and stared out of the window, thinking of my friends and the night we'd spent in London.

It seemed only a few minutes before we arrived at the farm, and there was Aunt Bridget hurrying towards the car even before it stopped, wanting to open the door for me. She hugged me first, and then Father and Elly hugged me again, and Arthur kept banging me on my back, and we all stood just looking at each other and smiling and crying. And then Bran raced up to us. Bran! We'd been given him a year or two before the war, when we were still at Hardwick, but I was often away so I didn't get to know him well. But he remembered me, and as soon I picked him up and felt his warm, soft coat I found myself weeping even more. I had been wary of every dog in India, but I let Bran lick my tears.

I looked at the farmhouse and could not believe it was so small and low. My memory was of a big house with tall chimneys.

Father carried my kitbag indoors, and we all followed him. What I needed most was to wash and to change my clothes, so after more exclamations of welcome and surprise I took my boots off and went upstairs to the bedroom I'd last slept in when I came here on leave from Chiseldon almost exactly four years ago. Though tiny, it contained a bed, a rug, a chest of drawers and, covered with a thin white cloth, a jacket on a coat hanger on a hook behind the door.

From the little square window I could see, just beneath me, Aunt Bridget talking to a neighbour in the garden. I could tell from her gestures and happy expression that she was talking about me. Her hair was going grey, and I'd forgotten how slim she was.

The lane led off to the left towards Bury, in the direction we'd come from, and to the right it went towards Flempton. The field furrows were dark brown, the trees almost bare, the puddles sky-white. A neat hedge and ditch edged the lane. Everything was so familiar and so new. I watched two young women cycle past.

Women. At the thought of women I sat down on the bed, my head in my hands.

"Lawrence, would you like Elly to bring up a basin of water for you?" called Bridget.

"No thanks. I'm dirty, so I'll come and use the outside tap."

"There's a towel down here for you. You can have a bath later on."

I stood up, took off my jacket, and went downstairs, ducking to avoid hitting the low ceiling. A cold wash in the cold yard woke me up, and I went back upstairs refreshed and beginning to think about food.

But what was I to wear? The clothes I had on were quite past it, but amongst the debris in my kitbag all I had was a well-worn shirt and a dirty pair of trousers. I looked round the room, went over to the chest of drawers and opened the top drawer. It held underclothes and socks. In the second drawer were two folded shirts and a pair of trousers. In the bottom drawer were two more shirts and another pair of trousers. I could not understand why, after all I had heard about the shortage of clothes, Uncle had so many spare things.

I needed to get warm, so I chose a pair of trousers and tried them on. They were for a man of my own height but of sturdier build. That was odd, for my uncle was taller than me and had never carried much weight.

Opening the drawer again, I saw some trousers I recognized as my own by a burn near the pocket. Then it occurred to me that Aunt Bridget, or Mother, or the two of them together, must have decided to store things here for my return. For *our* return. None of these clothes was Uncle Arthur's. They were mine and Conrad's. The clothes were waiting for us to come home.

As my own clothes no longer fitted, I pulled on a pair of Conrad's trousers and one of his shirts. I took the protective cloth off the jacket, put it on, picked up my dirty clothes and went downstairs. I could smell something very good.

"Ah. A new man," said Uncle. "How do you feel?"

I paused by the door. How did I feel? I wasn't sure, but everyone was looking at me expectantly. "Tired. Tired out. And very happy to be home with you all."

My father's face, more lined than I remembered, seemed both anxious and hopeful. He urged Elly to take my clothes into the scullery, then gestured me to take a seat.

Aunt Bridget brought in the sort of meal we Londons had dreamed of so often: roast lamb, carrots, cabbage, potatoes, gravy. She jumped up and down from the table, making sure everyone had enough of everything on their plates.

Father said a silent grace, as he sometimes used to. Arthur tucked in to the food, sometimes looking up and smiling at me. Elly hardly took her eyes off me. The five of us ate in near silence, each thinking our own thoughts. Occasionally two people would start speaking at once, and they would both stop and one would let the other one say whatever it was they wanted to say. In the gap between the main course and the pudding, I saw Father tug his handkerchief from his pocket, take off his glasses, and wipe his tears away. It was a bitty conversation and I had little desire to talk and nothing to say. Each of us was very aware that though I was here, Conrad and Mother were not.

After the meal I slept for hours.

January 1920

Somehow we got through the anniversary of Hattie's death, and then it was Christmas, and we even managed to celebrate. It was marvellous to have Lawrence safely with us. I was looking forward to helping him decide what to do next. He gave no indication of having thought about the future, but it was early days. He needed us, but he also needed to be alone, and he needed time. He slept, walked and read popular books that held no interest for me at all. It gave me great pleasure to see him play chess with Elly, although I noticed that he was teaching her Crown and Anchor, a betting game with dice he'd learned from the Londons.

I wanted to hear more about India: the mountains, plains, temples, the people, the buildings. Even the farms, for I knew that Arthur would be interested in those. I wanted him to tell me more about camp life and the events at Amritsar. But he seemed to prefer being quiet. Indeed, I'd go so far as to say that he was withdrawn, even unsociable. Whole meals passed during which he said nothing at all. After his lively letters, this surprised me and I looked forward to seeing him smile and laugh as he used to do so readily.

I was disappointed and saddened that he hardly spoke to me about his mother. If I made a simple comment, such as, "Hattie would be astonished to see how much you've grown," he would give a quick nod of acknowledgement, but otherwise nothing. He found it far too difficult.

But at least he soon began to look better than when he arrived, not least because he bought some clothes that fitted him properly. Also, he was rested, he was eating well and his rash had completely healed up. I grieved that Hattie could not see him.

One day I persuaded him to come over to Hardwick House with me. I knew that Mr Cullum would be pleased to see him and the drawings he had done in India. I tempted Lawrence by saying I could show him books containing beautiful botanical illustrations.

We were given a lift to Hardwick, and Lawrence was able to see for himself how the place had changed. We looked through what had been the gardens and saw the now dry fountain, the indoor riding school (its floor churned up, unraked and covered in dung) and even the thatched sheep pens.

We went to the house which used to be ours.

"My God. It's sad," said Lawrence.

"Yes."

"Will it be repaired?"

"I doubt it."

"Why not?"

"I don't think Mr Cullum will invest more in Hardwick."

"So what'll happen to it?"

"I don't know."

Lawrence wanted to go inside so I waited while he pushed open the damaged door to our house. He cracked his head on the lintel as he went inside, and swore loudly.

After only two or three minutes he reappeared. "We could never come back here. It's ruined. Whoever it was who was here, they've ruined it. And I hadn't realized how small it was. How did we all fit in there?"

We were warmly greeted by Mr Cullum. He commented on how Lawrence had shot up and invited us to join him for tea. Lawrence's drawings interested and impressed him. He identified some of the flowers, then sought them out in various books and showed us the work of several artists whom Lawrence immediately admired.

"Your work could be as good as that of these professionals," said Mr Cullum, gesturing to the cover of an elegant volume. "I'm sure that in time, with more practice and some tuition, you could contribute to a book like this one. Mind you, you'd need to learn all the Latin names as well as the English ones. But you're a lucky man, for your father would be the perfect assistant!"

I was obviously delighted to hear Lawrence praised so warmly, but he did not seem as pleased as I expected when Mr Cullum asked him to leave his drawings so they could be displayed at the next meeting of the Suffolk Horticultural Society. In fact, asked Mr Cullum, would Lawrence like to attend? People would be most interested to meet him. But instead of taking up this warm suggestion, Lawrence declined.

I was so disappointed. Why turn down such an opportunity? It might have led to all sorts of things. He shrugged off my opinion but on our way home I urged him to think about developing this interest in botany. Mr Cullum was right, I could help him with the Latin myself. Lawrence had detested Latin at school, but I assured him there was no need to study Caesar or Horace now, or even grammar. All he would need to know would be the names themselves. It would be a project we could enjoy together.

But by the time we reached home Lawrence had told me quite sharply that he would not be taking the botany idea further. Indeed, now that he was back in England, he might never draw a plant again. And then he grew annoyed at my other suggestion that he should get on his bike more often. I could not understand this, for he had enjoyed it so much in the past.

January 1920

In the paper there was a cartoon about the New Year. A nurse was presenting Old Father Time with a new baby clothed in a shawl marked 1920. Through a window, several boys could be seen fighting each other. Old Father Time was saying, "Ah well. Let's hope this one is more of a credit to me." I thought it was a very good cartoon.

I too was hoping for a better year. At least with Lawrence back it was off to a good start. He was tall and strong, but he spent most of his time just sitting and smoking, or snoozing on the sofa. If I ever lay down like that, especially in the daytime, I was told off. But no-one complained to Lawrence or about him. Nor did anyone seem to mind Bran settling in the crook of his knees, although Aunt Bridget was always cross if *I* let Bran jump up on the sofa.

Having my brother with us made a real difference to the house. Even when he was asleep upstairs we were all aware of him. I often wished Mother and Conrad were here too, and in a way they were because I thought about them so much, especially Mother. Sometimes I almost believed that I could make her appear through thinking about her.

So Lawrence passed his time slowly. Uncle Arthur let him be, and Aunt Bridget positively enjoyed running round after him. I was getting used to him, but he didn't talk to me much and the only thing we did together was to play chess and Crown and Anchor. I liked Crown and Anchor because it makes you laugh. We played for buttons, but Lawrence said the soldiers always played for money.

It was only Father who was impatient with him. Father had always believed in the importance of a daily routine and he had taught me to stick to one too, especially after Mother's death. I was perfectly happy to go along with this, and it was by now my second nature. But Lawrence would clean his teeth in the middle of the afternoon, or make himself a sandwich only half an hour before lunch. He had no pattern to what he did, and this infuriated Father.

One day when I was ironing in the kitchen I heard Father begin to talk to Lawrence about work again. What sort of work did he want to do? What did he think he might be good at? Had he had any ideas about his future while he was in India? Now the war was over, there would surely be plenty of opportunities for a bright young man like him. He had had a good education. He was fit and healthy. He was one of the lucky ones who had his whole life ahead of him.

I couldn't hear Lawrence's reply, but whatever it was, it was short. Father spoke again, and then I heard Lawrence say, "I really don't know."

"But you can't do nothing for ever."

"I won't. I promise I'll do something. But not yet."

"What's the matter? You're finding fault with everything."

"I feel hemmed in. I need some space. Things are too tight."

"What do you mean?"

"The fields, the lanes, the hedges and trees. This house. They're all closing me in."

"They're the same as they always have been. Nothing's changed."

"Can't you see that *I've* changed?"

"Yes, of course I can, and I'm trying to help you."

"Leave me alone! Don't try to help me. I'll be all right, but I need space."

"Conrad would just be getting on with things."

"*Conrad*?" yelled Lawrence. "What's *he* got to do with it. I'm not Conrad. Can't you see that I'm Lawrence? Your second son? You might well prefer to have Conrad back, but you've got me."

Father came into the kitchen, glanced at me but walked straight through and out of the back door, grabbing his old coat from the back of the chair as he did so. It was very rare for him to be as cross and upset as that.

A few minutes later I carried the finished pile of ironing upstairs. As I passed the sitting room I could see Lawrence stretched out on the sofa as usual, with his legs sticking out over one arm. His eyes were closed and there was a bruise on his forehead from where he'd hit his head on the lintel. Bran was snuggled up against him.

February 1920

Arthur felt for Eric. He knew that, had he had a son return from war, he too would want him to get on with things rather than sit around and let life happen. He heard Eric try to interest Lawrence in going to university, which is what he might have done if there had been no war, but now had no desire for. Unexpectedly, he seemed to show less spirit in his person than he had done in his letters.

When he asked how Lawrence felt the answer was always, "It's too difficult to explain."

"He'll come through," said Arthur to Eric. "Trust him. We don't yet know much of what he's been through, but we can be sure it's more than you or I have ever had to deal with." He put his hand on his brother's shoulder. "And he's lost Conrad and his mother. We shouldn't be surprised if he finds it hard to settle down. Come and have a drink."

One afternoon an unexpected visitor came to the house. Bridget called Arthur in from the farm because Mr Edward Lake, the managing director of Greene King, had arrived in an elegant black car. In fact, it was Eric and Lawrence Mr Lake wanted to see, not Arthur. Luckily Eric was ambling back from posting a letter, and Bridget sent Elly upstairs to call Lawrence down from his room. In 1916 Mr Lake had visited to pay his condolences in respect of Conrad, and he greeted everyone warmly, shaking their hands in a most friendly manner. He knew too that Hattie had died, and now he expressed his sincere sympathy. Assuming they needed privacy, Arthur left them all in the sitting room.

Later he heard from Eric that Mr Lake had stated that he was very conscious of his own good fortune, for all of his six sons had returned unharmed from the war. Conrad, he said, had been an excellent employee who would have gone far, and he profoundly regretted his death along with the deaths of the twenty-one other Greene King employees who had fallen.

He had come to ask whether Lawrence would like a position at the brewery. Mr Lake was confident that, coming from the same home and having had a good, solid education at King Edward VIth, he would have the same positive attributes and abilities as his elder brother. There were various openings and possibilities, so he was sure there would be something to suit Lawrence.

It was a marvellous, generous, unsought opportunity, but Lawrence had immediately thanked Mr Lake for his offer, and said that he was sorry but would prefer not to accept it. At this, Eric interrupted and urged his son not to be so hasty. Mr Lake, in some surprise, looked from father to son and asked if Lawrence had other plans.

No, he hadn't any. So what was he going to do? He did not know. What, no idea at all?

"Not at present."

Mr Lake looked at him. "But you'll be playing cricket, at least?"

"Yes, sir. I expect I shall."

"You know we're having a new pitch prepared in Bury? Out towards Nowton? It's going to be called the Victory Sports Ground, for obvious reasons. Just now it's little more than a ploughed field, but it'll be ready for the summer. I look forward to seeing you play there."

As Mr Lake walked back to the car with Lawrence and Eric he said, "Ah, well. What a pity. I'd hoped you'd be joining us, not least because I like my employees to be good sportsmen." Before getting into his gleaming car he shook hands again with Eric and Lawrence. "Let me know if you change your mind. Take a week or two to think about it. And discuss it with your father. He'll give you good advice." Turning to Eric he said, "Advising one's sons after a war is quite a responsibility, isn't it? Not something we'd ever imagined we'd be doing. I'm finding that some of my boys are taking longer to settle down than others.

"Anyway, I'm sure young Lawrence will come round to seeing that my offer is a damned good one."

Later, when Eric described to Arthur what had happened, Arthur had never seen his brother so angry. Lawrence, he complained, had been off-hand, ungrateful and even disrespectful to a gentleman who wanted to help him. He had turned down the best offer he could ever hope to receive. If he went on like this he would get nowhere in life. He had changed from being cheerful and pleasant to being lazy and selfish. Although it was mid-afternoon Lawrence looked as if he had just woken up, which was probably the case, and had not even bothered to comb his hair before coming downstairs. Hattie would be as disappointed and ashamed as he was. And although he felt bad saying it, he knew that Conrad would never, ever have behaved like that, so why did Lawrence? And he had absolutely no idea what to do about the situation. No idea at all.

Arthur abandoned all thought of the tractor's gearbox which needed mending, and continued to give his full attention to Eric as he repeated the story in slightly different words, emphasising Lawrence's lack of appreciation and his own embarrassment. Finally, when Eric covered his face with his hands, Arthur pushed him gently into a chair, fetched them both a cup of tea, and sat with him in silence.

February 1920

Lawrence and Elly were on the train on their way to see their grandmother at Downham Market. Lawrence had not seen her since his return, and Elly had only seen her twice since the funeral over a year ago. Hattie's sister Kitty had brought Grandmother from Downham for that painful occasion, and then taken her back there, for that was where she now lived permanently. It had been Eric's intention to ensure that he and Elly stay in contact with Hattie's family, but the distance between them made visits difficult so they only kept in touch through letters.

So, when Lawrence suddenly announced, out of the blue, that he would like to visit his grandmother, Eric was both surprised and pleased, and when Arthur heard of the proposed visit, he suggested that Elly went too, an idea that everyone agreed with.

The plan was that they would walk to Ingham station early in the morning, then take the train, changing at Bury and Ely.They would be met by Uncle Stan at Downham.

They had the carriage to themselves. Once on the main part of the journey Elly stared out of the train window and noticed the agricultural land gradually becoming wetter, until, somewhere past Newmarket, they approached the fen washes. Wide shallow lakes on each side of the railway were dotted here and there by flotillas of geese and ducks. At Ely, Lawrence pointed to the river with the cigarette he was just about to light.

"That's the Ouse. Did you know the Lark feeds into the Ouse and then flows north to King's Lynn? That water could have passed under our bridge near the farm. In fact, it could have flowed under the Abbot's Bridge in the Abbey Gardens. In the old days we could have come all this way by river. This railway line follows the Ouse the whole way to the Wash."

This was one of the longest utterances Elly had heard Lawrence make since coming home. He continued, "You should see the Indus. It's vast. It flows from the mountains in Tibet all the way down the western part of India, until it empties into the Arabian Sea at Karachi. Do you know where I mean?"

Elly shook her head.

Lawrence held his cigarette in the corner of his mouth while he searched in his jacket for a pencil and something to draw on. He made do with a margin of his newspaper.

"Right. Here's India. Here's Tibet. And here's the Indus, making its way all the way down to the sea. Look, it's not just a single river, because it keeps splitting up into thinner strands, but in reality they're not thin at all. They're very wide. And Karachi's here."

Elly looked at the map carefully. "And where were you?"

"Where were we? God, we were all over the place, but mostly up here." He indicated the extreme top left of his sketch. "Hang on, I need to draw it differently."

Lawrence found another blank place in the paper and began to draw a more elaborate map. "Damn. I should have started further over. Never mind. This'll give you an idea. Now, this is where we began: at Bombay.

The rest of the journey sped past. Lawrence showed Elly almost everywhere: Zam, Tank, Jandola, Dera Ismail Khan, Manzal, Jullundur, Thal, Amritsar.

"Were you fighting in all those places?"

"Most of them, and other places too. I can't remember all the Afghan and Indian names."

The train let off steam as it drew into the station at Downham.

"On the way home will you tell me more?"

"Depends what I feel like. Look, there's Uncle Stan! Hurry up!"

They stayed for a week. Lawrence slept on the floor, ("Don't worry Aunt Kitty. It's far better than sleeping on a rock, knowing I might be shot at by a mad tribesman.") Elly slept in the bedroom of her older cousin Hugh, who had fought in France, been a prisoner-of-war for ten months but was already married and doing well as an engineer in King's Lynn. Grandmother was already hoping for her first great-grandchild.

Uncle Stan was a medical officer in Downham Market and would be retiring soon. In the evenings he sometimes snoozed by the fire but there were times when he asked Lawrence about India. Lawrence was happy to answer him and spoke more about himself in a week than he had done in over two months in West Stow.

Aunt Kitty talked to him about Mother. She cried a lot and so did Lawrence. He put his arm round Kitty and comforted her, and soon Elly was crying too, and they were all holding on to each other. But they cheered up when Kitty told them about some of the things their mother had done when she was little. They didn't know she had brought two frogs into the house, and put them into the kitchen sink in warm water (for it was a cold day and she thought they must be cold). They didn't know that she walked to the shop on her own when she was only four, and asked the shop lady for some tobacco, because it was her grandfather's birthday.

These stories made Lawrence laugh as he used to when he was a boy. Elly had forgotten that Lawrence used to be a real joker, fooling around and getting into trouble at school and at home. She remembered a time when he took a baby rabbit into church. It was supposed to stay inside his shirt, but he thought it might suffocate, so he undid a couple of his shirt buttons and let it poke its head out. She got the giggles, and then Conrad saw it and snorted with laughter. In the end Father had taken Lawrence outside and sent him home. He wasn't allowed sweets or puddings for a week.

Somehow, Uncle Stan and Aunt Kitty brought out the best in Lawrence. They didn't expect anything from him and in their company he relaxed and thrived.

They wandered round the market, admired the clock with its four dials and saw the men building the base of the war memorial. Then they strolled to the iron lattice bridge over the Ouse, waited for the infrequent barges and watched them pass beneath. Elly liked knowing that they were heading in the direction of Bury St Edmunds, though few even made it as far as Ely or Mildenhall.

One day they borrowed bikes and rode, pushed along by the wind, to see the sluice at Denver. It was difficult to see how it worked and they were more impressed by the constant calling of wildfowl and the dark grey sky stretching in every direction.

"This is more like it!" said Lawrence.

"Like what?" asked Elly.

"Like what I want! Openness and space and air!"

Cycling home was hard work, for they were facing into the north wind. Elly's eyes were watering even though she tucked herself in behind Lawrence. But he was revelling in the challenge and even welcomed the first drops of rain with a yell of delight.

At dinner that evening Aunt Kitty asked, "And now you're home, what are you going to do with yourself? Have you made any plans?"

"I haven't decided yet."

"University, perhaps?"

"Not for me."

"Well, it's about time you made up your mind, or you'll get keen on some girl, propose to her, and she'll turn up her nose at you."

The next day, on their journey home, Lawrence and Elly shared their train compartment with other people, so they did not talk. They both gazed out of the window. It had been a good week.

February 1920

Chelmsford to Montagu April 12

General Dyer … is in a very bad way, and his condition is such that the doctors fear that any prolonged excitement may cause haemorrhage of the brain. Consequently, the Commander-in-Chief the other day, when he had an interview with him, had to confine it to a very brief space of time. He told Dyer that our judgement on him was that he had acted in excess of the requirements of the occasion at Jallianwala Bagh, and that he must therefore call upon him to resign. He also told him that it would be impossible for him to again hold command of troops in India. Since them General Dyer has resigned his command and gone home by Troopship on medical certificate.

February 1920

Father was waiting for us at Ingham, and at once Elly ran up and hugged him. She had enjoyed our visit, but was glad to be home. Father welcomed her hug, then turned to me. I too found myself pleased to see him, and I stretched out my hand. He took it eagerly, and we shook hands. It was strange, but for some reason the days away had made me feel less resistant to him. For some reason I had not resented any of Uncle Stan's or Uncle Arthur's questions as I did Father's. I acknowledged that it was me who caused this difficulty – deliberately - and being away had suddenly made me realise that I did not have to be like that. It was unfair and pointless. After all, it wasn't Father's fault that I felt depressed and unable to make decisions and get on with things, and, given how I had been behaving, it was not surprising that he might have preferred having Conrad home rather than me.

Suddenly, I wanted to do something active. There and then I resolved to get my bike out, check it, oil it, pump up its tyres and go for a twenty-mile ride. Although I had no idea about my long-term future, at least I had a plan for the afternoon, and I counted that as progress.

But in the evening Uncle Arthur came in with bad news. Lennie, the farmhand, had hurt himself badly while sawing some branches. His right arm was in plaster, and would be for at least several weeks. This was particularly unfortunate because the next month, March, was a key one for the farm. Already the first new lambs were being born, and there was all the sowing and planting to be done. It was impossible for Uncle Arthur or any one man to do all that work alone.

On the spur of the moment I said, "Can I help?"

Uncle Arthur and Father looked at me in astonishment.

"Yes. You certainly could. Thank you."

So, the next day, I found myself feeding pregnant sows, getting to grips with a tractor, and going with my uncle to see the land he'd just bought for sugar-beet. He's quite excited about this. Once harvested, the beet will have to go to the sugar factory at Cantley, on the Yare, and Uncle's expecting to get it taken there by train.

At the end of the day I was tired and well aware that since coming home I had done little in the way of physical exercise, so had lost much of the muscle I'd developed in India. After our evening meal I sat on an easy chair with Bran while my father read and Aunt Bridget and Elly knitted. It was only then I realised that my uncle, who was sitting at the cleared table as he often did in the evenings, was not reading but working. He was checking prices of feed and fertilizer, and recording his expenditure and earnings. There were five of us in the house, in *his* house, and he was the only one bringing in an income. Father had told me that though he himself made a modest financial contribution, Arthur was the real breadwinner.

There and then, sitting comfortably because of someone else's generosity, I knew what I had to do: I had to work for my uncle every day until Lennie came back.

The next morning I was up early to learn how, under Uncle's supervision, to milk the two house cows. Although

I'd watched this being done when I was a child, and seen plenty of natives milking their goats, it wasn't easy to sit with my shoulder shoved into the cow's flank, ensuring the bucket wasn't kicked over, while holding and squeezing the teats. Later I cleaned out the cowshed, and as I filled a wheelbarrow with dung I recalled the numerous Indian women I'd seen crouching on the ground making cakes of dung for fuel. I was exhausted at the end of the day.

Wednesday was market day in Bury, and we set off in the van with wicker containers of chickens. Everyone seemed to know Uncle Arthur, and he introduced me as "My nephew Lawrence, back from the North West Frontier." But, out of all those he spoke to, only one person knew where the North West Frontier was. Most guessed it was part of the Western Front. Someone thought it was in Turkey.

Why wasn't it known about? Apparently there had been no news about it in the Bury Free Press, perhaps because it did not feature in the London papers. But why not? It seemed that during the war nearly all the news had been about France, especially the Somme. People found the main European part of the war easier to understand than the activities going on at sea or in truly foreign places like Palestine or Mesopotamia.

On March 20th we went to the Memorial Service for the men who fell while serving in the Suffolk Regiment. It was a big event, held in St Mary's Church in Bury. We had to wait outside in a heavy snowstorm, stamping our feet in the cold until we could follow the numerous dignitaries, clergy, soldiers, officers, choirs and bands as they entered the church. The speakers attempted to turn grief into pride, but no address, hymn or bright flag could free us from the deaths of seven thousand men, especially as everyone was wearing black.

From where we were, we couldn't see the Cenotaph itself, but there was plenty to watch and listen to. At one point we became aware of a strange sound, like a low rumble. It gradually became louder and we all fell silent as it seemed to enter our bodies like a living thing. It was a drum roll – an extraordinary drum roll which took its time rising to a crescendo, then diminishd by slow degrees until all we could hear was a mere echo. I had never heard anything like it.

After the service, people queued up to see the Cenotaph with its flags and wreaths. On it, secured in a glass case, was a book of Heroes listing every Suffolk man who had fallen. It was open on the title page which disappointed Elly as she was hoping to see Conrad's name although she knew it might not be there. We filed out into the street and walked along towards Chequer Square. I looked at the monument there with fresh eyes. Who or what did it commemorate? Might one day people look at the Cenotaph in St Mary's and not know who or what *it* commemorated?

Names were being recorded on the columns and plinths of individual village memorials which were appearing everywhere. Each week, the Bury Free Press reported two or three more unveilings. They had already had them in Pakenham, Cockfield, Stowlangtoft, Risby, Livermere, Bardwell and more. All over the place. When I commented that the names of the fallen were being written down in books or in stone throughout the whole of Suffolk and Norfolk, and throughout the British Isles, Father pointed out that the same sort of memorials must be being built in France and in many other countries.

I resented the fact that the ceremonies and celebrations being held locally did not mention what we Londons and others had been doing in "our" war. It was as if we were invisible. No-one seemed to know that we had existed, and certainly no-one gave a thought to 1/6th Battalion Suffolk Cyclists.

But the more I worked on the farm, the more my depression lifted. Every day I learned something new: poultry disease, foot rot, potato clamps, machinery, lambing, pig feed, ridging, staking up, hoeing, when to call the vet, rainfall. I realised that though I had lived in Suffolk for almost all of my life, I knew little of what happened on farms. When, as a child, I had come to West Stow regularly, I had not taken much interest. I preferred climbing trees, fishing, looking for birds' eggs.

Now, with crops of sugar beet in view, Uncle was thinking particularly about irrigation. Would we need more water or less? The land he had bought was in good heart now it was spring, but at certain times of year he expected it to be either too dry or too wet. We began to look at advertisements for pumps and pipes, and as we did so I was reminded of the mills we had so willingly and deliberately destroyed in India. Now I questioned the pleasure we had had in smashing them up.

I kept on being reminded of India. Each time I walked from the farmhouse along the lane to Beddy's Field I passed a house being re-thatched. They had got to the stage where the thatcher was up on the roof hammering away at his pegs while his boy carried up another load of straw. In my mind's eye I had an image of Harry running round with a burning brand and setting fire to the homes of natives. We used to cheer when the dried grass roofs flared up and left a smouldering shell, a bitter scent.

I didn't tell anyone what I was thinking, but I wished I could, for I missed my London friends. We had all promised to stay in touch, but my only contact had been a few Christmas cards and two letters from friends I had written back to but heard nothing more from.

March 1920

Daily Mail May 4th 1920, reporting on Dyer's return to England

I shot to save the British Raj – to preserve India for the Empire, and to protect Englishmen and Englishwomen who looked to me for protection. And now I am told to go for doing my duty – my horrible, dirty duty… I had to shoot. I had thirty seconds to make up my mind what action to take, and I did it. Every Englishman I have met in India has approved my act, horrible as it was. What would have happened if I had not shot? I and my little force would have been swept away like chaff, and then what would have happened?... No-one in authority condemned me for it. On the contrary I was given command of another operation, as a result of which I was complimented… If I have done anything wrong I should be court martialled, but there has been no suggestion of that. I have never been heard in my own defence.

May 1920

Life has improved! Lawrence is transformed from the man he was when he first came home. He is enjoying working hard with Arthur, he is out on his bike when he gets a chance, and – best of all – he is opening up to me. Gradually, he is telling me about what he did in the North West Frontier. It's worse than I imagined. He had not told us about the very worst things in his letters because he wanted to protect us and even now he just tells us what happened, but not how it happened. He has not told us what it was like to bayonet a man, or to see a friend knifed, and I confess I do not want to hear the detail. It was strange to recognise that my son was now protecting me rather than the other way round. But he described how a soldier we had read about earlier had fallen into the Indus by accident, and how he could not be saved because of the heavy kitbag on his back. Lawrence told me, "As he tripped he turned, and he was looking up at us as he hit the water. I can still see his open mouth, his hand grasping his rifle tightly. We had to leave him there, leave him sinking to the bottom of a river in a foreign land. There was nothing we could do."

Lawrence also told me how the men had at times laughed together and at times spoken of their lives at home, and worried themselves sick about their parents and their wives or girlfriends or their children. I was not expecting him to say, "And when I heard Mother was ill it didn't occur to me that she might die. But she did, and I felt so bad because I had not taken her illness seriously enough. And I still feel so, so bad."

He was weeping like a child, and I pulled him towards me, hugged him and told him he was not bad. His mother knew he loved her, and she loved him.

One evening, as the weather was beginning to warm up, he and I strolled along the road for a smoke.

Unprompted, he announced: "Out there, we sometimes wondered what we were alive *for*. The people who had a strong belief in God could answer that, but I couldn't. At least, I couldn't come up with a real, important reason. It was only when I was doing some specific task that took all my attention that I could make any sense of it. I remember two of us hauling some baggage up a cliff. The baggage was urgently needed by the men in our camp at the top, and we were exposed and could be shot at any point. At that moment I knew I was alive for one precise purpose: to get the baggage up there. Nothing else mattered, as long as I achieved that. Not my family. Not the war. Not my future. The only thing that mattered was getting the baggage to the top.

"Now I ask myself if that action was important at all? How important was the baggage? Or our camp? How important was anything that we were doing?

"I still don't know what my life is for. The best I can do is to break things down into small tasks, and work my way through those. Is that enough?"

I cannot express how my heart leapt at hearing him coming out with such thoughts. I remained silent while we ambled along towards the church where bats dived past us.

"I don't know if it's enough. Perhaps it's enough to help others and enjoy what one can."

"Isn't there more than that?"

"There might be. But your strategy is a good one."

"Right now it's good to work on Uncle's farm, so that's what I'm doing. There's nothing else I'd prefer to be doing."

"That's fine."

"But you wanted me to go to Cambridge."

"Yes, I admit I did. But I don't think that now. I can see it wouldn't be right for you."

"Elly should go there. She'd do well."

I was astonished. "Elly?"

"Yes. She's the cleverest of us three, the cleverest of our family... She'd do well."

As we walked home I thought seriously, for the first time, about the possibility of my daughter going to Cambridge. I'd never met any woman who'd actually studied at Cambridge and obtained a degree, though I knew of Girton and Newnham colleges. I suddenly remembered I'd promised Elly that I'd think about the possibility of her having a career, but it had gone completely out of my head. I should probably go and talk to her head mistress.

June 1920

Lord Stamfordham, George V's Secretary to Viceroy

You will, naturally, understand how much public opinion has been aroused by the outcome of the Enquiry (set up in November 1919 to examine the principal witnesses for the events at Amritsar) and the action of General Dyer. Upon the latter, judgement is divided, and while on one side he is condemned for what is regarded as heartlessness, callousness and indifference to the value of human life; on the other side there are many who sum up their opinion in the words, "Dyer saved India". This latter view is strongly held by the Military members of the Army Council, and I have heard it repeated by thoughtful men who have lately returned from India.

Westminster Gazette: No British action, during the whole course of our history in India, has struck a severer blow to Indian faith in British justice than the massacre at Amritsar.

Morning Post: He did his duty.

June 1920

Lawrence is doing very well. Much better than I expected. He's quick to learn, he's prepared to work hard and he does everything I ask, without question. Perhaps that's because he's used to taking orders. But I'd like him to trust his own judgment and use his own initiative more. I can see he's always going to defer to me because I've a lifetime of experience on the land. In respect of growing cereals, keeping pigs and sheep, he's clearly unlikely to disagree with my practices and opinions.

So I'm going to give him some responsibility. It was Bridget's idea, and it's a good one. I'm going to put him in charge of my new venture: sugar beet. I'll give him a budget and a free hand. He'll need to work out what to buy: seeds, machinery, fertiliser. And he'll need to develop methods for everything from sowing to growing, harvesting to transporting. I'll be behind him, but my advice will be limited as I'm new to beet. Bridget thinks it'll be the making of him.

To start him off, I'm sending him up to Norfolk where they've been growing beet for a while. I've a couple of contacts near Swaffham. Lennie is back at work now and that's helping free Lawrence up.

And I've been thinking about Elly, too. She does a lot of schoolwork – far more than I ever did when I was her age. Possibly more even than Eric, though he was a scholar. Most Saturdays she goes with Lawrence to wherever he's playing cricket. Last week his team was short of a scorer, and she stepped in. Apparently she made a very good job of it. But the main reason she goes is because there's usually a group of young people there. Bridget is wondering if there's a boy she's keen on, but that's nonsense. She's not even fourteen years old! Lawrence is the one who's more likely to be thinking about that sort of thing, but I must say I haven't seen a hint of it. All in good time.

This weekend he's taking Elly and a friend of hers to see a film called "Tarzan of the Apes."

June 1920

In February there was a terrible murder. A tram driver killed a woman (she was a tram conductress) in Ipswich. The trial was held this week. It took up an entire page in the newspaper – columns and columns of it. I didn't read it all. In the end the man who'd been arrested was found guilty, so he'll be executed, which is awful.

Lawrence read the whole thing and he was surprised because there was so much reporting about it. He said that one person had killed, and one person had been killed, so why did there need to be so much in the paper? In the war hundreds of thousands of men killed or were killed. Each of them was just as important or unimportant as the two in the newspaper, but no-one wrote column after column about them. He was quite angry and said, "The world would be jammed full of words if this happened every time someone killed someone."

I overheard Father saying to Uncle Arthur that Lawrence would never have said that before the war, and that his saying it showed how much he had changed in these last years. Then I heard Father give a big sigh, and Uncle said, "Lawrence is coming through, isn't he? You must be feeling proud of him."

Murder is different to war, but I wondered which was worse: a killing in a war, or a murder? They're both bad, but in different ways.

I like being with Lawrence. Recently it was Aviation Week in Bury, and he suggested we went with Father for a flight. It was expensive, but Uncle Arthur is paying him a wage now, and he and Father bought the tickets together. We parked at Eldo House Farm. When it was our turn it was amazing to look down on the town. We could see the Abbey Gardens, the centre of the town, the Cathedral and other churches, trees and gardens, Hardwick House, little roads and even the railway line. It was so strange, so magical to be above the earth. People were looking up at us. I bet they all wished they could go in a plane. And when I looked along, instead of down, there was countryside stretching out into the distance and miles and miles of sky.

And then we did a loop-the-loop! My stomach turned as the plane rolled over, and some people screamed. I made myself look out of the window because I wasn't going to miss a moment! When we were level again everyone was gasping and saying how they had felt. It was wonderful! More than wonderful! As soon as we landed I wanted to go up again. I wanted to see what it would be like to fly over a forest, or the sea, or mountains.

Last week we went to see *Tarzan*. It's about an English baby adopted by an ape growing up in the jungle. They say it's a romance, but it wasn't very romantic. Some of it didn't make sense. For example, when an English sailor appears in the story, at the point when Tarzan is a boy (not a baby any more), they can talk to each other. But how would Tarzan know how to speak English if he's only ever communicated with apes? The fight between Tarzan and the black man is good, even though Jane makes stupid faces while she's watching it (she's supposed to be terrified that the black man might win and carry her off, but of course he doesn't).

I started to tell Aunt Bridget about *Tarzan*, but she wasn't interested. She had just heard that the Honourable Lady Wood, from Hengrave Hall, had been appointed as a magistrate.

"That's no job for a woman! Even if she's very brave, she'll have to be protected from all those criminals."

I told her that at the beginning of *Tarzan*, when a woman said she wanted to go to Africa with her husband, she was told that people who went there had to be coura- geous, and she had asked "Is it only men who can be courageous?" and in the end she was allowed to go.

"But that's just a made-up film. I'm talking about the real world."

"Mother believed that women could do everything if only they had the chance."

"Well, I can't imagine why any woman would want to be a magistrate," sighed Aunt Bridget. "Work like that should be left to men. For goodness' sake, imagine what would happen if there were even more women in men's jobs than at present? I mean, who would go to a woman dentist? Yes, women can be drivers and teachers but they can't do everything that men do. They're just different. Can you imagine a woman vicar, or a soldier? "

I don't think she's right. It's true that men seem to be able to do any job, and women don't. But does this mean that they *can't*? And if not, why not?

June 1920

Yesterday, Saturday, I received a letter. It had five Indian stamps on and my heart beat fast because I knew at once that it was from Pal. Deenpal, my Sikh friend! It was in a flimsy envelope, so I opened it carefully. The writing was spidery and rather faint.

May 13th 1920

Dear Lawrence,

I hope you remember me. I am sending you greetings across the world. Please forgive mistakes in the letter. Writing English is difficult. I copied your address from the paper you wrote it nearly one year ago.

I am home now, after much travelling. I am with my wife and her family and my boys, and that is good. My wife is fat because she will have another baby soon. I am working at a railway station.

Many Indians died in the war, including some of my friends from this region. Do you remember I told you my cousin in a hospital in a palace in England? Sadly, he died and was burned on a funeral pyre with other Sikhs who died the same hospital. I heard that important visitors come to see the patients and in 1915, the King and Queen came. Lord Kitchener also, but the visitor my cousin was most happiest to see was Sophia Duleep Singh, one of the daughters of the Marharajah. She cared much for Indian soldiers. Did your father meet her when she was young?

But I am thinking about you. Have you found a wife yet? I hope so. You must not become old without wife. I married when I was 18. You must be 24 or 25 already. If there are no women you like in England, come here, for there are beautiful women here. They are good to make babies and cooking.

Do you think about India and the Frontier? Do you speak about it? I find it difficult to talk, so I stay without words. I have told my brother only about Amritsar, for when I begin to remember, I cannot sleep or eat. I know the newspapers write about General Dyer, and people argue him and what he did. I liked him, but he was a very bad man. He says he tried to save India, but I think he tried to kill it. I wish I had been more strong against to shoot in the Jallianwala Bagh. I wish I did not shot people. The memory screams will always be inside me.

Please give greetings to your parents. You told me many things about your home, and I remember your brother was killed in France. May he be at rest. I hope your mother and father and sister are in good health. I hope there is peace in your home.

My friend, please come to India one day. I would like to meet you again. I have told my wife about you and she also would like to meet you.

Your friend,
Deenpal

Lawrence looked at the address on the back of the envelope. At first glance it was unreadable. He examined the two pale stamps. Each bore the head of George V, and the words *India Postage*. The value of each stamp - Two Annas and Four Annas – was printed below the king's head. There were also words written in a script he could not read.

He read the letter again, then hurried outside to find someone to share his joy with. He found his father snipping at the front hedge with shears, and thrust the letter in front of him, but he was not wearing his glasses, so Lawrence read it out to him, faltering when he came to the part about Amritsar and the reference to his mother.

Eric could see what the letter meant to Lawrence, and it gladdened him. He had heard a little about Pal, and now he recognised the importance of the friendship.

"You must write back."

"Yes, I shall. Why on earth haven't *I* written to *him*? I have his address. I shall write today."

Lawrence looked again at the address Deenpal had written on the back of the envelope. Gradually, he made it out. It wasn't a house address, but the name of a railway station. It must be where Pal worked.

At that moment a car drew up. In the front was a neighbour, Wilfred, in cricket whites, and his girlfriend. In the back was a girl Lawrence did not recognise.

"Come on," called Wilfred, "Aren't you ready? We're late as it is."

"Is it time? Sorry. Give me two minutes."

Still holding the letter, Lawrence sprinted indoors, up the stairs and into his room. He pulled off his working clothes and pulled on his whites. Still full of excitement, he stood the letter on the shelf, leaning on the mirror. Then he ran down, grabbed his bat from by the back door and hurried to the car.

He opened the rear door, got in and slammed the door.

Wilfred's girlfriend in the front passenger seat turned round and said, "Sadie, this is Lawrence. Lawrence, Sadie."

Lawrence shook hands with the girl next to him, then looked out of the window thinking about Pal and his letter. As they passed fields full of young wheat and leaf-thick trees his breathing calmed down. He shut his eyes and imagined being on a train on a track crossing a bare mountainous landscape, then drawing into a hill railway station, somewhere like Dharamapur. He imagined climbing down from the train onto the platform and being greeted by Deenpal, proud and smiling in a spotless uniform of white turban and dhoti, and vivid red trousers.

August 1920

I had only been to Elly's school a few times. Two years ago I had seen a production of *Midsummer Night's Dream*, in which Elly had been Peaseblossom, and last year I saw an exhibition of arts and crafts. The best of Elly's knitted scarves had been on display before she gave it to Lawrence when he came home.

Today, at four o'clock, Elly and I had an appointment with Miss Pitcher.

We were welcomed in warmly. "Thank you for coming, Mr Bailey. Please sit down."

"As you know, I've been thinking about Eleanor's future. She's an intelligent girl who's well ahead of her class in almost every subject. She's doing particularly well in Arithmetic, Algebra and Geometry, in English Language and

Literature, and in Geography. Her History is good, as is her Science. It's really only her French and Latin which need attention."

I nodded, pleased to hear such good comments.

"Have you had any thoughts about what she might do? I know she won't be leaving school for several years, but it's never too early to begin to think about things for a girl such as your daughter."

I shifted in my chair. "I confess …"

"Of course, the sad death of Eleanor's mother must have been such a shock… I'm so sorry.."

I tried to sound positive. "Well, I think my wife had real ambitions for her. I don't know what, exactly, but I know she wanted her to do something useful in her life. More than just getting married and having a family, important though those are."

Miss Pitcher turned to Elly. "What sort of things interest you? What would you like to study at university?"

University? Did Miss Pitcher really think Elly could go to university?

"Perhaps you'd like to learn more languages, so you could be a teacher? Or Classics, though you'd have to improve your Latin considerably. But you're lucky, because I know your father is a scholar! You'd help Eleanor with her Latin, wouldn't you, Mr Bailey?"

"Of course."

But Elly said, "I don't know. I don't know what there is to do."

Miss Pitcher looked at me, and I felt her silent criticism of me for not even telling Elly about what possibilities existed. She must have thought me a detached father who had no ambition for his daughter.

There was a short pause.

Then Elly suddenly announced, "I want to be a pilot."

"A pilot?" repeated Miss Pitcher, in surprise. "What sort of a pilot?"

"One that flies aeroplanes."

There was another pause, during which Elly stared across the room at the portrait of the last headmistress.

"But why?" asked Miss Pitcher. "Whatever gave you that extraordinary idea?"

"I think it would be exciting. And interesting. And important."

"But, Elly," I said. "Women don't fly planes. They can't."

"Can't they? They drive cars and buses and tractors, so why can't they fly planes?"

"My dear," said Miss Pitcher. "They're not allowed to."

"Who said?"

Miss Pitcher smiled wanly. "That's just the way it is, I'm afraid. Except in America, but it's different over there."

I could feel Elly hovering on the edge of rudeness in the way that Hattie used to, and I willed her not to tip over into outright disagreement.

"Well, Mr Bailey, can I suggest that you explain to Eleanor the advantages and pleasures of obtaining a university education? We can have another discussion, perhaps in six months' time? I may have been a little hasty, but no harm's done.

"The school would be so proud if Eleanor joined the small number of girls who have gone from here to Cambridge. Or to Oxford, of course. But as you were at Cambridge yourself – am I right? – and it's so near, I'm sure you'd prefer her to go there. It looks very likely that within a year or two women will at last be eligible for full degrees."

Miss Pitcher stood up and opened the door. She held out her hand and gave me a firm handshake while looking at me in a friendly manner. "And don't forget the Latin, will you? Even a couple of extra hours each week would make a difference. I'm sure you'll both enjoy getting your teeth into '*Gallia est omnis divisa in partes tres*'."

I smiled at Miss Pitcher using the familiar quote as we left the room. I like her. She certainly wants the best for Elly, and Hattie would have appreciated that.

September 1920

I had hardly noticed my first meeting with Sadie, but the second was much better. One Wednesday I was in Bury, at the market with Uncle Arthur. He had sent me to the Round House with some papers, and on the way back I made a detour to the area with the deadstock where I was hoping to find a coal scuttle. The handle had broken on the one at home, and I had promised Aunt Bridget to try to find a decent second- hand one. I couldn't see any, so I edged my way through the crowd and back in the direction of the livestock.

And there, completely unexpectedly, was Sadie. Although I had not seen much of her at the cricket match, I recognized her dark, shining hair. Today it was wound up, but before it had been loose like a mane. She was right in front of me looking at second-hand cycles and a man was trying to persuade her to buy a rather worn out lady's model.

"All it needs is a lick of paint, a new chain, and perhaps a new saddle. You can see for yourself that the pedals are fine, and the brakes work well, and these tyres will do you for years."

Sadie stared at it doubtfully.

"Why don't you have a ride on it?" said the man. "It looks the perfect size for you, but we can put the saddle up or down if you want."

Anyone could see that it was not a good bike, so I stepped forward and said, "Sadie, hallo! Excuse me, but can I help you? I know quite a bit about cycles."

She looked at me gratefully, "Lawrence! Thank you so much. I need one but I've no idea what to buy."

"I'll take you to a bike shop. You'll get much more choice there. They repair all the second-hand cycles they get before they sell them, so you know they're in reasonable condition."

The man huffed in annoyance at having lost a sale, but I didn't care. Sadie was clearly delighted that I had turned up, and I realised immediately that I was very pleased to have bumped into her. I had to go back to my uncle at once, but she agreed to tell her mother that I was going to help her find a bike. We arranged that on the following Saturday, I would meet her and her mother in Bury, take her to choose a cycle, and accompany her home in case there were any difficulties. Her mother would take the bus back to Brandon.

I found myself willing the days to pass. She reminded me of someone I knew but I couldn't for the life of me think who. No-one in West Stow, or in Bury, or at a cricket match. Whoever it was completely escaped me.

But on Thursday a note came from Sadie, via a friend who was visiting West Stow, saying that she had to go to

Ipswich with her sister and would not be able to look for a bike this Saturday. I was very disappointed. As she did not mention fixing up another date I concluded that she had changed her mind about seeing me. Perhaps she'd even made up the story about going to Ipswich in order to avoid me.

So I threw myself into the farm, working early and late. I was enjoying it, and I was well aware that both my father and my uncle were looking at me with respect. Then, one morning when I was having a cup of tea with Uncle in the kitchen, I had a surprise.

"Lawrence, what do you think I should do with the farm when I'm old?"

Of course I had given this some thought. I assumed that he would sell up and make enough money for him and Aunt Bridget to live comfortably in a smaller house in the village. Years ago Conrad and I had wondered if Uncle Arthur might leave the farm to my father, which might mean that we inherited it one day in the future.

"Do you think I should sell it? Or should we keep it in the family?"

I didn't know what to say. I wasn't sure what he meant by "keep it in the family" and I didn't want to presume anything, so I found myself stuttering, "But who.. ?"

He cut me off. "You, of course. Would you want to take it on?"

"I .. I don't know .." I was both astonished and hesitant.

"Well, you should think about it. If you don't want it I'll have to think again, because there's no-one else."

I paused and thought carefully before I said, "Yes, there is."

Uncle looked at me fiercely. "No there isn't. Not in the family. Not now."

"There's Elly."

"Elly? My God, what's the world coming to when an older brother makes way for a younger sister in business? *No*. Not Elly. Elly can be part of it, of course, just as Bridget is, but it's you I want to run it. Elly's very intelligent, but she knows nothing of farming. And she's a woman, for God's sake!"

Apparently my father had already been consulted about this, and within a few weeks a formal will was made nominating me as the person who would inherit the farm. I found myself bowled along by events that I hadn't set in motion, but I was very happy about it and it boosted my confidence.

September 1920

Third meeting! On the Saturday of our final match of the season I tied my bat onto my crossbar and set off to Brandon to play the Heath House team. In the distance ahead of me, going in the same direction, was another cyclist. I decided to catch him up and sprint past him, but as I got closer I realised it was a woman. It was Sadie! She was riding home from visiting her grandfather in Flempton. She was on an old bike which clanked and creaked. I didn't comment on it, or on our last meeting or our failed plan to meet.

But she did. "Lawrence, I feel so bad about .. you know.. when I was meant to ... "

"It doesn't matter at all. There's no need to apologise."

"Yes it does. My mother was worried about my sister who's becoming involved with an unsuitable man, and that means she now worries too much about me, too."

I couldn't help saying, "But your mother was going to be with us, wasn't she? She would have seen that I was a reasonable person."

"I know. Of course, yes. But it's too complicated to explain. I'm afraid I just did the easiest thing and agreed not to meet you."

We rode on, two abreast on the empty road. I imagined her mother as a scaly dragon, and perhaps there was a scaly dragon father just behind her.

Sadie said, "I don't think mothers worry about their sons as much as they do about their daughters. You're lucky."

I swerved to avoid some loose gravel. "I'm not lucky. My mother died just as the war finished."

"Oh, I'm sorry. So, so sorry. I shouldn't have said that."

"You weren't to know."

We rode on in silence. Then a car approached and I hung back so I was riding behind Sadie. The sun was glinting on her hair. Just as I came level with her again there was a clang, and she was thrown forwards as her wheel skidded and stuttered. Her chain had broken.

She half fell from the saddle but was on her feet almost immediately. I suggested she sat down on the grass because her ankle was bleeding, and the palm of her left hand was badly grazed. As I moved her bike off the road she said, ruefully, "That's the last time I borrow a bike."

"There's nothing wrong with borrowing a bike. But you ought to have it checked first. Couldn't your father have had a look at it? Or your brother, if you have one?"

"My father died when I was thirteen and I haven't got a brother."

I felt terrible. "I'm sorry…"

"Don't be embarrassed. How could you have known?"

I sat down beside her, reflecting on the coincidence that each of us had lost a parent already. It felt a vitally important connection.

We were both silent. We watched a wagtail drinking from a puddle, and listened to an insistent blackbird.

But I wanted to get Sadie home, so I hid her bike in some bushes from where I could pick it up later, and inspected the damage to her hand. The bleeding had already stopped, and although she had torn the hem of her dress, she said that of course she could manage the last mile to Brandon. So we set off at a leisurely pace, me pushing my bike on the outside, and Sadie walking by the grass verge. I'd be late for the match, but what did that matter?

We talked about everything from her interest in gardening, her cat, her mother (who had become over-protective since losing her husband), her wish to go to London and her fussy piano teacher, to my work on the farm, my family, my joy of cycling, my time in Waziristan, the 25th Londons and Pal.

That was it! Pal! That was who Sadie reminded me of! They both had thick, dark hair. I had seen Pal's when he washed it, when it was not wound round by his turban, and here was Sadie's, in front of me. I was delighted by the similarity, but I said nothing as I thought she might find it strange to be told that she reminded me of a man.

We walked for about half an hour but it seemed that we reached her house within only a few minutes. I could have gone on walking and talking with her all day. And there was Mrs Finney, her mother, thanking me for bringing Sadie home and offering me tea and generally being quite unlike a dragon. I accepted an invitation to call in on the following Sunday.

But I couldn't let my cricket team down, so I said goodbye, stood on my pedals and sped to the pitch feeling on top of the world. My exhilaration was noted by most of my friends, but I did not tell them why I was as I was. I wanted to savour this feeling of heady excitement, so I just told them that I'd been held up on the farm.

I made twenty-three runs, and we won by a good margin, but as I rode home I hardly thought of our victory. All I knew was that life was very, very good.

November 1920

Arthur, the previous week, had read in the *Morning Post*

A Debt Acknowledged

A soldier's honour has been vindicated, and the stigma of national ingratitude been to some extent removed.

Many of the subscriptions that have been received by the Treasurer of the Fund have been accompanied with the words: "To the man who saved India."

Today Arthur was searching in the paper for Dyer's response to being sent a cheque for the amount subscribed by the public. Those who contributed believed him to be a man they felt deserved thanks and not criticism.

"Ah, here it is. How astonishing! £26,626 6s. 2d. Over £25,000. That's a fortune!"

"I'm not surprised," said Bridget. "Let's hope the whole sorry business gets forgotten now. It's gone on long enough."

I am proud to think that so many of my fellow-countrymen and women approve of my conduct at Amritsar, and I accept the token of their approval in the spirit in which it is offered. On my part my conviction was, and still is, that I was bound to do what I did, not only with a view to saving the military situation and the women and children, but with a view to saving life generally. No hesitating or half-hearted measures would, under the circumstances, have served the purpose. The act I was called upon to perform filled me with horror, but the great sympathy and approval accorded to me by thousands strengthened my convictions and were a great help at a time of extreme strain. The thousands of letters received by you as treasurer of the Fund, and by myself privately, form a memorial which I value very highly, and I would take this opportunity of expressing my great regret that I cannot answer them all personally. I am very grateful for the splendid support given me throughout by the Morning Post, not only in upholding the cause, but also in opening its columns to the Fund and so enabling a better estimate to be formed of the general trend of public feeling in this matter. It is difficult to find words in which sufficiently to thank all those who have helped me, and I can only hope that others in similar difficulties may meet with an equally generous response from their fellow-countryman.

Your obedient servant, R. E. Dyer.

"Well, he's set up for life now, isn't he?" said Arthur. "Mind you, I don't begrudge him one penny."

December 1920

Lawrence has been home from India for just over a year, and things are going better than I could have expected. I only wish that Hattie could see how he has recovered his equilibrium and even joie de vivre. Much of this is down to

Arthur. He put his trust in Lawrence, and could not be more generous towards him. And Lawrence has a nice girlfriend, too.

Elly has her sights set on winning a special prize at school, and has a good chance. After the interview with Miss Pitcher we talked about working at some Latin and one evening I unearthed a copy of Book V of *De Bello Gallico,* and read it for the first time in years. It was packed solid with military strategies and events – ghastly stuff. I immediately shied away from it for we'd had enough of war.

Within a day or two I had turned from Caesar to Virgil. What gentle joy! Much of the poetry of the Eclogues dealt with rustic and rural events: birds and streams, flowers and farming. Even though there was also exile, poverty and loneliness, I knew that any one of the Eclogues would be much better for Elly – and for me - than anything Caesar had written. With some excitement I began flicking through the ten sections, looking for suitable passages. This was going to be most enjoyable.

Two hours later I was still looking, but at least I had a list of page numbers. I told Elly what I'd been doing and she smiled at my enthusiasm.

"Shall we begin tomorrow?" I asked.

"Yes. That's fine."

"Elly," Laurence called across at us from the other side of the room. "I should thank you for diverting Father's attention from me. You'll be a far better student than me."

Elly laughed. "Don't you remember any Latin from school?"

"Yes. I can decline *mensa* and *puer* and *bellum,* and I know *amo amas amat.*"

Elly shook her head in astonishment. "Is that all?"

"Well, I expect I could remember more if I tried. Yes, I'm sure I could. I wasn't as bad as Farrow or Rush. They were completely hopeless at everything. Oh, and I know *Tenex et Audax*. That's the motto of the 25th Londons. It means tenacity and boldness. I'll never ever forget *Tenex et Audax*."

"Nor will we. You must have told us that hundreds of times."

Lawrence bent to stroke Bran. "I haven't thought of Farrow and Rush since I left KEGS. I wonder what happened to them."

February 1921

"Is this yours?"

Lawrence came into the room carrying a box which he held out to me. "I found it at the bottom of the cupboard in my room."

I recognised the box at once. It was the one given to me on my birthday a few years ago. I hadn't seen it for ages.

"Pity it's locked, because when you shake it you can tell there's something inside."

"Hang on, I might be able to find the key."

I left Lawrence and Sadie by the fire and hurried up to the room I used to have. I had swapped rooms with Lawrence soon after he came home, but had forgotten all about the box. When I ran my hand along the ledge behind the Lord's Prayer, something fell to the floor. I ran downstairs shouting, "Found it!"

"So, what's in your box?"

"Just my autograph album, I think. It was my box for secrets and special things."

"Sounds interesting. Come on, let's have a look. Open up."

I turned the key in the lock and opened the lid. Inside were several flints, some coins and the autograph album. Lawrence examined the flints and said they were good ones. Perhaps they were ones I had been intending to take to the Sturges. Sadie said that one of the coins was French, and I remembered that a patient at Ampton had given it to me. But it was the autographs which intrigued us the most. I recalled many of the entries themselves (the sketch of a haggis, the two portraits of me, several riddles) but I had forgotten almost all of the men who had written or drawn them. Lawrence went through it carefully from cover to cover, hoping to find an entry from a London or from any Cyclist.

He was disappointed and said he wished he'd got a book full of memories like mine. At that moment I thought of the drawings he'd done of plants, and reminded him of them, and he sprung out of his chair and went upstairs two a time to fetch them.

When Sadie saw them she was full of praise. "Lawrence, they're very good. You should do more." She turned the sheets over slowly, taking her time. "My mother would love to see these."

I picked up a scrap of paper on the floor and I was just about to put it in the fire when I saw it had handwriting on it. I gasped with embarrassment as I read it.

"What have you got there?" asked Lawrence. I resisted him trying to take the paper from me, but he grabbed it and held me at arm's length as he read aloud:

The army may be digging a tunnel from Elveden to France. If they do, English soldiers could go into France (a good thing) or German soldiers could come to England (very bad). This may not be true. But it might be. Signed Eleanor Barbara Bailey. May 16th. 1916.

He doubled up with laughter, and then Sadie joined in, and the noise brought Uncle Arthur and Aunt Bridget in, so Lawrence insisted on reading it aloud again. I put my hands over my ears. I felt so, so stupid.

But Aunt Bridget stuck up for me. "Elly wrote this years ago, when she was only ten. It's not fair to laugh at her."

But Lawrence kept repeating the phrases he found funniest: *"German soldiers could come to England (very bad)."* That's hilarious! And, *"This may not be true, but it might be".* Then Father came in and Lawrence read out what I'd written yet again, in a silly voice, and then Father recounted the incident when I'd gone into the Elveden estate and been brought back by the gamekeeper, and everyone laughed again. But when Sadie told Lawrence to stop teasing me, he did so and at last everyone left me alone.

I thought of Dan Hunt with his fishing rod and I wished I'd hit him on the head and shoved him in the river.

May 1921

Hardwick House was gradually being dismantled. Well, not the House itself, thankfully, but some of the carriages and the greenhouses were being auctioned. It saddened me, but at least I had seen it at its best. When, less than ten years ago, Mr Cullum was Mayor of Bury and had civic duties to carry out, he often needed my help and I came to know even more of his treasures than I had done earlier. As well as shelves and shelves of books, there were portraits, porcelain, objets d'art and his collection of autographs which included entries from popes, European aristocrats and even American presidents.

Recently I've been back to Hardwick House in search of more Latin texts suitable for my teaching. Since starting to coach Elly, Miss Pitcher has recommended me to several other parents. I now teach four children each week. The two oldest, both girls, are doing well, but the brother of one of them has not made one jot of progress. I am sure he would prefer to be playing football but dare not admit it for fear that I will tell his parents. Another younger boy is just beginning to get a grasp of the declensions and conjugations. On the whole I enjoy this work, and it earns me a small sum each week.

Lawrence is very keen on this girl Sadie. She is delightful and I am happy to see them enjoying each other. She's often here. But would she make a farmer's wife? I don't believe so. When I look at Bridget's life, I cannot imagine that Sadie would settle for it. She could easily deal with the business side, for she has a good head for figures and has been helping Lawrence with his sugar beet budget. But she needs people around her, and at present she's working in the Brandon branch of Gurney's Bank, where there are always comings and goings. However, if she and Lawrence were to marry, she would obviously have to give that up and come to live here.

Bridget has been thinking along the same lines. Last week she commented on Sadie's good looks, and on her lively nature. She stands out in a group, much to Lawrence's delight. I would be very happy to have her in our family. I've even caught myself thinking about grandchildren, especially as I am sure that Hattie would have liked her. And Hattie would be delighted to know that Lawrence was doing sterling work on the farm and was going to inherit it.

Today Sadie and Ursula her sister and their mother came to tea. Ursula drove, and through my bedroom window I watched her pull up and park in the yard. Within seconds Lawrence was there to greet them. He opened the front passenger door and a tall lady, obviously Mrs Finney, stepped out. Sadie and Ursula got out at the same time. All three ladies were wearing summer dresses, and all were smiling. Even from where I was, I could see Lawrence was delighted.

For the first time this year, we had tea in the garden. Elly went backwards and forwards to the house, insisting that Bridget stayed at the table and enjoyed the company. Sadie said less than usual, but Ursula, who had an opinion on everything and a great sense of humour, made up for it. I asked Mrs Finney about Brandon, and we discovered we had acquaintances in common. Her husband's mother, it turned out, had once worked in the Maharajah's household.

We talked about the War Memorial to be erected in Bury. A public meeting had been held on May 1st, at which every aspect of the proposal was discussed: subscriptions, size, style, location, cost, inscriptions, designers. Apparently the idea of a Celtic Cross gained a good level of support. It will take quite a few months to plan and build, but at least the process is being set in motion.

After tea we all ambled round the garden. Lawrence had Sadie on one side and Ursula on the other. From behind I saw Ursula's fair crop tied with a blue bow, Sadie's sunhat and Lawrence's short curly hair. These two sisters were very different in both looks and character. And then Elly came running up. She was waving at them to wait for her and I suddenly caught a glimpse of Conrad in her gesture. How did such things get passed on in families? Had she seen Conrad make that gesture, or had she always done it? I couldn't recall seeing it before. And where had Conrad got it from? Me, or perhaps Hattie?

September 1921

The summer passed easily enough. The farm was doing particularly well, thanks to Lawrence's efforts.

Eric fussed around his Latin lessons happily, but was increasingly concerned about Mr Cullum whose health was deteriorating. Eric had always appreciated being welcomed into our household at West Stow, especially since Hattie's death. He often said that he was "rich in relations", and he regretted the fact that Mr Cullum did not seem to have any close family. Or, if he did, he did not have much contact with them. Because Eric had been connected to Mr Cullum for many years, he cared about him and these days he often returned from his weekly visits to Hardwick in sombre mood, and spoke increasingly of the passing of the pre-war way of life.

He was right. Things were changing, not just at Hardwick House or in West Stow, but everywhere.

Elly and Sadie got on well and often spent whole afternoons chatting by the side of a cricket pitch. Sometimes they missed one of Lawrence's feats of skill: a difficult catch, a maiden over, a particularly good innings. On one such occasion, when I heard Lawrence complaining that Sadie had failed to notice something important, she replied,

"We can't watch every minute of a game that lasts for hours. No-one does. And I'm sure you'd never watch every minute of any game I was in. Did you watch every minute that time Ursula and I played tennis?"

Sadie was quite capable of arguing back, and I hoped this trait would not cause problems between her and Lawrence. I noted how Elly observed the couple as they became closer and wondered what she was thinking.

Bridget was expecting Lawrence to propose to Sadie at any minute. Indeed, she was looking forward to it. I thought back to my proposal to her in 1873. I had known her and her family for well over a year but I was nervous. Her father was very ill at the time but told me he would welcome me as a son-in-law, though he doubted that he would be a father-in-law for long.

That spurred me on, and in the afternoon I suggested to Bridget that we went for a walk, despite quite heavy clouds. We set off at a leisurely pace, but after ten minutes it began to drizzle, and we took shelter under a huge beech. In this green and leafy canopy I took her hands and told her I loved her and wanted to marry her. But she said nothing.

"Say yes," I begged, "Please say yes."

"But you haven't asked me!"

So I did, and she said yes.

October 1921

Alison had moved away to London, and Libby was in a different class to me but I had made other friends too and it became much easier to see them at weekends because some of their families now had a car, and some even a telephone, as we did. Uncle Arthur and Lawrence were used to tractors, so driving a car came easily to them, and indeed to Sadie. I would learn as soon as I was allowed, but Father and Bridget didn't want to learn.

I decided to work hard at school and then go to university. While I was there I would find out about how to become a pilot. I've asked lots of people, and not a single one knows. But I've won a prize for Industry and Scholarship (partly thanks to Father's help with the Latin) so that's a good start.

I was sure Lawrence and Sadie would get engaged, and I hoped they would because I thought they suited each other. They were together most of the time when they weren't working, and they were always holding hands, but not in front of Aunt Bridget because she disapproved. Like my father, she seemed to think that people ought to be as they were before the war, but that was *years* ago. Seven years ago, in fact. Although Uncle Arthur kept saying things like, "Well, you won't get change from half-a-crown for anything these days," or "Travelling isn't as it used to be," he wasn't saying that the new things were wrong or bad, but that they were different.

Aunt Bridget was just old-fashioned, and always would be. But I liked her. She was very kind, and she did not have to work so hard now because she and my uncle decided to employ a woman to help with the housework. I thought at first that Bridget would find fault with Sheila, who was young and had two children. Her husband had been badly injured in the war and couldn't work, and during the war Sheila worked at the rabbit skin factory, but when Lingwood's took it over they gave her job to a man. I knew my uncle and aunt paid her well for what she did, for life was difficult for her. One of her little boys had rickets.

I was glad I was young when the war ended. Even if there was another war, it obviously wouldn't happen for many years. No-one who had been through this war would ever get involved in another one because they knew how bad it was. And yet people still had wars. Did they forgot how bad they were, or how many people died or were killed? If I were a man I would refuse to fight, even if people said I was a coward. I'm not sure if Lawrence and Conrad were right to join the colours, but Lawrence said there was no doubt at all. Despite all the deaths, they were definitely right. Otherwise, he said, it would all have been for nothing.

But I wondered if it was exactly that: all for nothing.

November 1921

Lawrence gazed up at the towering memorial on Weather Heath, just a few miles from Icklingham. It was far higher than anyone had expected. His father said he thought it even higher than both Nelson's column in London and the Britannia monument in Great Yarmouth, but he doubted his memory for he had not seen those since well before the war.

The November cold bit into the group which had assembled to officiate at the unveiling. Field Marshal Sir Henry Wilson, the new Bishop of Bury and Ipswich, and Earl Iveagh stood together on a raised platform. Nearby, the ladies were trying to prevent the hems of their coats from whipping their legs. Lawrence found it amusing that some of the most elegant wore hats rather like turbans. Turning round, he noticed his father in conversation with a man he did not recognise but who was clearly Indian. Could it be one of the Duleep Singh family?

During the speech reporters scribbled notes while others took photos. Every passing motor car slowed down, their drivers curious. The large expanse away from the road was filled with parked carriages, motors and numerous bicycles. Pedestrians were still arriving, many from Elveden, where Earl Iveagh had given all his employees a day off. Three choirs, one from each village, took up their places, as did soldiers, a band, several buglers, the Fire Brigade and a group of VADs.

As the Reveille was played Lawrence looked round at the crowd. He knew many people by sight and nodded a good morning to a mother and daughter he knew from Lackford, a couple from Thetford, two brothers from Wordwell. There were several disabled men, one of whom was Sheila's husband.

Why had the earl decided to build such an impressive memorial when those in most other villages were simple? Was he doing his best to commemorate the three parishes, Icklingham, Eriswell and Elveden, which virtually belonged to him? Or did he want to display his wealth? Not that he alone had paid for the column, for numerous tenants and local people had contributed too.

He thought about the men whom he had been so close to for several years and was now so far from. Sidney, Albert, Sandy. Cyril, Wally, Ted. Given that the men whose names the column recorded were dead, did Earl Iveagh's reasons matter? Everything was down to luck. His own name could be on this memorial, and it was only chance that he was alive. He could so easily have been killed. What was important was that these men should be remembered.

Recently he had gone into the cathedral where a plaque now commemorated the thirty-two former pupils from

King Edward's who had been killed. He recognised almost all the names and had a picture in his mind of what many of them had looked like, or what they had done at school: a couple of outstanding sportsmen; a boy who was often the butt of jokes; several brainboxes; a class clown; even a pair who had had parts in the Bury Pageant in 1907. He remembered them all except for two. He searched also for other names, and was pleased when he could not find them. Perhaps they had survived the war or spent it doing something useful in England.

But the names on the plaque formed a permanent list of those who had gone for good. As well as the names were the dates of the war and the school coat-of-arms, and the words: *They loved not their life unto death.* What did that mean? Lawrence read the phrase again: *They loved not their life unto death.* Of course they had loved their lives.

Sadie held his hand firmly, and led him towards the banks of flowers. Well over a hundred bouquets had been laid down and even now more were being added. The messages accompanying them were simple and poignant. *"To Harry, in ever-loving memory, Annie." "For Ernest, Never forgotten, from your very own Nancy." "To our dear brother Wilfred, from Doris, Joan and Madge."* Despite the wintry day, their scent permeated the air.

Or perhaps Earl Iveagh wanted his column to symbolize a reaching, a soaring towards God?

The speeches over, the crowd sang *Oh God our help in ages past.* Then Sir Henry Wilson stepped forward purposefully towards something that Lawrence, despite his height, could not see. A few seconds later three Union Jacks unfurled simultaneously, so revealing the names of the fallen. The crowd, still respectful, began to jostle gently towards the base of the column, but stood stock still when the Last Post was played. Then they moved forward again, and began to mingle and get into conversation. Lawrence observed his father standing with Arthur and Bridget. He seemed older than he had done at the beginning of the war, and of course he *was* older. He had lost much of his hair and now wore glasses all the time, and his expression showed that he was suffering. Who, given what had happened to his son and his wife, would not be? But Lawrence had managed to have a quick word with him to ask whether the man he had been talking to was indeed a Duleep Singh, and it turned out to be Prince Freddy, one of the Maharajah's sons, which had pleased Eric greatly.

An additional reason for his father's low mood was the fact that Mr Cullum was said to be close to death. No-one knew what would happen to Hardwick House, but a little discussion had taken place about it after the church service the previous Sunday. A friend of Arthur's had suggested that if there was no heir, the house and estate could be put up for sale. But what if, in these difficult times when running a big estate was so expensive, no-one wanted it? Another voice said that it could be pulled down, couldn't it, and so free up all that land for something useful. Lawrence witnessed his father's shock and dismay at the thought of Hardwick House being demolished. No, he had declared adamantly. That would never happen, could never happen.

And Elly. Lawrence had gone to India when she was nine, and now she was fifteen. She stood calmly, almost elegantly, pushing her hair back when the wind blew it across her face, listening to her father talking with the vicar. What would she make of her life? She was turning out to be the one with the brains. He watched her edging towards a group of five or six boys and girls slightly older than herself. She obviously knew them, and they welcomed her as she approached.

Still hand-in-hand with Sadie, Lawrence cast his eyes across the crowd again. There were plenty of middle-aged and old people, and the young women obviously included the wives and sisters of the fallen. There were not many men of his own age present. The Bowen brothers were not there; nor Jack Hooper; nor Ted Wallis. Nor those forty-seven men whose names were on the new column. And of course Conrad wasn't there either.

And nor was Mother. Given the circumstances, Conrad's death had been half anticipated, but Mother's was completely unexpected. Who expects to lose their mother while they themselves are at war? If only he had recognised that she was seriously ill. If only he could have said, or even written, goodbye. But things were as they were. Perhaps he shouldn't be so hard on himself. Mother was buried in the churchyard at Hawstead, and Conrad's name, rank, regiment and birth and death dates were on a small plaque inside the church. His parents had particularly wanted this because he had no known grave, and, so far, his name was not on any memorial.

Thank God he and Sadie had found each other. Thank God he had found the right woman so easily, in the right place at the right time. He put his arm round Sadie's waist and hugged her gently. He used the words *Thank God* out of habit, for he did not believe that God organised their meeting, or war or peace, or anything at all.

Was it foolish to hope for better things? Might all his and Sadie's hopes for their unborn children, the farm and an apple orchard be overtaken by events they could not control? Did everyone just have to get on with things despite what might happen, accepting good and bad? There was no other answer than *Yes*.

The band started to play the National Anthem and in an instant Lawrence found he had let go of Sadie's hand and was automatically standing to attention.

Soon after that, the crowd gradually thinned out. People began to leave on foot or return to their cars, carriages and bicycles. Arthur walked ahead towards where they had left the motor. Lawrence opened the front passenger door for his father and made sure that Elly, Sadie, and his aunt and uncle were squeezed safely into the back. Then he settled himself behind the steering wheel.

No-one spoke as they drove home.